"Susan Grant's sexiest story yet!"
—*New York Times* bestselling author Gena Showalter

"Dang, but Jared was a hot hero! Susan Grant is an author I sincerely wish I hadn't waited so long to discover!"
—Shannon McKelden, author of *Venus Envy*

"Charming, witty and sexy as all get out!"
—RITA® Award-winning author Linnea Sinclair

"Susan Grant proves once again...she is Master of the Futuristic Genre. Jared and Keira's heat burns up the pages!"
—Award-winning author Colby Hodge

YOUR PLANET OR MINE?

"One of the best books of the year!"
—*New York Times* bestselling author MaryJanice Davidson

"Wow! This book just has everything and I found myself laughing out loud; [Susan Grant has] a real gift for comedy."
—*USA TODAY* bestselling author Lindsay McKenna

"A cute, quirky otherworldly romance that's totally delightful to read."
—*Fresh Fiction*

"I love Susan Grant's books and this one was simply incredible. I loved the characters, the story and the whole premise behind this fabulous book!"
—*The Best Reviews*

"The pacing is so effortless and the humor awesome! But most of all? [Susan Grant] has the romance totally nailed. I love their chemistry, and there's something very sweet about them, even though it's totally hot, too."
—Deidre Knight, bestselling author of *Parallel Heat*

THE SCARLET EMPRESS

"Exhilarating...adrenaline-filled...shocking twists and turns keep readers enthralled."
—*Publishers Weekly*

SUSAN GRANT

MOONSTRUCK

HQN™

ISBN-13: 978-0-373-77259-9
ISBN-10:   0-373-77259-9

MOONSTRUCK

www.HQNBooks.com

Printed in U.S.A.

Dear Reader,

Every once in a while, a story sneaks up and grabs me by my heart—and my throat—and demands that I write it. *Moonstruck* was one of those books. It was the kind of story that exploded onto the pages, not losing any of its intensity in the transfer between the imagination and the typed page. In fact, I actually was slated to pen a different tale when Finn, the soldier hero from *Moonstruck,* sidled up to me dressed in his Drakken armor (which can be quite scary), easily charming me with his boyish grin as he brought his lips close to my ear and murmured, "I'm afraid your plans have changed...."

Needless to say, I put the other story aside. When seemingly only a short time later *Moonstruck* was done, I sat back, breathless, and thought: wow, now *that* was an experience. Dear reader, it is my sincerest wish that when you finally turn the last page of *Moonstruck,* you, too, will share that feeling. So please sit back, get comfortable and let me tell you a story that begins far away beyond the stars....

Susan Grant

P.S. As always, I love to hear from readers. Please visit me on the Web at www.susangrant.com and at www.myspace.com/susangrant.

Author's note: *Moonstruck* is the first book in the all-new Borderlands series, which is based loosely on the same world as my Otherworldly Men trilogy. While you may meet a character or two from the past, *Moonstruck* is more intense emotionally and darker without sacrificing all the adventure and fun you've come to expect from my stories. I invite you to experience the Borderlands for yourself at www.the-borderlands.com.

Infinite thanks to: Carolyn Curtice and Cindy Feuerstein for the early reads—your eyes save me every time; my editor Tara Parsons for your endless support and for sharing my excitement about this book; my agent Ethan Ellenberg, consummate professional; Gena Showalter, an über-talent and cover-disaster picker-upper; the readers at Paranormal Romance—wow, look at us now!; the sisterhood at Romvets—you awe me, girls; Connor and Courtney—for lighting up my life with your love and laughter, Mom loves you; and Linnea Sinclair, extraordinary woman and friend— I dedicate this one to you, kid.

MOONSTRUCK

CHAPTER ONE

BRIT WOKE SLOWLY, luxuriating in silken sheets as she took a drowsy accounting of her circumstances: One, it was morning. Two, she was naked. And three, she was lying in a strange bed.

A real bed. Compared to the one in her quarters on board the CSS *Vengeance,* the bed was lavish, big enough for three or four. It appeared, however, that only one other person shared the mattress. What was his name again?

Brit rolled onto her side to view her bedmate. Did it matter what she called him? She'd tolerate his company for perhaps another night or so before he became another pleasant memory from shore leave like all the others before him.

She reached out and moved a curl from his forehead. No lines of worry marred that perfect, golden skin. He'd never needed to block out the screams of battle, nor grimaced at the horrors of war. No, this man existed in a sort of perpetual shore leave: all pleasure, no pain. He was almost pretty, she decided, but well-built—she would not have chosen him otherwise. His dark hair was tousled; his lips were full, stopping *this* short of feminine. She preferred a more manly mouth. Ah, but he'd used it well. There was time for him to use it again, too, before she deserted him for breakfast.

On her belly, she slid closer and licked his jaw. "Wake up…" *Whatever your name is…*

He stretched and smiled, then rolled her onto her back. Two long, thin slashes marred his shoulder. "I scratched you," she murmured as he nuzzled his way down her neck to her breasts. She hadn't remembered clawing him; she normally wasn't violent in bed. Well, not this violent. But it had been too long between shore leaves this time, and she'd been hungry.

Hungry to forget…hungry to remember.

With this stranger between her legs, she could cast her memories back and pretend he was Seff and she his young wife, innocent, full of hopes and dreams, all the things she wasn't now. They were only teenagers, married less than two years when Hordish marauders came. With this pretty stranger and all the others before him she could lose herself in the sex, almost believing in those moments of blinding, no-strings-attached passion that she was still human. That she could still feel.

"Come here." She took his head between her hands and kissed him roughly. He returned the kiss with equal intensity, crushing her to the pillow, but something wasn't right. Something's missing, she thought. *Of course it is, you fool. His passion is staged—it's what you bought him for. Yours is real.*

She swore under her breath, grabbing his shoulders and digging in as she trapped him close. She wanted him inside her—now—thrusting hard, before her thoughts, her self-analysis, went any deeper.

From the bedside table, her Personal Communicator Device rang.

"Blast it," she hissed, twisting from under him to grab the PCD.

Her bedmate playfully pulled her back and threw her down to the mattress. "Whoever it is can wait."

"Release me." The snarling command came out in her admiral's voice. The man-toy backed off immediately, lifting both hands. White, soft palms, she noted. He hadn't done a day of real labor in his life. Why, when there was nothing to do but service wealthy, privacy-craving clients on this pleasure dome of a resort planet? He was an attractive, empty shell of a man looking for a day's pay earned with his cock. It was quite nice as cocks went, true, she thought with a brief, almost longing stare at the man's hefty equipment standing at attention between his legs…until the communicator rang again, diverting her attention.

Brit sat up, swinging her hair over one shoulder. "Admiral Bandar," she said curtly into the PCD as she hooked the secure-signal communicator over her ear. Several tones told her that her voice required authentication before the identity of the person trying to reach her could be revealed. The procedure was typical for high-priority, classified calls. Except that Brit was light-years off the beaten track on a vacation planet. The connection could take a while.

In the corner of her eye, she caught the sparkle of her midnight-black, crisply pressed officer's uniform hanging in the closet next to an iridescent, gossamer-lace poolside cover-up. Who would dare to bother her on shore leave? This was supposed to be a few weeks' respite before she returned to the helm of the *Vengeance* to hunt down increasingly desperate Hordish pirates in the Borderlands. The war might be over, but there was cleanup to do.

The war...over. It had been several months, and Brit still couldn't wrap her mind around the concept. Yet long ago, before time began, the galaxy was whole. The worlds of the Drakken Horde were the original cradle of the goddesses. Then, under threat of religious extermination, the goddesses were forced to flee their home. They found refuge on the ice planet Sakka, where they formed a new government, the Coalition, and essentially split the settled galaxy in two. The two sides, Coalition and Drakken, had warred ever since. Every schoolchild could recite that bit of history.

What no one considered, however, was the sheer number of faithful living across the border under

Hordish rule who worshipped the goddesses in secret—undocumented believers, billions, even trillions of them. When the young goddess Herself, Queen Keira, killed the Drakken Horde leader Lord-General Rakkuu to escape capture, she in effect broke the dam holding the faithful back. The warlord's blood hadn't even cooled when those secret believers began pouring out of the shadows. Thus, in an almost bloodless coup, the Drakken Empire had come crashing down, bringing peace to a galaxy that remembered nothing but war.

Peace with the Horde? Bah! It would never last. The only trustworthy Drakken was a dead Drakken.

Brit shot to her feet. Pacing away from the bed to find privacy for the call, her hair swinging just above her buttocks, she felt her bedmate's eyes on her nude body. She was older than him by a number of years, she was certain, yet, nearing forty, she looked better than women almost half her age. Then again, she allowed herself no excesses. She was disciplined, focused. She knew what she wanted, and that was to kill Horde.

"Authentication verified," a computer announced.

A familiar voice came on next. "My sincere apologies for the interruption, Brit," soothed Prime-Admiral Zaafran, her commander-in-chief. "However, it is with good news that I do."

She closed the veranda door behind her. "The treaty has broken down." Her hopes soared.

Zaafran's deep chuckle crushed those hopes. It didn't sound as if he shared them, either. *He doesn't have the reasons you do.* "I have orders," he said. "A new ship—brand-new, state-of-the-art."

A bolt of surprise shot through her. "And the *Vengeance?*"

"She's being retired."

Her warship had the best record out there, winning more battles than any other. She loved that hunk of luranium; it was as much a part of her as her skin and bones. The merest whisper of the word *Vengeance* struck fear in the hearts of the Drakken. They knew that she, Admiral Brit Bandar, was in command. They knew that she held no mercy in her soul for them. "Admiral Stone-Heart," they called her.

The nickname amused her.

Over the years, countless Hordish war leaders had lusted after her capture. Oh, the things they'd dreamed of doing to her, most of them related to sex and torture—she'd learned a few choice scenarios from listening to Drakken prisoner confessions during interrogations—but they'd never caught her. Now they never would. The entire Drakken realm lay vanquished at the Coalition's feet. A victory that for Brit wasn't satisfying at all. She wasn't done with the Drakken yet. No, nowhere close. "It will seem odd, commanding a new ship, Prime-Admiral."

"One foot on the bridge and you will change your

mind. I've seen her. She's more impressive than any ship in our fleet, even your beloved *Vengeance.*"

"I look forward to you convincing me of that, sir," Brit quipped, though an expanding ball of tension sat cold in her gut. Regardless of the reason, Zaafran planned to remove her from her ship. Even if she was trading up, as he'd implied, it was an unsettling event. It would be for any captain of any ship, let alone tearing her from her beloved *Vengeance.* The warship had been the closest thing to home since Arrayar Settlement.

"Convince you, I will," Zaafran assured her.

"What is the ship's name? Give me that, at least."

"Have patience, Admiral. Report to the Ring. I'll tell you the rest."

Patience—bah. Brit frowned as he ended the call. A summons to the Ring to trade ships seemed odd. The usual procedure for a new ship captain was to proceed directly to the shipyard or port, run through the usual change-of-command formalities if taking the bridge from someone else and be off. Yet, the Prime-Admiral wanted to see her in person. He was hiding something. But what?

She let herself back inside the room and shoved the veranda door shut. Morning sunshine streamed between the slats of shuttered windows. The Ring was the Prime-Admiral's headquarters, a space station orbiting Sakka, the Holy Keep of the Goddess and the seat of the Coalition government. Of late, the

Ring had been the location of the *Unity* Peace Conference where Coalition and Earth leaders were meeting to determine the fate of a vanquished Drakken Empire and its newly liberated citizens. And, Brit surmised, carve up what was left of any value for themselves.

It was a giddy, hopeful time—for everyone else but her. While the galaxy celebrated the Drakken surrender, Brit had prowled the bridge of the warship she commanded, cursing it. Dreading it. She wouldn't know what to do in peacetime. She wasn't ready for it. Peace meant unfinished business with the Horde. She could never reverse what they'd done but she could keep it from happening to someone else. She'd spent her entire career doing exactly that.

Now they were taking her ship away, replacing it with a new one. Taking her mission and replacing it with…what? The mighty *Vengeance* was to be retired. Would *she* be forced into retirement next? Brit tore the PCD off her ear and stalked back to the bed.

"It's about time," the man-toy murmured with come-hither eyes. But it was a wasted effort. The mood had passed.

"Get dressed." Brit reached into the closet and removed a few extra credits from the safe. She'd paid the man in advance, but his performance last night warranted a tip. She tossed the credits on the table. "And be gone before I return."

She closed and locked the bathroom door, and

stepped into the shower, letting the streaming water fool her into believing the moisture on her face wasn't angry tears.

WARLEADER FINNAR RORKKEN paused in the entrance of a dilapidated eatery and bar, waiting until his eyes adjusted. Inside, it smelled like sweat and sex and blood—like any typical Hordish haunt. A few dead bodies littered the stone floor. Finn stepped around them, his boots muddy from the hike from the ship to town. This planet had been badly bombarded during the Great War, probably several times. Spring rains turned scarred hardpan into mud. All week, downpours had continued unabated. He'd never seen so much damn rain.

Water dripped from his ponytail and earrings, his leather overvest and trousers. His wool sweater stank, and was two sizes smaller than when he'd bought it. He was tired of being wet, tired of being hungry more often than not, tired of…

Blast it all, he was just tired!

The tang of cheap alcohol hung heavy in the muggy air. Finn waved off the expectant glance of a bar wench. He didn't want a drink; he wanted a warm, dry room and a good square meal—simple needs but harder than ever to satisfy. Worse, there was more than his belly to fill. He had a crew of fifty-two to look after.

As an Imperial Fleet warleader, he was paid in

scrip that he divvied up amongst the crew. In port, they'd exchange scrip for real money. The implosion of the Drakken government had rendered the scrip worthless. Finn had to dig into his own funds to support the ship and crew. There hadn't been much in the way of funds. Now he was liquidating ship furnishings, liquor and unneeded weapons, anything he could barter or sell. To slow the hemorrhage, he'd resorted to raiding. It was like the old days.

He'd given up piracy (more or less) upon his promotion some years ago to Warleader. He'd turned a new page in his life. He'd thought he'd found a new career, a respectable one. Now, he'd fallen back on old ways. Desperation did that to a man. The skills honed during his reign as Scourge of the Borderlands hadn't vanished. A recent haul from a raid in the Borderlands had been sizeable enough to keep them fed. Life had turned good again, relatively speaking, until the *Pride*'s plasma core acted up, forcing them to put down on this scum pool of a planet for repairs.

Finn had paid dearly for the privilege. No one was supposed to fix Drakken ships anymore without Coalition knowledge. Almost all the remaining raid money went to bribing a mechanic to circumvent the new rules. Rationing supplies would be necessary all over again, something he hadn't yet had the heart to break to the crew. No, not until he learned more about the mysterious summons to the Ring of the Goddess.

A body slammed into his side. Finn spun, his dagger in his hand. Hooking his boot under a leg, he threw a large man to the ground. The stench of alcohol rising up from the drunk was almost strong enough to make his eyes water. With the distraction of the drunk, someone who hadn't grown up on the streets as he had might not have felt the light touch of fingers on the empty leather money pouch attached to his belt. He had the pickpocket in his hands and off the ground in a half breath. Through the red haze of anger, he saw two eyes going wide with fear.

He dropped the thief to the ground, making sure he saw the glint of his blade. "You'd better run, boy." The child dashed away. "Run!" he shouted after the waif, old memories whispering. He'd been in those shoes before; he knew what it was like, being so hungry that you were immune to risk.

Finn exhaled as his pulse slowed. A pickpocket this time; a thief with more murderous intent the next. He was a target. The men and women in his crew were targets. No matter how tattered their uniforms, they were several levels up from what most people wore around here. Any one of them could be ambushed at any time, ending the day lying on their backs in a pool of blood for the price of what little of value they had in their possession. The Border-lands had always been a dangerous place. Now there was an air of acute desperation.

But Finn might have a way out of this dead end

spiral, an escape. *An escape or a trapdoor?* He didn't know. His mysterious summons from Coalition Headquarters commanded that he show up at the Ring next Septumday. The accompanying message was a personal one, issued by Chief of the Coalition Naval Command, Prime-Admiral Zaafran, as if the idea of Finnar Rorkken, formerly the Scourge of the Borderlands, aboard the Ring wasn't surreal enough. Good gods, what was next, a love letter from Admiral Bandar? The way things were going, he wouldn't be surprised to see ol' Stone-Heart herself sitting there when he arrived.

He almost wished she were. After all the games of hide-and-seek they'd played in the Borderlands, he felt as if he knew her. A more worthy opponent he'd never encountered. If he ever had the chance, he'd buy her a drink and brag about all the times she'd thought she'd had him in her clutches, only for him to slip away again. He respected her, aye, admired her, but he had to admit the male in him was more than a little curious about the woman at the helm of the *Vengeance.*

No one knew what she looked like, although there'd been many guesses bandied about. No one who'd met her ever returned to pass along the juicy details. They were either dead or scraping luranium out of the mines on a prison asteroid. Not him, oh, no. He'd led her on one merry chase after another across the Borderlands until she'd been called away for more pressing duties: battles more critical to the survival of the Coalition than catching a pesky pirate.

The war, over—it was damned hard to imagine. Now that he was out of a job killing her people, and she was out of a job killing his, maybe they'd have time for that drink after all.

You're delusional, Rorkken. Aye. Something told him that Stone-Heart didn't view him in quite the same way he did her.

Smirking, Finn clamped a nano-pic between his teeth as he scoped out the noisy, crowded, shadowy bar. Bioputers spread through his mouth in a refreshing wave, eliminating any sourness. The pic was a welcome little novelty found amongst other, more important supplies taken on that Borderlands raid. The Coalition had lived with high-tech for generations. The Drakken lived with whatever they could steal or, rather, appropriate. Other than their machines of war, their weapons, they were centuries behind the Coalition in technology.

There was a newcomer to this two-sided game: Earth. When it came to tech, Earthlings made the Drakken look downright advanced. Luckily for Earth, it was protected under its new status as a Holy Shrine, thanks to it being the birthplace of Queen Keira's consort, quite an achievement for such a far-flung, water-covered little rock.

A burst of singing drowned in angry shouts. Glass shattered. Someone cried out. Finn rolled his eyes.

It was time to haul his crew out of the bar before they were too drunk to find their way back to the ship. Then he'd tell them the news.

The musical tinkle of female laughter drifted over to him. A group of women stood off to the side, giggling and ogling him, waiting for a signal to come closer, one or all of them. An image of their naked bodies writhing under and over his lasted only seconds and barely registered between his legs. Zaafran's orders and what they could mean commanded too much of his imagination. If the outcome was as good as he hoped there'd be plenty of time for such sport soon, for him and his crew.

With a sly, regretful glance in the direction of the women that got them tittering all over again, Finn crossed to the rear of the bar. He found his second-in-command leaning heavily on a grimy counter, his eyes glazed over with a telltale fog. "Gather the crew, Zurykk. We're off."

"We've only just gotten started, sir."

Finn circled his hand. "We've got orders out."

"Orders?" Zurykk dropped his boots. The skinny little wench wrapped around him protested. She was small, hollow-eyed. A girl that age should be in school, not a soldier's bar. Problem was, the last years of Lord-General Rakkuu's aggressive campaign to topple the Coalition had frayed what little was left of society's edges. Unnecessaries such as education had been the first to go. People were too busy reeling from the horrors of war, too numb to salvage their humanity in the shadow of unbearable atrocities.

Would the treaty with the Coalition make things better or worse? Who knew? It was a time of change. Finn intended to land feetfirst like he always did.

"What orders, Captain?" Zurykk repeated.

"We're to dock at the Ring of the Goddess no later than Septumday morning."

"The Ring?" Zurykk searched his face and choked. "Gods, you're serious."

"As a plasma burn, aye."

"We're gonna run for it, though, aren't we? We're not going to show up." Zurykk absorbed Finn's determined expression and downed the last of his drink. "You're crazy."

"An optimist."

"A fool!" In the glare of Finn's disapproval, the man added, meeker, "Captain, sir." He slammed his glass to the counter and exhaled loudly. "The question isn't whether you'll be executed, Cap'n, but whether it'll be public or private."

"Private, I hope. If that smart-noose curls around my neck, I plan to spend my last breaths on obscenities raw enough to make Stone-Heart blush."

"You need blood to blush," Zurykk pointed out.

Finn chuckled. "Aye, you do, that." Blood was something that cold bitch surely didn't have. "Gather everyone up, Zurykk. We're off."

Finn took a watchful position by the door as his second-in-command yanked the crew off chairs and out of cots, tearing them from the arms of lovers or from bowls of greasy, cheap, but belly-warming stew. Rakkelle, his latest pilot, pulled her shirt over surprisingly white and delicate breasts. A few red splotches on her skin told him she'd been engaged in activities that had been anything but delicate. Finn hated to interrupt any of it. Without battles to do the job, a crew needed a way to vent energy. Finn would rather it be sex than bar fights that could leave them dead or, worse, badly injured. These days, with medical supplies hard to come by, they needed to preserve what little they had.

With the crew grumbling all around him, Finn walked out into a cold and soaking drizzle. Rakkelle strode alongside him. Again he thought of her breasts, and felt a twinge in reaction to the thought of tasting them. Lusty little Rakkelle wouldn't mind, but Warleader Finnar Rorkken didn't sleep with his subordinates. He still had a few principles that went along with his hard-won title. A few.

Fewer principles by the day, he thought, reminded of his precarious situation.

"Zurykk says we're heading out, Captain," Rakkelle said.

"Aye. We're been ordered to the Ring."

She let out a husky war cry, spinning around to face the others. "The Ring! We're going to the freepin' Ring! We'll slice off their wee little Coalition balls and crack 'em like gornuts!"

The crew roared like they did before a battle.

"Shut your traps!" Finn bellowed. He rested a hand on the butt of his pistol, glaring at the noisy men and few women who knew he'd use that weapon if provoked. "I've been summoned to appear by Prime-Admiral Zaafran."

Boos and curses came in response.

Finn drew the pistol. The laser sight streaked along the foreheads of the suddenly silent crew. His aim was deadly, and they knew it. It was no different from his pirate days: a strong arm kept a Hordish crew in line. "Disrespect of our military orders is to disrespect me. Who dares more disrespect?" He armed the pistol. "It will be your last mistake."

"But, sir, they're Coalition."

"And so are we." That generated more growls of protest, quickly self-extinguished. "We are one now, one world. We either accept this, or we flounder and fail. I will not fail." He twirled the nano-pic between his tongue and teeth, glaring at the men and women surrounding him. He counted to ten before he spoke again, quieter. "Am I clear?"

"Aye," the mumbles went around.

"I didn't hear you."

"Aye!"

Finn jerked his chin to the dock. "Let's move out."

Ahead, his warship glinted darkly, evilly, a giant

amongst the smaller ships in port. His ship, his pride, he thought. *Finn's Pride.* With most Hordish vessels bearing monikers such as *Blood Wrath, Scourge of Death,* and even *Stench,* his ship's name was the source of ridicule at first. One by one, his disparagers learned the consequences of that. Now his ship commanded respect, wherever they went.

Finn strode on ahead, letting damp, cool air wash over him. He was going to have to fight to keep his ship, fight to keep his career. It was nothing new. He'd struggled for everything that had come his way, from the moment he was born until now, fighting for every gods-be-damned bite of food, it sometimes seemed. From skinny street urchin to opportunist pirate, to working his way up the ranks of the Imperial Fleet from unwilling conscript to decorated Warleader, he'd busted his ass for it all.

He threw a grateful glance at the heavens in thanks for all the near-misses, lucky breaks and last-minute saves over the course of his life. Someone Up Above took pity on his sorry soul. The gods had been generous with him, aye, but they'd made him sweat for every blasted bone they'd thrown his way.

What is granted can be taken back, no matter how hard you've worked to win it. Finn had learned that lesson well. He threw a dark, regretful glance at his ship. Ah, but it had been good while it lasted....

As if reading his thoughts, Zurykk ventured quietly, "What of the *Pride,* Captain? What of us?"

"I have nothing more to tell." Finn was well aware that the ears of the crew were hard-tuned to his every word. "Zaafran refuses to explain until I am on board the Ring. Only then will he reveal his news." *History-making, ground-breaking, life-changing news* had been the Prime-Admiral's exact words. Finn wasn't sure what to believe. News might mean a promotion, or the commencement of his war crimes trial. "I asked for more than that, I did, but he told me to have patience."

The crew was vocal in their disappointment. Of course they wanted to know more. Their fates were tangled with his. In these dark times, the loss of their warleader would be devastating. He was all that separated them from hunger and homelessness. For morale's sake, he'd keep the pitiful state of the ship's vault to himself now that he'd coughed up what he owed for the plasma core repairs. For the same reason, he'd keep private his nagging reservations on his summons to the Ring. Zaafran's "news" was either incredibly bad or incredibly good. Finn had his bets on the former. His heart held out for the latter.

CHAPTER TWO

"I SMELL HORDE." Brit sniffed as she exited the airlock connecting the *Vengeance* to the Ring. Hands clasped behind her back, her posture perfect, she strode forward as Lieutenant Hadley Keyren scurried to keep up with her. "They all have that peculiar stink."

Hadley wrinkled her nose. It was clear by the girl's silence that the cloying stench didn't bother her. Brit would never forget it for as long as she lived.

The Drakken were here, inside the Ring. *Blast this treaty, letting barbarians sully our highest military offices.* "Find out where in the VIP wing I am to stay, Hadley. Set up my quarters as always."

"Yes, ma'am."

"Other than the prime-admiral or you, I do not wish to be disturbed once there. Screen all my calls."

"Yes, ma'am."

A group of officers passed them in the bustling corridor. "Admiral," they greeted with respectful nods. "Goddess be with you."

"Gentlemen," Brit replied, scanning their faces.

Coalition uniforms mostly with an Earthling or two amongst them. But no Drakken. No Horde.

Brit's hands flexed at the small of her back. Her stomach muscles clenched with tension. "Download the names of my new staff. Include their military history and war records."

"Yes, ma'am."

"I do not want any unknowns serving under me."

"No, ma'am."

"Have the data waiting for me with dinner."

"Broiled rainbow fish, tropical fruit medley, wine—Kin-Kan Vineyards, vintage 6763. Is that right, Admiral?"

"Sixty-three? Yes. Very good, Hadley."

"Thank you, ma'am."

Brit stopped in front of Prime-Admiral Zaafran's suite of offices with a click of her polished, booted heels. An aide scurried into the labyrinth to announce her arrival. "And, Hadley…"

"Yes, ma'am?" The lieutenant's intelligent blue eyes lifted expectantly, awaiting her next orders. The young officer's blond hair was knotted in a chignon at the base of her neck, above the rim of her uniform collar as regulations dictated. Once, Brit had been just as sweet and eager to please. But that was before… She set her jaw. "I hope you enjoyed what little there was of your shore leave. It may be some time before we see another."

"Yes, ma'am." Then, softer, "Good luck in there."

"Luck favors those who don't depend on it, Hadley." Brit turned, steadied herself and entered the office of her commander as if she owned it.

GORGEOUS BABE, TWELVE O'CLOCK. With his gaze locked on the slim blonde, Major Ruben Barrientes smoothed a hand over his Air Force blues, wishing he was wearing his flight suit. His USAF Thunderbird insignia always impressed the ladies, but chances were the hot little number in Coalition blacks didn't speak or read English, and had never heard of the USAF flying demonstration team, a coveted slot he'd vacated when this even more coveted slot was offered to him.

You don't need no fancy jet patches to make you hot, he reminded himself. Centering the blonde in his target, he rolled in for the kill.

"Girl, you don't deserve that," he said low and in her ear, causing her to whirl around. Those blue eyes were even more gorgeous up close. He wanted to kiss the circle of surprise right off her soft pink lips.

"I don't know you," she said.

"You do now." He flashed what he knew was a killer smile and extended his hand. "Ruben Barrientes. At your service." Curiosity and wariness filled her narrowed eyes. And attraction, he was sure of it. She wanted him already. "Just call me Tango. Everyone does." He'd wound up with that call sign because he was Argentine by birth—no matter that he had blond

hair and grew up in Texas, it didn't matter, he was
Tango as soon as the squadron heard the remains of
his Spanish accent. The pretty little lieutenant wouldn't
know where Texas was, let alone Argentina.

She didn't take his hand. Instead, her fist landed
in the center of her chest: the Coalition version of a
greeting. He'd screwed up; he should have done it her
way. Months of crash courses in everything Coalition
hadn't polished away all the rough edges. He'd keep
working on it. He, Tango, was synonymous with
smooth. He aimed to keep it that way.

"I am Lieutenant Star-class Hadley Keyren."

"So, Hadley—"

"Lieutenant Keyren," she corrected.

She wanted to keep her distance. That was okay,
it wouldn't last long. She was a good girl; he could
tell with one look. Good girls always fell like ripe
apples, right into his hands. "So, *Lieutenant,* is
General Grouch always like that?"

"Pardon me?"

"'Get me this, bring me that.'" He sniffed in imi-
tation of the other woman's rapid-fire demands,
hoping his accent didn't make him too tough to understand. "And you scurrying after her, all sweetness,
like the girl in that movie *The Devil Wears Prada.*"

Hadley's look of perpetual surprise deepened.

"The Devil Wears Prada..." Did the words even
translate? The closest thing to devil was "god of the
Dark Reaches." And Prada? Shit, forget that. In prep-

aration for this assignment, Tango had spent the past twelve weeks in a total immersion course, learning "the Queen's tongue," aka "QT," the language of both the Coalition and the former Drakken Empire. Unfortunately, if the blond babe's expression was anything to go by, he might as well be speaking Chinese the way he mixed American slang with her words. "Girl, all I gotta say is that you handled that ruthless bitch pretty damn well. Me, I wouldn't have been so nice."

Hadley stiffened. "She is my commanding officer."

He laughed. "My condolences."

Hadley's powder-blue eyes turned dark and humorless. Furious. "That was Admiral Bandar."

"No way. That was Bandar…?"

"Yes. *Admiral* Bandar."

Tango's heart dropped. Bandar was his new boss. Bandar was to the Coalition as General Patton was to the United States—and he'd just dissed her in front of her assistant. *Good going, Tango*. He shoved his hand through his fresh haircut and swore. He hadn't recognized the admiral. The military headshot photo he'd seen was nothing like the reality. He wasn't sure what he'd expected, but it wasn't this—a tall, sleek, comic-book superheroine complete with patent-leather dominatrix boots and a black commando uniform. All that was missing was a bull whip and he wasn't so sure the admiral didn't have one tucked in her belt somewhere; he'd been too busy looking at Hadley and feeling sorry for her.

If he had a tail, right now he'd be tucking it between his legs at the thought of being on the receiving end of Bandar's displeasure. It was gonna happen, though, sooner or later, so he'd better be ready. His charm wouldn't work on Bandar. He wouldn't even try. She'd rip his balls off and spit them out. Unconsciously, he brought his legs together, just in time to hear Hadley in the midst of chewing him out.

"You speak of her with disrespect when you aren't even worthy enough to utter her name, Earthling." Her voice had dropped to an angry hiss. "Admiral Brit Bandar is one of our greatest war heroes. She's *my* hero. She's a living legend. Many of us owe our lives to her. She'd give hers to save any of ours."

He lifted his hands in surrender. "Look, I know. I'm sorry. I fu— I screwed up. I was just trying to be funny—to break the ice, since we're going to be serving together."

"What do you mean?"

"You work for Admiral Bandar, right?"

"I'm her executive officer, yes."

"I'm one of the pilots assigned to the *Unity*. We're going to be stationed together on the same ship."

"I don't know what you're talking about."

It was no joke; her confused expression attested to that. How was it possible for her not to know? Unless she and the admiral had just arrived, and...

Tango swallowed. "Do you want the good news first, or the bad news?"

Hushed mutters nearby drew their attention. Hadley's eyes widened as a tall Drakken crossed the corridor trailed by two black-suited Coalition security goons. The Drakken wore knee-high boots over leather pants, and a leather vest. His white shirt was more than halfway unbuttoned, held in place by a crisscrossing of rugged weapons belts. Streaks of tattooing and tanned skin peeked out in between the well-worn straps. His expression was hard, his eyes wary, and he needed a shave. Or maybe the ponytail and beads were what made Tango gladly take a step out of his way as the Hordish officer strode past, beads and jewelry clinking. He caught a faint whiff of leather and something that smelled like cinnamon. "There goes Jack Sparrow," Tango murmured to Hadley.

"Who?"

"Jack Sparrow, *Pirates of the Caribbean.*" Explaining was futile. "It's another Earth movie. I brought it with me. I've got a suitcase full of magazines and DVDs, three thousand tunes on my iPod and plenty of time over the next year to give you a crash course in Earth culture."

Hadley wasn't listening to him at all. Her full attention was glued on the Drakken as he disappeared into the waiting room for the prime-admiral's offices. "Another one of our shipmates, I guess," Tango said.

"He *is?*"

"Why else would he be here?"

Hadley's eyes closed. "Goddess..." she whispered and sagged against the wall.

THE PRIME-ADMIRAL'S headquarters commanded a sweeping vista of the outer ring. Hundreds of thousands of portholes glittered, making the enormous, circular space station look like a jeweled band hovering in space. Zaafran was standing in front of his wall of windows, his index finger pressing a PCD to his ear, when Brit entered his private office. "Have him wait in the briefing room once Joss is done with him," he was saying.

"Admiral Bandar, sir," one of the security guards announced.

Zaafran ended the communication and strode toward her, his white teeth flashing. She allowed him to hug her. She'd known him for too many years not to.

"Kin-Kan wine before lunch?" the prime-admiral offered.

"You remembered," she purred.

"Always."

The table was set for a meal. Set for three, she noted. Hmm. There was to be another guest. Who else would be joining them? She kept her silence— and her impeccable military bearing; the prime-admiral would tell her when he was ready.

Side by side in front of the wall of windows, they sipped the luscious, deep-ruby-hued wine and admired the view. Brit left it up to her superior officer to begin the important conversation or make small talk.

"I want to discuss your new command, Admiral."

So much for small talk; he was going straight to business. She preferred it that way.

"Brit, we've followed orders all our military lives. Some have been easy, some difficult."

"Of course," she said.

"Our duty takes us from our loved ones. It takes our own choices, our personal freedom. Yet, we serve because we are a special breed, a breed apart."

"With all due respect, sir, this is a conversation one might have with a new, untried ensign on their maiden voyage. I'm your most experienced commander. My loyalty, my devotion to duty is something you should expect without question."

Zaafran compressed his lips as he studied her.

"Without question," she repeated.

"I know, Brit. You, more than any other officer. But I… You…" He sighed. She'd never seen him speechless. "Better that I show you this first." He activated the holo-vis. "Display triad." A silver triangle appeared in front of them, three-dimensional and glowing as it spun slowly in midair. Each edge was a different color. "From the reunification hearings comes this—our future. The Triad. Planet Earth, us and the former Drakken Empire—" he pointed to the blue side of the triangle, the black and finally the red "—form the Triad Alliance. The Coalition as we have always known it is no more."

Surprise exploded inside her, but her military bearing remained supremely confident and unflinching. One hand cupped her glass of wine; the other she kept pressed behind her, elbow bent, just so. Her shoulders were back, her chin up and her expression serene. In the end, her only reaction to Zaafran's bombshell was the barest lifting of her left brow. So this was what they'd been cooking up all these weeks during closed-door hearings. She'd suspected as much. Hearing it was another story.

"The Coalition will provide most of the resources and infrastructure for stability in these early stages of reorganization. Earth is too small and backward, of course, and the Drakken Empire is in disarray."

"So, what you're saying, Prime-Admiral, is that we're still in charge."

His slight smile gave her the answer she wanted. "As it should be," she murmured, comforted by the knowledge that some things, the important things, hadn't actually changed. The Coalition had, after all, won the war.

Her commanding officer spoke to the holo-vis once more. "Show next." The triangle disappeared, replaced by a warship beyond her wildest dreams. It was half again as large as the *Vengeance,* with what appeared to be a double plasma-drive core, overlapping weapons portals and many more decks.

"She's magnificent."

Zaafran beamed with pride. "She's every bit as much a symbol of our future as the triangle I just showed you. Feast your eyes on the first Triad Alliance ship, the TAS *Unity*. Congratulations, Brit. She's yours."

"The *Unity?* Bah. What kind of self-respecting battleship is given such a weak name?"

"A new kind of battleship. A ship for a new era. A ship for *diplomacy*."

Her brow went up again. She was a soldier, a warrior. Not a diplomat. Was this what he was so reluctant to tell her?

"She symbolizes the Triad's first steps toward the future, united as one. As her captain, you will command a crew consisting of Coalition, Earth and Drakken."

And Drakken. So there it was. "I see…" Brit took a delicate, controlled sip of wine, rolling it on her tongue before swallowing. "How many of them?"

"You will command a total of two hundred and twenty officers and enlisted personnel. Of that, our initial mandate requires approximately sixty percent Coalition, thirty-five percent Drakken and five percent Earthling."

"I'll simply assign the bulk of the Horde to the propulsion room belowdecks and out of sight. The overflow will go to the ship's load master. They can work on keeping the cargo bays polished. As for the Earthlings, I can't decide if their number is too small to be of concern or just enough to get in the way."

"No, Brit. The crew will be integrated, not segre-gated. We're going to make peace work. We're going to prove everyone can get along. And if you don't feel up to the task, Bandar, I'll remove you right now and send you back to the *Vengeance*."

Shock vibrated through her with the unexpected reprimand. She deserved it; she'd angered him with her impertinence. The prime-admiral's intensity reminded her of the times they'd sat around a war table in their younger days, planning strategy to thwart Drakken onslaughts. He'd been one of the Coalition's greatest tacticians before moving into positions of power that took him off the bridge of a warship. For that reason, Brit had refused to follow in his footsteps. She wanted to be close to battle. She wanted to hear it, to feel it. She would not be denied the satisfaction of victory. The creation of the Triad wouldn't change that. Serving with Horde wouldn't change that. It would just…complicate it a little.

She squared her shoulders, keeping the knuckles of her left hand pressed to her back. "That will not be necessary, sir. I'll take the assignment…and obey your orders." No matter how much she'd prefer serving on the *Vengeance* to taking part in an ill-advised political experiment that would never work! "You have my word."

Zaafran's expression gentled unexpectedly. He took a few pacing steps away and drove a hand through thick salt-and-pepper hair. Once more, he seemed to struggle with what he wanted to say. "Gods, I'm sorry, Brit. My gut told me this may have been asking too much of you—or of anyone who experienced what you have. Your ties to the Arrayar Massacre… Gods, Brit, any normal person would—"

"No." She almost showed emotion. *Almost.* Her posture was perfection, her expression utter serenity. "We will not speak of that."

"It was a terrible tragedy—"

"The subject is closed." True to her nickname, her tone and her expression were cast of stone. "Sir," she added, conscious of how close to insubordination she skated. Zaafran would know what few others did. Only a few high-ranking officials had access to her personnel records and a need-to-know regarding her life prior to her selection as a cadet in the prestigious Royal Galactic Military Academy. Zaafran had every right to doubt her ability to carry out his orders; her connection to Arrayar Settlement cast her objectivity into doubt and thus her ability to function as captain of the *Unity.* She wouldn't fail, however. Her career was her life. Blast it all, her career was all she had left. She wouldn't let the Drakken destroy it whether directly or indirectly.

"I am not unbiased when it comes to the Horde," she conceded. "Who amongst us is, Prime-Admiral, after all these years of war? Yes, I may have more reasons than most to distrust them, but I will not let it interfere with my duty. I regret that my flippant remarks regarding shipboard assignments led you to believe otherwise. I will complete this mission as ordered." She shot him a sly glance. "You never said I had to like it, though."

His mouth twitched at her intentional humor. "There's something else not to like, I'm afraid. Your new second-in-command. We've chosen Finnar Rorkken. He holds the Hordish rank of Warleader."

"Rorkken?" The blood drained from her head. Rorkken, that bastard, that thief. The wily brigand who'd evaded her every effort to ensnare him. "He's the Scourge of the Borderlands!"

"Was," Zaafran corrected.

"*Was* one of the most notorious pirates in the disputed territories, I'll have you know. I came close to capturing him once or twice. Had my primary focus not been on protecting Coalition worlds from the Imperial armada, Rorkken would have been mine." Oh, how she'd longed for that face-to-face encounter: her triumphant, him in wrist and ankle cuffs. She'd have made him pay for the secret admiration she harbored for the man. "It's been years since I've heard his name. I assumed he was dead. Though in truth, I haven't given his pitiful soul much thought."

"He accepted a commission in the Imperial Fleet seven years ago. He's commanded a medium-size battle-cruiser ever since."

"But you mustn't forget what he was. Of all the Hordish officers to choose from, this is the best you could do?"

"He's the only Drakken of any respectable officer rank who isn't dead, in hiding or on trial for war crimes."

"My, what impressive qualifications—last cookie at the bottom of the box, and a broken one, at that."

"Or, if you'd rather, we can return you to the *Vengeance* while it sits in retrofit on Ninfarr."

Ninfarr. Not that damn stink pit. Brit drew her shoulders back. "My ship is not in need of a retrofit."

"Any ship can use a thorough go-over. One never knows what one will find that will require extensive repairs."

The prime-admiral's amusement at her indignation didn't quite cover the fact he was dead serious. Unless she cooperated, Zaafran would make her sit in Ninfarr for who knew how long, stuck in a locale she'd hate, out of commission and useless. "Your alternative is even more unpalatable than sharing the bridge with a Drakken."

"My hands are tied, Brit," he said, softening the blow. "The reunification laws governing the *Unity* insist that she be commanded by a former Coalition officer with a Drakken officer as the second. Rorkken was the best we could find for the reasons I've already stated. He's a good officer. I think you'll be pleased in spite of your reservations."

"Good, eh?" *The only "good" Drakken is a dead Drakken.* Brit took another, controlled sip of wine.

A noise at the office entrance signaled an arrival.

"Ah, he's here." Zaafran gave her upper arm a cautionary squeeze before striding away to meet the newcomer.

Two security guards entered the alcove across the spacious office. Then a barbarian stomped inside in heavy boots and stopped. So this was the Scourge of the Borderlands. Brit sneered, studying him in profile. His Hordish attire and adornments fluttered, tinkled and clanked in contrast to the clean and silent black uniforms of his escorts. He was formidable in build: lean, powerful, broad shouldered. His nose had a small hump where it was probably broken at some point. Other than that, he seemed to be clean-featured, even handsome in a raw, compelling way. *Good looks, wasted on a barbarian.* Like most Horde, his clothing revealed a good bit of skin. His tattooed flesh wasn't filthy or sweaty as she was used to seeing on his kind, but golden and smooth, although his uniform, if one could call it such, was faded and quite obviously mended by hand in several places. Brit couldn't imagine life without self-repairing nano-fabric.

Upon seeing Prime-Admiral Zaafran approach, the Drakken came to attention, bringing the knuckles of his right hand to his forehead. "Warleader Finnar Rorkken reporting as ordered, sir."

Zaafran answered with a fist over his chest. "How was your journey?"

"Long, sir."

"And your in-briefing?"

"Also long."

Zaafran chuckled. "I'll pass along kudos to Star-Major Joss for a job well done. Come, I want to introduce you to your new commanding officer."

Brit assumed an at-ease but impeccable posture as both men turned and walked in her direction. Rorkken slowed, noticing her for the first time. His eyes crinkled at the edges as they narrowed at her: warm, thickly lashed brown eyes under a pair of neat, dark brows that drew together in boyish inquisitiveness at the sight of her.

Her breath caught. *Seff.* Oh, gods. He looked like Seff.

Brit's heart convulsed like a wounded animal, her mouth going dry. How could this be? The Drakken resembled an older version of her long-dead husband, the love of her life, lost so long ago that she could hardly remember his face, the feel of his arms, the sound of his voice. Now he was here, standing before her in the very form of the monsters who took him from her.

The wine in her glass sloshed. She put the glass down on a side table with an overly loud clatter. Prime-Admiral Zaafran glanced at her with surprise. Rorkken, the shrewd bastard, contemplated her with a gaze that was far too penetrating and perceptive for her liking.

She couldn't seem to rip her focus from his face.

She knew exactly what he'd look like if he threw his head back and laughed. Grief simmered inside her, along with shock and joy, and attraction—physical attraction.

No. Damn it all, not that, anything but attraction for a Horde. There was only one kind of lust she was capable of feeling for a Drakken, and that was a lust for vengeance.

The bands of control were now clamped so tightly around her chest that she could hardly breathe. Her heart raced; perspiration prickled her skin. Brit Bandar was a mess.

Admiral Bandar, however, would reveal nothing.

She dragged her attention away, keeping her narrowed eyes averted until she'd gained control over what was displayed in them. Rorkken's resemblance to Seff was slight at best. Yes, of course it was. The barbarian was taller, and older. He was bigger boned; even the skin tone wasn't the same as her late husband's. In fact, the more her shock abated, the more she realized the differences she should have noticed in the first place. Yet that first impression had been enough to rip open the old scars, allowing her to feel what she'd worked so hard for so many years not to.

By the time she'd let go of the wineglass, resuming her impeccable military bearing only seconds later, she was certain no shock registered in her face. She was less sure about what she'd exposed in that moment of being caught off-guard, though. The warleader peered at her in bewilderment, as if he were unsettled himself. What had he seen?

Brit made the first strike, a defensive measure. "You're staring, Warleader. Do you not know who I am?" Her brow went up. "Or is it that you do?"

The warleader stopped to think before answering. Smart man, that. Prime-Admiral Zaafran interrupted. He seemed anxious to regain control of the proceedings. "Admiral Brit Bandar," he told Rorkken, introducing them. "The commanding officer of the *Unity.*"

Shock flickered in the Drakken's golden eyes. *Stone-Heart.* She saw him think it, as clear as day. Her mouth formed into a not-quite smile she knew he didn't miss.

Rorkken brought the back of his hand to his forehead in a salute. She'd expected he'd recoil in fear meeting her, to be somehow less than a man in her awe-inspiring presence.

Not Rorkken. The knowledge of her identity only intensified his interest, it seemed. She wished she could erase what she'd revealed to him but time could never be turned back. She of all people knew that.

"Admiral," he said. She was acutely aware of the tilt of his head and the timbre of his voice—*hell*—and the way he watched her with Seff's eyes—*double hell.* That damned physical attraction. How dare the barbarian make her think of Seff? How dare he make her respond to him as a male? "It is an honor," he finished.

He said it as if he meant it in the most respectful way possible, and yet…he pondered her as no man had dared ponder her in more years than she cared to remember. *He makes you feel like Brit again.*

She stiffened. Insolent bastard! Yet, she couldn't condemn him for disrespect if the interpretation of what she saw in his gaze was all hers. For the first time in her long career, she didn't know how to react. She chose what had always worked best: cold silence and a haughty glare. Her trademark, some said.

Rorkken's expression was unflinching. He seemed to be working hard to read her. "I don't expect you to feel the same about serving with me," he said.

"As a matter of fact, I'd rather cough up blood."

"And waste good blood? We Drakken would rather use it for a nice, warm bath."

Outrage boiled until she met his eyes and realized his remark was meant as a self-deprecating jest. He'd teased her. No one teased her. She was Admiral Bandar. No one would dare.

This Drakken dared.

Heat flared in her cheeks at the realization. Her reaction swung between hate, surprise and respect— hate for his kind, surprise that he recognized how society viewed the Drakken and respect for what appeared to be brash self-confidence moderated by self-awareness and intelligence, traits she didn't expect from a Hordish barbarian. Murderers, all, but she was going to have to find a way to tolerate this one. For duty's sake.

For her *career's* sake, she qualified. *"Any ship can use a thorough go-over. One never knows what one will find that will require extensive repairs."* Zaafran had given her no way out. It was either work with Rorkken or sit with the *Vengeance* in dry dock, far from the front lines. The choice was clear. Rorkken. Dry dock would give her too much time to think.

CHAPTER THREE

WHAT IN FREEPIN' HEAVENS just happened? Finn blinked, shaking his head. That was one hell of an introduction. It felt as if he'd been stunned by a plasma grenade. First the woman acted as if she recognized him. Then came the pain. In a flash of a moment, a half breath, her soul had been exposed for him to see. His reaction had been visceral. The snap of physical attraction hit him hard.

Finn couldn't merge the woman who'd locked gazes with him with the reality of who she was. *Stone-Heart.* She was gods-be-damned Admiral Bandar, and all he wanted to do was freepin' strip off that impeccable uniform of hers and put his hands on that sweet-as-sin body. *"Hey, sweetheart, why don't we get the hells out of here and find someplace to be alone?"* That's what he'd like to say. He could imagine how *that* would go over. This wasn't a Borderlands drinking hole, and Bandar wasn't just any female. He had to behave; he had to stop thinking of her as a woman, to stop thinking with his cock. To stop noticing her long, graceful neck, or the deep curve under her full lower lip that he wouldn't mind suckling.

To stop thinking about kissing her senseless.

Good thing he hadn't known what she looked like back in the old days, or he might have *wanted* to be caught. But it wasn't the old days any longer, and his worries ran far deeper. The loyal band of men and women on his crew were depending on him to come through. As first officer on the *Unity,* he had a shot at bringing everyone serving on *Finn's Pride* with him. He'd told them as much. He'd better hold up his end of the bargain.

Then what were you thinkin' telling the most infamous Coalition officer that you bathe in blood?

It had been a gut reaction to her pain, compelling him to lighten the mood with a joke, to put her at ease, to see if he could make her smile. Her name might be synonymous with war, but Brit Bandar *the woman* had been badly hurt. Whoever was responsible for that hurt, she still loved.

Finn had gone through life wringing humor from often-depressing circumstances—at times it was the only way he'd made it through with his sanity intact— but blast it all, he damn well knew when to be serious. This was one of those times. He needed this gig.

Unfortunately, his remark fed into what Bandar already believed about him: he was a barbarian. Closed-off and haughty, she fixed him with a glare, wearing her hatred for the Drakken like a war medal.

It was obvious she'd decided to pretend their initial reaction to each other had never happened.

He'd play along. He'd play almost any game with the prospect of starvation staring him in the face.

Nevertheless, he returned Bandar's cold gaze without insolence and without fear. He'd survived this long relying on his gut. Those instincts now told him an apology would be a mistake.

She'll see it as weakness.

"Please, let us eat." Zaafran waved almost too eagerly in the direction of the dining table. It was clear the officer sensed tension between them.

Turning on the heel of one flawlessly polished boot, Bandar glided after her superior. Nothing wrong with admiring her, ah…assets, Finn decided as he walked in trail. What man wouldn't? More than her beauty, he admired her grace. From the curve of her long, slender back to the sway of a very sexy bottom, every move was pure elegance. Street rat beginnings, a hardscrabble life, years in the military, he'd never been around a woman like her. A real lady.

At the table, Prime-Admiral Zaafran waited until Bandar had taken her seat at the table before he did the same. The officers' chairs glided to the table, subtly adjusting height and angle.

Smart chairs, Finn thought with dismay. He'd experienced the likes of one once already at his shipboard in-briefing and orientation with Star-Major Joss. It was not something he cared to repeat.

Finn remained standing, both in deference to the other two officers' higher rank and his not wanting to reveal his ignorance on advanced tech. Smart chairs were programmed to adjust to hundreds, maybe even thousands of individual seating and comfort preferences. Finn's wasn't one of them. Those occupied by the two admirals clearly were, but the one he'd occupied earlier had acted anything but smart.

He sized up his chair like he would an opponent in a fight. With as much of an air of cocky confidence as he could muster, he lowered his rump into the seat. The chair rocked, sliding sideways and almost colliding with Admiral Bandar's before Finn caught the edge of the table to stop himself. "They're not used to Hordish asses yet," he said with a chuckle.

A sidelong glance at Bandar revealed her expression of disdain. She thought him a barbarian; that much was obvious. His unfamiliarity with advanced tech served only to shore up that opinion he'd already reinforced by the bathe-in-blood joke. By the gods, he'd damn well prove himself worthy to be here, to serve with her. Just as he'd fought all his life to hold on to what rare good things came his way, he'd fight to hold on to this.

I'm skilled with a few things I guarantee you'll remember more than a chair, sweetheart, he thought, then jerked his wandering mind away from visions of sin with his new commander.

Zaafran waved off Finn's clumsiness. "The smart chairs on the *Unity* will obey you, Warleader."

"I damn well hope so, sir." Or he'd consider dismantling them all and tossing the scrap out the airlocks.

Black-uniformed aides circled the table, pouring wine. They, too, were clean and well-fed. Finn tried not to stare in wonder. Everything he'd seen so far while in Coalition hands was shiny and clean. It was truly the Realm of the Goddesses. The contrast to his world was sharp. *Your old world.*

The amazing feast so tempted him that he fisted his hands in his lap to keep from grabbing a helping until served. If only Zurykk and the rest of the crew were here with him. The food displayed on the table was far more than three diners could consume. Maybe he'd take some back for the crew.

You're not a street urchin anymore, living in a basement of a warehouse with a pack of other children. These are not stolen spoils brought into the den to be grabbed by ravenous hands.

Aye, he was a Triad Alliance officer now with certain behaviors expected of him. Triad soldiers did not stuff their pockets full of food. They didn't need to, Finn realized as he breathed in the aromas. Every day he'd be able to eat like this, and soon his crew, as well, gods willing. Rumor had it that the Coalition had plenty more where this came from. Now he knew the legends were true. They fed their warriors well. Hot meals would no longer be a luxury. If anything, Finn would have to be on guard against overindulging and going soft.

"Moor-steak?" an aide asked politely.

"Thanks be," Finn said, almost on a sigh, fists on his thighs to restrain himself as fragrant, grilled filets were added to his plate. It took all he had not to start eating before the meal was fully served.

He couldn't wolf down the meat like he wanted. He'd need to use proper utensils; he needed to make a good impression. At least until he got his sorry ass and his crew's sorry asses on that ship. Once everyone was aboard, it would be that much harder to get them off. Between now and then, he could afford no mistakes.

Finally, the aides backed away and left them to their meal. Finn's right hand was almost shaking in anticipation by the time he took hold of his fork. In the corner of his eye, he observed how the other two officers used their utensils and handled the consumption of the various types of foods.

He cut a slice of meat and slid it inside his waiting mouth. *Praise be.* He was a self-admitted carnivore; the taste and texture of the moor-steak nearly had him singing aloud. Another slice followed quickly, and then another.

He'd not had a meal this good in a long time. Perhaps not ever. Well, except for maybe the time they raided the prison warden's pleasure vessel on Indra.... Ah, well, he'd best not share that now; there was more than food to be sampled that night. Smiling, Finn took the largest socially acceptable bite of meat he could.

Chewing, he glanced up to find Bandar watching him with hooded, observant blue eyes while she sampled a delicate bite of a kind of fruit he'd never seen. Again, curiosity surfaced about the pain she'd revealed and the reason for it. Her eyes were a solid wall, allowing no hint of the woman he'd glimpsed earlier. It was almost as if he'd dreamed it. Maybe he had. A former Drakken street rat dining with two top Coalition Fleet officers on board the Ring could easily be explained away as a hallucination.

Enough thinking. Back to eating. Hungrily, he lifted a hunk of fresh bread to his mouth when Bandar interrupted. "When was the last time you ate?" she asked.

Finn worked his jaw. His first impulse was to lie. He detected no pity, yet to admit he and his crew had been existing on the brink of starvation wasn't something he took pride in. On the other hand, lying to her seemed distasteful on several fronts. "Yesterday. It's been weeks since we had a hot meal, though."

"Weeks?" Zaafran put down his fork.

Finn did the same with his bread, but gods, how he wanted to dredge the crust through a puddle of gravy on his plate and shove it into his mouth. Hordish tradition was to devour first, talk later, if they talked at all during a meal. Drinking, on the other hand, loosened tongues. That's where the talking occurred, not at mealtime. Dining was linked too closely with actual survival. "I've not had the money to feed my crew. The Imperial Fleet operated on a scrip system. We'd exchange scrip for legal tender. Now the scrip is worthless. I used up what real money I had left and most of the food and liquor last week bartering for repairs."

"You were forced to choose between repairs and food." Was Bandar appalled? Saddened? What? Why did that perfectly neutral blue gaze irk him so? *Because you glimpsed what is there underneath.* Aye, he was a pirate at heart. Once a pirate got a peek at the treasure, he wouldn't rest until it was his.

"I'm not the only captain having to make that choice. It's happening across the Borderlands, and across what's left of the Empire. They don't trust the Coalition, and what they'll face when they come into port. They'd rather risk starvation than spend their years rotting on a prison world. But with money running out, and the scrip worthless, it's getting mighty desperate."

"Desperation leads to instability," Zaafran said.

"And instability leads to war," Bandar put in. Finn had the strangest feeling she wouldn't be sorry to see peace collapse. "What do you suggest we should do, Warleader?"

Rorkken took a moment to ponder the rich meal in front of him, a feast that would remain an elusive dream for most eking out survival in his old haunts. "We make an effort to reach out to rogue Hordish ships and lure them into the Triad with the promise of food and fuel and a blanket pardon."

Bandar gave a soft cough, bringing her glass of wine to her lush lips. "Pirates serving on Coalition ships, and pardons for Hordish criminals," she muttered. "What is next?"

Stone-Heart laughing at one of my jokes, naked and in bed? Finn willed his tongue to stay put.

Bandar took a double-take at him. It was almost as if she read the mischief lurking behind his eyes. A flicker of pain showed in her face, and for a breath he thought her composure might falter again, but she replaced her glass carefully and returned her attention to her meal. To avoid looking at him, he suspected, but to his relief, at least they were back to eating. He hurried through what was left on his plate, in case they stopped again for conversation.

"I say a timely move would be to have the *Unity*'s first deployment be to the Borderlands, Prime-Admiral," Bandar said, continuing to dine, thank the gods. "I'm familiar with the territory, and we know Warleader Rorkken is. The warleader and I can discuss ways to lure rogue Hordish vessels out of the shadows." Her eyes met his. "A blanket pardon is out of the question. That will have to be decided on a case-by-case basis."

"If you're looking for a clean record, Admiral, you won't find it."

"The fact that you are my first officer proves your point, yes?"

"Aye, I'm the best of the worst, they tell me." He let out a self-deprecating chuckle. His chair rocked precariously. He grabbed the edge of the table to steady himself. Damn chair. "But before this voyage is over, you'll consider me the best of the best, Admiral," he vowed.

"I expect no less from any member of my crew, Warleader."

"Speaking of a good crew…" Finn took a breath and said what he'd come here to say. "There's space for seventy-seven Drakken on the *Unity*. I understand from Star-Major Joss that you're in need of seventy-six more. With the situation in the Borderlands unpredictable, do we want to delay here, waiting to round up stray Drakken?" He didn't wait for them to answer. "I have fifty-two on my ship. I would like to bring them aboard with me."

Zaafran sat back in his smart chair. "I don't know. I have some concerns about taking on a whole crew. Fragmented, their loyalty would be to the Triad and Admiral Bandar. Intact, their loyalty is to you."

"I'll talk to them, sir," Finn offered. "I'll explain what we require. They'll listen to me. They're hard workers." Without this chance they'll go hungry, he wanted to put in, but he'd better play the sympathy card as a last resort only.

Zaafran rubbed the side of his index finger across his chin. Food was once again forgotten. By now Finn was too concerned over the fate of the men and women who waited for him back on board the *Pride* to eat. "I assume you agree, Admiral," Zaafran said to Bandar.

"Actually, I do not."

They both glanced at her, surprised.

"Their loyalty to Rorkken may prove to be an advantage." Her plump lips closed around another berry. She chewed carefully, swallowed, the slender column of her throat moving. "They answer to Rorkken, who answers to me. If there is a problem, Rorkken remedies it. But there won't be any problems, will there, Warleader?"

She wanted this to fail. He saw it then. She wanted someone on his crew to start trouble, and they'd be off her ship, all of them.

"There won't be trouble, Admiral. I give you my word as warleader."

Which meant little to her, he sensed.

"I'll hold you to it, Rorkken."

"I won't fail you."

Something flickered in her eyes with his quiet tone. She dropped her gaze to her plate. Again, the wall had almost parted. Every time, it did something to his gut.

She turned to Zaafran. "I'll take Rorkken's crew, if that's acceptable, Prime-Admiral."

Zaafran waved a hand at the admiral in relief. The man was one step closer to getting them launched and out of his hair.

Finn folded his arms over his chest, his armor creaking. He'd won. Instead of celebrating that he got his crew on board, he was thinking about what a gods-be-damned long voyage it was going to be. First, there was something going on between him and Bandar that he couldn't figure out, but it had something to do with hate and hurt and one hell of a mutual sexual attraction. Combine that with patrolling the Borderlands with her wanting to hunt down rogue Drakken to arrest them, and him wanting to save them. If he were smart, he'd leave now.

Problem was, Finn had been hungry more than he'd been smart. He needed this job. He'd waged worse battles against worse odds than the one between his heart, his cock and this hands-off woman.

CHAPTER FOUR

SEVEN...FIVE...THREE... Standing shoulder-to-shoulder with Rorkken, Brit counted decks, willing them lower and faster. The ride in the lift from the floor that housed Zaafran's offices Ring level down to where the *Unity* was docked at gangway level was interminable. Brit never knew how long mere minutes could stretch out. Each one was an eternity. In the hours since lunch, her reaction to the warleader hadn't faded. It was more than a passing resemblance to Seff; Finnar Rorkken radiated what could only be described as presence. She could close her eyes and know he was there.

That was unacceptable, of course.

Finally, the descent was over. The door slid open with a soft hiss. Brit strode out first, hands locked behind her back, trying to give the impression she was employing a purposeful stride, not running away. Instinct urged her to flee Rorkken; attraction made her want to have him at her side. She boiled with self-loathing and lust, hating that she thought of him, a Drakken, as a man at all.

She'd spent a career serving with males. Few turned her head, few inspired more than a passing notice. Why this Drakken?

He looks like Seff. Yes, of course that was it. Why else would she be so drawn to him?

"Drawn" is an understatement, and you know it. She wanted him in her bed, inside her body, which was utterly unacceptable. Such an attraction must be eradicated.

She was a sexual being. Now those signals were misfiring, pointing her to the wrong target. If not for the interruption of her shore leave and playtime with the man-toy she hired she wouldn't be wrestling with such pent-up hunger in the first place. The fault was Zaafran's—yes, his and the entire Reunification Committee's—for taking her from the *Vengeance* and forcing her to take command of a freak show of a crew.

Heavy boots caught up with her. She gave Rorkken a sidelong glance if only to remind herself of what he was. *Not a potential lover. A Drakken.* Skin peeked out from under worn leather straps—the curve of muscle and bone, scars. She sped up to escape the sight.

Rorkken easily maintained her pace. He smelled of leather, and clean skin, spicy sweet, and faintly like that peculiar odor all Drakken carried. It made her want to retch. She was used to Drakken stinking like animals. There was that underlying smell they all had that she couldn't define. All she knew was it lingered wherever they were, and wherever they'd been.

"Shall we tour the bridge first?" he asked. "Or belowdecks?"

"The bridge."

"I'd hoped you'd say that."

She stiffened at the deep, almost intimate timbre of his voice. How many like him had purred in similar tones as they slit throats, or raped, and murdered little children? *Don't think of that.* She gritted her teeth until they ached. Arrayar was a long time ago, in another life that hardly seemed like it had ever belonged to her. But it had.

Rorkken's armor creaked, and the beads in his hair tinkled. A Drakken with Seff's eyes. She couldn't look at him.

You have to. He is your first officer. You can't talk to his boots. But she didn't trust what he might see if their eyes met. *Control, Bandar. You didn't become an admiral because you are soft.* Yes, she had to rise above her emotions. They had no place in this job. "My crew—my former crew—have been told to upload their gear to the *Unity,*" he continued. Everyone would stay on board tonight, even though no launch date had been set.

"Admiral Bandar."

Brit's heart leaped in relief at the reassuringly familiar voice as Lieutenant Keyren walked up to them. The girl had the misfortune of an open, honest face that couldn't conceal anything. Hadley glanced from her to Rorkken with clear concern and amazement. The only other times she'd seen Brit this close to a Drakken was during prisoner-of-war transfers.

Brit went through the formalities of introduction. "Warleader Rorkken, this is my executive officer, Lt. Hadley Keyren."

They exchanged greetings. "Nice to meet you, sir," Hadley said.

Her executive officer, calling a Hordish pirate "sir." The galaxy had changed overnight.

The next sight underscored that thought. The area around the gangway was crowded. Dozens of Drakken bustled about uploading supplies and equipment. Hairstyles of all descriptions, jewels and tattoos, outfits of leather and frayed fabric that could be considered uniforms only in the broadest sense: the sight of them hit her senses at the same time as their stench.

She halted, Hadley bumping up against her. "Sorry, Admiral."

The Drakken in the corridor turned to stare. "Stick your eyes on your work," Rorkken growled.

They went back to loading the ship, but dozens stole glances at her and Lieutenant Keyren. Hadley watched the scene as if it were a badly edited horror holo-feature. Perhaps in their new Triad uniforms the Drakken would look less like Horde, and more like…braided, beringed, tattooed Horde wearing Triad uniforms. Brit swallowed a groan. "I'll hold you responsible for any contraband brought aboard the vessel."

"Onto the *Unity?*" His eyes crinkled with a hint of amusement as they did each time she refused to call her ship by such a wimpy name. She despised that she amused this man. Did he have to be so damn attractive?

"Yes, the…" The name was too pitiful to utter. "No stolen goods. No stowaways. No hallucinogenic substances."

"As long as sweef doesn't fall under the category of hallucinogen, I can vouch for the contents of what they're bringing aboard." He wore that half smile again, as if teasing her.

She pretended not to notice. Sweef was distilled from the berries of a type of conifer and mixed with an additive used in robot hydraulics fluid. Homemade stills abounded on military ships. It was cheap, easy to make. Abuse rotted the teeth not to mention various internal organs without widespread use of nanomeds to reverse the damage. "I don't know how you Drakken tolerate the stuff. It's poison."

"Aye. But sometimes, a little poison is better than the alternative."

"And what is that?"

"Thinking. Thinking too hard."

Something in the Drakken's voice grabbed at her. She knew all about thinking too hard. She'd plunged herself into her career to avoid doing just that. She avoided thinking…thinking about the past. *Must never fall into that trap.* She swallowed, squaring her shoulders. "I want you to report to the ship's physician ASAP. Arrange for a full exam."

"I assure you, Admiral, I'm no alcoholic."

"I assure you, Warleader, had I suspected that you were, you wouldn't have set foot on…my vessel." The *Unity,* his glance insisted. "You have a cut on your right middle finger, on the knuckle."

"Ah. So I do. I think I'll survive without a doctor's visit," he added dryly.

"I should hope so. The fact that you have a healing cut at all indicates the low level of nanomeds in your system."

"More like no nanomeds."

Brit had never before spent time contemplating how the Drakken warlord had treated his own citizens. In the Coalition, health care and education were universal rights throughout the queendom. Not so in the Drakken Empire, apparently, where technology was hoarded by the rich and powerful. High-ranking Drakken she'd taken as prisoners over the years had shown high levels of nanomeds of various types in their bodies. Yet, this warleader had little or no protection from disease or injury. "You have full access to Coalition med-tech now. You and your crew will receive physicals and the proper maintenance nanomeds. You first. The rest as their work schedules allow."

"I am—we are—deeply grateful."

"Gratitude is irrelevant. I must have my crew in

top form for our mission. We can't afford downtime due to sickness. A physical body healing on its own is inefficient." And downright primitive. To deny citizens basic care was unimaginable. A crime.

Many Drakken carried some sort of stiff fabric draped over their arms. A whiff as they went by told her the fabric was the source of the terrible smell. "What are those?" she asked Rorkken.

"Their sleeping skins. Rakkelle!" He pulled a "skin" from the hands of a thin young woman with dark hair and a pretty face and unfolded it for Brit to view. It was the texture of sausage casing, transparent, but thick and lined with grommets.

It stank. She wrinkled her nose, found Rorkken watching her with that strange look again, his boyish eyes gone soft. "We hang them from the ceilings for sleeping," he explained. "They're then filled with blankets and pillows."

"On a modern warship there is no need for hammocks. There are bunks."

"The skins are more comfortable than bunks, ma'am," the girl broke in.

"Rakkelle," Rorkken growled under his breath with a shake of his head before Brit had time to reprimand her for speaking out of turn. "Ask permission to speak."

Good that the warleader didn't hesitate to discipline his crew. *Your crew.* Brit sighed quietly through her nose. Yes, they were hers, too, since she couldn't very well shove them through the airlock, as much as she would like to.

"Request permission to say something, Admiral Stone—" The girl reddened at her near error. "Admiral Bandar."

"Speak."

"Skins move with a ship. Bunks, they be land-folk beds, ma'am, rooted to the ground. A true spacer sleeps in a skin."

"Young lady, in my military, when you speak to a commanding officer, you do so giving your name and rank."

"My error, Admiral," Rorkken interjected. "This is Rakkelle of Pehzwan."

"Yes, ma'am. That's me."

"Doesn't she have a rank?"

"I'm the pilot."

"Your military rank…"

"I don't have one."

"She's *civilian?*" Brit thought of all the excuses she had to walk away from this mission now. Only, stubbornness and honor wouldn't let her use any of them. Instead, she assumed her trademark glare and focused it on her second-in-command. "Explanation, please, Warleader."

CHAPTER FIVE

FINN SWALLOWED A GROAN at the way Bandar's elegant brow lifted as she turned her appalled gaze to him. His plan had been to launch first, explain later about the patchwork nature of his crew. It was this gig or taking their chances in the Borderlands, hungry and on the run. Sure, the Triad seemed open to giving assistance to Drakken, but Finn didn't care to risk testing that generosity so soon after the war's end. Better to work with what he had: a miraculous invitation to serve on this ship. That meant talking fast and honest or risk having Rakkelle and the others blow his good intentions.

"I lost my pilot in a dockside skirmish just before the end of the war. I needed a pilot. Rakkelle was available. She's flown cargo freighters most of her life." And four different pirate ships. Best he leave out that part.

"I'm good, too!"

"Say, 'I'm good, too, *Admiral*,'" he instructed through clenched teeth.

"Admiral, ma'am." Rakkelle nervously slapped her knuckles to her forehead in a sloppy salute.

Finn rolled his eyes. "Get out of here, Pehzwan. Load the rest of your gear." He shoved the skin back into her hands. Her fingernails were dirty, he noticed. Bandar probably had, too. He thought he'd told Rakkelle and the others to clean up before coming aboard. Then he remembered that she'd been helping unload cargo. Well, she'd have a chance to wash soon enough. There were washrooms aplenty on this ship, some even in a crewman's own quarters. He knew his would have one. Utter luxury. He made a mental note to check their hands before the upcoming meal.

Rakkelle swaggered off, swaying her ass for the entertainment of the men in the crew as she draped her sleeping skin over her shoulder.

"She's an imp," Bandar observed. To his surprise, she sounded amused, but not in the bitter way she was with him.

"Aye, she is that."

"A little imp who'll be flying my ship. And she needs a bath."

"I'll make sure she gets one—all of them." He wanted to prove they weren't barbarians. Though all he'd been thinking about all afternoon was holding Stone-Heart's sexy ass in his hands and acting anything but civilized.

She pressed a finger alongside the bottom of her

nose. "The stench of those…skins is intolerable. Dispose of them."

He'd known the smell most of his life. He had to work hard to notice it. "Skins are a space-faring tradition. It's what every Imperial sailor knows."

"They'll sleep in beds, Warleader. Like soldiers, not pirates."

Rorkken almost fought her on that, convincing her that they had rights based on the Triad, that she couldn't convert them to Triad overnight. But he backed off. There would be other battles. A lifetime of fighting had taught him the bigger ones were better worth the fight.

Not to mention that he needed this gig. His crew needed this gig. If it meant painting their toenails pink to keep it, he'd freepin' consider it. The prospect of full bellies offset the small amount of ego lost in any concessions required to stay in Bandar's good graces long enough to launch this ship—with all of them aboard.

"I'll see that the skins are removed from the *Unity*," he said.

"Now, let us continue to the bridge, Warleader."

"Give me a moment with the crew, please, Admiral."

Bandar answered with a nod and continued down the corridor, trailed by her loyal lieutenant. "See that my shipboard quarters are set up," he heard her tell Keyren. "We won't be sleeping on the Ring tonight. All hands will sleep on board tonight, and until we launch."

Zurykk sidled up to him and murmured in his ear, "Don't expect me to start following you like that, Captain."

Finn laughed. The man would die for him. That was all he needed to know. "She doesn't want the skins aboard," he said when the admiral was out of earshot.

The crew met the news with grumbles. Finn's hand went to his sidearm—new, Triad issued. "Enough. We are on this ship by the goodwill of the gods. Don't push your luck. We sleep in bunks like they do."

"Why do we have to be the ones to give in?" his apprentice engineer Simi asked.

"Because we lost the war, fool," Zurykk grumbled.

Bolivarr spoke up. "It's more than that. If we want to stay here, we have to adapt to their rules."

He gets it, Finn realized with pleasure. Then again, sharp perception and willingness added weight to Bolivarr's claim that he'd been an Imperial Wraith before they'd found him unconscious and bleeding in a back alley with no memory of how he got there, thanks to several years' gap in his memory. The former elite commando was now a hitchhiker dependent on a captain's mercy. Bolivarr might understand Finn's reasoning for wanting to play along with Bandar's demands, but the admiral? If she was disturbed about Rakkelle, wait until she found out about Battle-Lieutenant Bolivarr.

"Besides, we're not to blame for losing the war,"

Bolivarr said with quiet conviction. "Our leadership, if you could call it that, lost it for us."

Finn sliced a hand through the air before any political arguments could start. "It's freepin' done. Over. The surrender is signed. Be grateful we're here, alive, warm and well-fed."

"When do we eat again, Captain?"

The grumbles changed to eager murmurs. They'd been grateful for the food he'd had sent down to them. "After the staff meeting. Food and drink for all. And it's best you no longer call me captain."

"You'll always be our captain, no matter what."

Looks of loyalty went around.

"Aye, I will, in more ways than you'll know. But we have a new captain—Admiral Bandar—and you will follow her orders as you will follow mine."

"Stone-Heart..." More grumbles.

"We'll follow her orders to the letter. As for bunks, that's what we'll sleep on for now—and like it. These aren't thin, lumpy, bug-infested mattresses, you oafs. We're talking luxury. A better night's sleep than these skins. Hot food, new uniforms, comfortable beds— we're moving up in the world, men and women."

Finn only hoped they could do so without losing who they were.

HADLEY SCRAMBLED to accomplish what Admiral Bandar had asked of her. The admiral's instructions had been curt and to the point. She wanted her quarters set up before the staff meeting. Everyone was being ordered to stay on board the ship tonight. It was typical of her commander to do such a thing. When you served under Admiral Bandar, you were her crew. You never doubted you were part of a team. Hadley wondered how the admiral was going to handle the motley crew she'd inherited. Apparently forcing them all to share the same finite space was one way to enforce crew unity.

Unity. Hadley liked the name. It was so much nicer than the rest of the ship names she'd seen, on both sides. Those nasty names were all posturing, in her opinion. Admiral Bandar needn't be alarmed by her new ship's name. The woman could command a toy bath boat and others would still steer clear out of deference or fear, depending whose side you were on.

Hadley dumped her personal possessions in a heap in the center of her new quarters. She'd unpack later, after making sure the admiral's captain's suite was set up to her liking. She was out of the room and back in the corridor a moment later, hoping the crate she'd ordered sent to the admiral's suite had been delivered.

An unfamiliar artificial voice thundered out of the ship's new comm system, echoing down the shiny new corridors: "Attention—all personnel. Call to quarters is in effect. All personnel will retrieve their personal items and proceed to their assigned quarters immediately. Attention—all officers. There will be a command staff meeting at oh-five-thirty standard ship-hours."

Hadley glanced at the digits glowing on her sleeve. That didn't give her much time to finish setting up the admiral's quarters. She hurried through the bustling corridors and almost collided with a group of Earthling officers on their way into the cargo area.

One of them was Tango. Sleeves rolled up and holding a box under one muscular arm, the pilot circled his finger at all the commotion. "Do you know what we call this at home, Hadley?"

She frowned at his use of her first name in public. "No, Major Barrientes—" she struggled with the pronunciation "—I do not."

"An ass-leaping-event, as in leap through your ass to get it done."

She put her chin in the air and ignored him. The Earthling pilot ran his hand over his short blond hair and laughed. "Man, there's nothing like an impatient admiral," she heard him say to his friends as he passed by. "They want everything now, now, now. They want to make their mark on the world."

Gods! He horrified her. He fascinated her. She waited until he'd walked by before she turned for another look, only to catch him winking at her over his shoulder, as if he knew she'd take a second peek. Oh, she hated him, too! Face ablaze, she turned back to the corridor ahead.

Tango's flirtation left her emotions roiling. She was relieved when she finally reached Admiral Bandar's suite of rooms at the end of a quiet corridor housing senior officers' quarters. One of the cargo rats—a crewman she'd served with on the *Vengeance*—was waiting outside the admiral's suite with the crate. "Got the admiral's things," he said.

"I'll let us in." Hadley submitted to the retina scan and walked inside.

The crewman slid the heavy crate through the door and straightened. "Gods, look at this. It's a blasted palace."

A palace to a space-hand, she thought, thanking him and shooing him out. Still, it *was* quite the suite, and with a view to die for. Hadley's quarters on the other hand had two square portholes. On the *Vengeance* she'd had one, so it was an improvement.

She made the bed with the admiral's sheets and blankets, plumping the pillows. Then she set to the unpacking. The crate held familiar items from Admiral Bandar's old quarters: several glass bowls and numerous holo-cubes from her travels. The images were exclusively scenery—the sea or sunsets taken on shore leave, never other people.

Hadley knew the admiral had family, but only because once she'd dared to ask. The admiral's parents were religious, extremely so. Admiral Bandar had been raised on a planet settled by pilgrims. Odd. The admiral was not a believer. Vehemently not a believer. Religion was a topic everyone around her learned not to bring up. It too often made the admiral irritable, and sometimes even pensive.

Hadley strived to do anything but upset her. Admiral Bandar was her hero. She remembered the emergency drills, growing up on her home planet. Then one day the drill was real. They were under attack. The Drakken ships were destroyed by a warship under the command of Admiral Bandar when she was still only Star-Commander Bandar. The admiral had saved Hadley's planet. From then on, Hadley was determined to model her life after the admiral's. She was the first female from folksy, clannish Planet Talo to win an appointment to the Royal Galactic Military Academy, and the youngest graduate to be selected as the admiral's executive officer. The miracle of Hadley's existence was having the honor of serving in a capacity to make the officer's life easier. Although it was her dream to someday rise up through the ranks and captain a ship of her own, she learned so much from watching in her day-to-day routine as Admiral Bandar's assistant.

Hadley's thoughts returned to the Earthling pilot, and his disrespectful words. With four brothers at home on Talo, she knew he'd been trying to show off. That unsettled her almost as much as his rude observations of her boss. Maybe even more. It wasn't often she was in a position to be flirted with. On the *Vengeance,* most of the other junior officers were intimidated by the fact that she was Admiral Bandar's exec. What did they think—if they broke her heart she'd turn them in? It was her darkest secret that she was still a virgin. It would stay her darkest secret, too. What twenty-three-year-old was still a virgin? Maybe now on the *Unity*, she'd finally have a chance to expand her social horizons.

With the Earthling? He was handsome. He was exotic, too, being from Prince Jared's homeworld. If only he wasn't such an ass!

With reverence, Hadley placed Admiral Bandar's items around the suite. The admiral would no doubt fine-tune the arrangement, but after so many years of working with her, Hadley had developed an almost infallible sense of what the woman liked. She reached into the container for the last item. It was a medium-size white engraved box she was used to seeing sitting on a shelf high above the admiral's desk. It was a pretty box, but ornate, and had seemed out of place with the admiral's taste for clean, unclut-tered decor. Hadley had always wondered about the box, and what was inside. It was larger than a con-tainer for jewelry, big enough for some items of clothing. She'd once guessed books or dinnerware but now she saw it wasn't that heavy.

Her hands slid over the lid's engraved surface. And stopped. It felt wrong, peeking. Head held high, she carried the box to some shelves by the admiral's new desk, placing it at the same approximate spot as on the *Vengeance.* She stepped back, admiring her handiwork. The admiral would be pleased.

Hadley's gaze traveled back to the white box. So much about her boss was a mystery. Would it be so wrong to learn a little more about her? In the end, it might help Hadley be a better assistant.

Biting her lip, she took the box down from the shelf and set it on the desk. Nervously, she glanced at the door. *All clear.* Then she lifted the lid.

A small folded blanket lay on top, hiding the contents beneath. It was soft and pink, nothing like a blanket the admiral would use. Cute, chubby marr-mice decorated the satin hem all the way around. It was a baby blanket, Hadley realized with a start.

Heart pounding, unable to stop herself, she lifted the blanket out of the box, even though she knew what she'd stumbled upon was a terrible violation of her commanding officer's privacy.

Under the blanket was a bracelet, a silver band. Hadley turned it in her hands. It was engraved. *Me and you forever. Seff.* There was an old, worn leather volume of the *Agran Sakkara,* the religious tome that formed the basis of their worship of the goddesses. But the admiral wasn't a believer… The bible was badly damaged, the cover torn, the pages crushed. Hadley ached to open it and see if anything was written inside, as some families were prone to do. She forced herself not to. It was bad enough she'd opened the white box.

Only one item remained—something small and wrapped in tissue paper. Fingers shaking, Hadley peeled the sheets away. Two tiny white shoes dropped into the palm of her hand. Tiny confections of utterly feminine satin and lace. Hadley held the fragile shoes cupped in her palm. They were too small to have fit anything but a newborn infant.

The admiral's daughter. Hadley gasped. It felt as if a hand had tightened around her throat. There had been a baby. Admiral Bandar's baby. Why else would you keep a baby's shoes if it wasn't your baby? A niece, maybe, but Hadley doubted it. If it was the admiral's infant, what had happened to it?

Hadley traced her finger over the engraving on the bracelet. Had it been a gift from the baby's father? Admiral Bandar's husband? What happened to them? Why hadn't the admiral ever mentioned either one?

A wave of guilt washed over her. These were the admiral's private things. Hadley never should have seen them.

Hurriedly, she put everything back in the white box, checking it twice before she closed the lid to make sure everything inside was arranged as she'd found it. She slid the box into place on the shelf, surrounding it with the holo-cubes that always circled it. Backing away, she fumbled for the entry door and her escape. She'd learned secrets she could not share with anyone else.

Brit's hands gripped each other at the small of her back as she stormed off the lift toward the bridge. She was used to having Hadley in tow. Even Haldran, her former first officer, would lag behind her. Not Rorkken.

Damned Rorkken. He matched her stride for stride, and without evidence of exertion.

All Brit wanted to do was retreat to her quarters. She'd ordered Hadley to set up her shipboard suite right away. A mental image of Kin-Kan wine chilling came to her. She'd down the first glass as fast as she could; the rest she'd savor.

She turned the corner and walked onto the bridge of the galaxy's newest warship. Her steps slowed as she took in the sweeping command center, the clean lines of the pilot and weapons stations. Outside the generous banks of viewports, the graceful arc of the Ring could be seen. She walked to the forward view window at the very bow of the ship, her heart singing despite her reluctance to take this position and all it demanded of her, and placed a hand against the cool, clear surface. She imagined a vista of stars. Ah, gorgeous.

Her hand closed into a fist. Damn Zaafran. He must have known how she'd react to this ship with the absurd name. It felt right here. Yes… She brushed fingertips along a polished railing. It was almost like coming home.

Rorkken stopped beside her, shattering the moment. The scent of his skin came to her, unwelcome, generated by the heat of his barely clad body. She'd ordered everyone to don their new Triad uniforms. Rorkken would, too, after their tour was complete. His transformation couldn't come fast enough. It was bad enough being constantly reminded he was Horde that she didn't need to keep being reminded he was a virile, well-built male, too.

She blocked the very thought.

"Gods, she's magnificent," Rorkken said. "The heavens have surely gifted us."

"You're a believer."

"You sound surprised," he said.

"You're Horde."

"Trillions of Drakken have been worshipping in secret under the warlords' rule."

"For all the good it did them," she muttered.

She sensed his surprise in the tensing of his body. "You're not a believer?"

She snorted softly, bitterly. "No."

"I didn't know there were those in the Coalition who weren't."

"Well, we've learned a little more about each other's cultures today, haven't we?"

"Aye…" His eyes, Seff's eyes, found hers. To her dismay, they glowed with gentleness, and that look of curiosity, the desire to know more—more about her. When was the last time any male wanted to know *her?* To know Brit? Shivery bumps raised on her flesh. Damn him. Damn him to the dark reaches and back. *Murderers, all.* "There is little time to waste, waxing poetic about a ship. Let us continue with our tour." She turned away from the viewport just as her PCD beeped.

"Incoming urgent message," a dulcet artificial voice announced in her ear.

Rorkken brought his hand to his ear, as well. Apparently he'd been fitted with a PCD, too—and didn't quite know what to make of the interruption, judging by his startled expression. *Welcome to the world of no privacy,* she thought, remembering her aborted shore leave. *Wherever you are, the Coalition Military will find you.*

Or, rather, the Triad.

The comm screens burst to life. Each one framed an image of Prime-Admiral Zaafran's face. *Secured transmission* scrolled underneath the image. "There you are," he said, finding them. It was a visual only. His voice came over their PCDs. "There's been a change in plans."

Brit knew him well enough to discern the tension tightening his mouth, and the fear—the *fear*—in his eyes. The man didn't scare easily. Neither did she, of course. Then again, when you had nothing left to lose, fear was rather futile.

Rorkken must have read Zaafran's anxiety, too. He walked closer to one of the screens in his heavy boots. "Sir?"

"We've already received reaction to the galactic press release sent out a short time ago announcing this ship and its diplomatic mission. That reaction came in the form of a generalized terrorist threat against the *Unity*. We have to take it as legitimate."

Brit sent a sidelong glare at the warleader. *Don't you people ever stop?*

"Intelligence is working on tracking the source of the threat. In the meantime, I don't want us sitting here, vulnerable—the entire Ring vulnerable. The Ministry of Intelligence and the Reunification Assembly approved an accelerated launch schedule. I realize we're shy of the mandated numbers of personnel. We'll deal with that, but not now. As long as you have exceeded the minimum complement required by space regs for a ship this size, you're good to go. And you do have those numbers. The *Unity* will depart as soon as all personnel are aboard."

"We're launching…" she confirmed with Zaafran.

"Now."

"Gods," Rorkken muttered.

Brit couldn't have said it better herself.

CHAPTER SIX

EVERYONE WAS ON BOARD. Launch was imminent. "I damn well want to know who you've brought aboard before we break dock with the Ring, Warleader," Admiral Bandar ranted inside the luxurious new command office Finn would share with her during the voyage. It had direct access to the bridge. That door was now closed. Finn couldn't help thinking this was Bandar's best and last chance to kick him and his motley crew off the *Unity*.

The terrorist threat hanging over their heads gave her little time to peruse the *Pride* personnel list he'd loaded on a borrowed data-vis: names, planets of birth, ages, past and present assignments, anything he could get out of them with Zurykk's help, but Bandar was taking time all the same.

She sat at her desk and scanned the data-vis with narrowed eyes. If the luck of the gods held, she wouldn't decide to send one or several of them home once she saw who was on that list. Hells, she wanted to send all of them home, him for sure. That much was obvious.

Bandar slid her elegant finger down the list, saying nothing. Her dark brows drew together in a frown. "Hadley, leave the warleader and I to confer for a moment."

"Yes, ma'am." The lieutenant walked away and out of earshot.

Finn folded his arms over his chest and stood before her, facing her across the desk. "Sit, Warleader," she said, tapping a light pen against her chin as she read.

"When the smart chairs on this ship stop being stupid, I'll sit."

She lifted those cool blue eyes. "Put in your preferences—hard or soft feel, a quick response, or slower and smoother. Everyone is different. What do you like?"

Hard and fast or slow and smooth? He swallowed. Gods. In his mind, they were naked and she was breathing those questions in his ear. He caught his thoughts and stopped them, but not before he saw a flash of heat in her eyes chased by alarm and that damned vulnerability again. It got to him every time. And heavens knew what she saw when she looked in his eyes if that's the reaction he conjured in her.

Her gaze was back on her gods-be-damned personnel list before he'd let out his breath. There was no denying the sexual pull between them. There was no denying they both found it damned inconvenient.

"I'll stand for now," he said hoarsely, avoiding the chair.

"As you wish, Warleader," she responded with equal huskiness.

He cleared his throat and tried to pretend he wasn't battling sexual fantasies starring Admiral Stone-Heart.

"There is an irregularity with a crew member named Bolivarr."

His Imperial Wraith. Finn gritted back a sigh. He'd really wanted the man along. His gut told him his knowledge of Drakken and Coalition intelligence would be useful—once the wraith remembered it.

"Is there no given name?" she queried. "Or is it his surname that is missing?"

"Bolivarr is his only name, according to him. He was an Imperial Wraith." It was best to jump right in with the truth. "I found him out cold in the street on Junnapekk Station, a mining world in the Haydes Belt. He'd been stripped naked and beaten. No ID, except for his wraith tattoos. No weapons. I believe he was left for dead. If it wasn't for the nanomeds in his body, he would be. He'd lost a lot of blood."

"You took him, not knowing who he was?"

"If I didn't take him, no one else would have. He'd have died. We'd lost a few space-hands in the weeks prior. Outside the injuries, Bolivarr looked strong and in good shape. I figured, if he lived, I could use the extra man."

"You list almost nothing between his years at the Imperial Military Academy and the time he came aboard your ship."

"He remembers nothing of that time."

She lowered the data-vis. "Or so he says. Wraiths are assassins, like our REEFs, only without the bio-engineered implants. Their activities were so covert, even your own military feared them. They are masters of deception, of survival."

"I hear what you're saying, Admiral, and gods know I thought the same, but I believe what he says. I'm a good reader of people. I can see a truth or a lie in a glance. It's served me well."

She'd gone pale with his admission that he read others well. He knew she was thinking about the look they'd shared, worrying what he'd figured out about her. He'd seen the pain, aye, but it didn't mean he knew the source of it, he wanted to reassure her. He kept his silence. To reveal what he'd seen would be a mistake.

"Admiral, Bolivarr has a deep hatred of the dead warlord and the Drakken government, and doesn't know why. He asked me for asylum, and I granted it. He's been nothing but a model officer ever since, a source of calm in crisis."

Again, she tapped the light pen against her chin as she pondered the information he had given her. He had the feeling she was contemplating him as much as she was the subject of Bolivarr. Finally, she said, "Your wraith might very well be of use to us, hunting strays in the Borderlands. More so if his memory returns."

"Our wraith," he reminded her.

"No. Yours, Warleader. I will hold you fully responsible for him and his actions on this ship."

Yes, he thought, breathing a sigh of relief. Bolivarr was on.

"I want both of you to see the ship's physician, Dr. Kell, for full exams after the launch. Have the medical reports sent to me."

"Aye, Admiral. And thank you."

At the gratitude in his tone, she frowned.

"I know," he said. "I don't have to thank you. I will all the same."

She slipped the data-vis in her uniform pocket. "Call an all-hands meeting immediately. I want to speak to the entire crew before launch."

He came to attention. "Aye, aye."

THE SMALL SIZE OF THE CREW was apparent when the number of bodies filled up only two-thirds of the main briefing room. Rather than speaking from a dais constructed for that purpose, the admiral paced the floor in her usual way: head held high, posture erect, her expression cold and observant. Finn was certain she'd already examined every man and woman's face in the audience, and had drawn opinions based on what she saw in them.

He shared the floor with her, on her orders. It was an important sight for the crew to see—a statement. He was Bandar's second, no question; he shared command of this ship. Coalition, Earthlings and his own crew would not miss the symbolism. As much as she seemed to despise him when they were alone, in public she acted almost civil, and certainly fair. She was a professional, that's why, a professional who no doubt regretted revealing her emotions to him in Zaafran's office earlier that day. Would she punish him for it all the rest of the voyage? Gods, that could be years. Or so he hoped. He was determined to make this gig last…. The luxurious quarters, the delicious food, the well-made uniforms, he thought, running a hand over his new Triad gear with its fancy commander epaulets. *Rorkken,* he thought with a sizzle of pride. *You've finally made something of yourself.*

He'd never known his mother (or his father, for that matter), but if she were in the heavens looking down at him right now, she'd be proud.

Bandar finished briefing the crew on the relevance of the terrorist threat. "We will launch immediately following this briefing. The official word, however, is that we'll be docked here for another week, awaiting personnel and supplies. We'll be light-years away from the Ring before anyone can make good on their threat of blowing us into plasma dust."

Noises of approval went around the room, evenly split amongst the various groups sitting separately by choice. It was less easy to discern the Coalition from the Earthlings, now that everyone was wearing Triad uniforms, but the Drakken still stood out with their jewelry, tattooing and hairstyles. Bandar would notice. At least they were bathed and clean. Aye, one step at a time.

"If you take one thing from this first meeting," Bandar concluded, "I want it to be that we are in this together. Together as the new Triad Alliance." Her conviction was evident in her voice if not her eyes. He alone knew what she really thought about the Drakken presence here: *"I'd rather cough up blood."* The professional in her didn't reveal her personal opinion to the crew. It was no secret why she'd gone so far in her career. One could be a great admiral but not a great leader. Brit Bandar was both.

"Those are our orders. And that is what Warleader Rorkken and I will enforce. If anyone on this ship has a problem serving with any of the groups aboard, speak now, and I will have you escorted off the ship. It will not reflect negatively on you in any way."

No one moved so much as a finger.

"Well then. Do you have anything to add, Warleader?"

"No, Admiral, I do not."

She nodded and turned back to the crew. "I'm sure you all are eager to take up your new duty stations and launch this impressive vessel." Her gaze flicked in Finn's direction. "The *Unity*," she added, meeting his smile with a withering gaze. "Before you do, there is some business to take care of."

She pulled the data-vis from her pocket. The Drakken crew list, he thought with a sinking feeling that increased when she called out, "Uroo Markar, Seljon Silubakk and Rakkelle Pehzwan, come forward."

The three looked confused. Finn wasn't. They were his three civilians. It was illegal to have civs on a military vessel performing military jobs. In the half-dismantled Drakken Fleet, it hadn't mattered. It mattered here. It mattered now.

He'd thought when she perused the list and asked about Bolivarr that she'd made the decision for the civs to stay, as well. He'd failed them because of that assumption.

Wasn't there a better way to dismiss the trio than in front of the entire ship? He ought to be the one to take care of it—in private—since it was his fault they were here. He tried to capture Bandar's gaze, but she ignored him.

He heaved a sorry sigh, placed his hands behind his back, striking a relaxed pose for show, and asked the gods above for mercy on his crew.

Rakkelle swaggered to the floor, casting hot glances at anyone who'd look, and there were a lot of looks. Markar followed her nervously, Silubakk in trail, sullen.

When the three stood in front of her, Bandar walked around them, inspecting their new uniforms. Markar was sweating. Even Rakkelle fidgeted where she stood. Then Bandar stopped, facing them, as cool and composed as stone, her namesake. "The *Unity* is a warship. Civilians are not allowed to serve on a warship."

Rakkelle visibly deflated. Finn could see the disappointment in her eyes. Like it was for all of them, this had been a big break for the pilot, an amazing stroke of luck. Rakkelle would not want to lose this chance any more than the rest of them would. The fact remained, however, that she'd never been in the military. She'd never even had any formal pilot training, learning through real experience with pirates willing to teach her to fly for gods-knew-what in return.

Finn sighed. He'd do all he could after the meeting and before they were evicted from the ship, but his options were limited if Bandar insisted on their dismissal. Aye, it looked as if he'd have to bid the trio farewell.

"Markar, Silubakk, step forward."

Yes, Admiral, Finn mouthed, coaching them as best he could from afar.

"Yes, Admiral," they chorused to his relief.

"You men now hold the official Triad rank of space-hand apprentice." She attached Triad rank to their shoulders. The men were stunned, but no more than Finn.

"Rakkelle Pehzwan."

"Yes, ma'am!" With the prospect of staying on board now looking promising, she'd perked up. She practically jumped forward to stand in front of Bandar.

"Your situation is different, I'm afraid. You're a pilot. In our military system, pilots are officers. I can't make you an officer with no training."

"Aye…" Rakkelle looked suddenly smaller, under-fed. Like a sad stray.

"I have another solution."

Rakkelle's eyes widened as Bandar fastened two small patches to her shoulders. "Cadet Space-class Pehzwan, your academic and military training will run concurrently with your service aboard this ship. Should you prove worthy, you'll be commissioned with the Triad rank of ensign."

Rakkelle whooped, pumping her fist.

Bandar's nostrils flared in disapproval, and Rakkelle blushed. "Sorry, Admiral. Sorry! I'm just so…" Rakkelle met Finn's furious glare and snapped to attention. Somehow, she managed a salute that wasn't half-bad. "Thank you, ma'am. I will prove worthy of my promotion."

Bandar returned the salute and dismissed the trio.

They returned to their seats where they were welcomed by a rowdy contingent of Drakken. Finn shook his head. Zurykk and Bolivarr quieted them, but not before they'd won dark looks from some on the Coalition crew. A treaty wasn't going to erase centuries of bad blood overnight.

Especially where he, Bandar's unwanted, Hordish second-in-command, was concerned. Why hadn't she informed him of her decision to promote his crew members? She had to have known the solution would please him. Did she intend to leave him out of the loop the rest of the voyage? *I think not.*

Bandar turned to him. "Have all hands prepare for launch."

"All hands prepare for launch!" Finn repeated, shouting the order to the entire room. Then he placed his body between her and the audience. "Admiral."

"Yes, Warleader?"

"I didn't know you weren't dismissing the three civs until you pinned rank on their shoulders. I didn't like the surprise."

She lifted that blasted brow. "You don't agree with the decision?"

"It was your making it without my knowing that I don't agree with." He didn't miss her surprise at voicing his disapproval before the chill returned to her expression. He was a fool to confront her before the launch and while there was still the opportunity to remove him for insubordination or any other reason she might choose. Yet, as hungry as he was for this job, he had no intention of being a figurehead while performing it. He had his pride—as an officer and as a man. "I do thank you for what you did, especially for Rakkelle. I am grateful, and so are they."

"Again, your gratitude is misplaced. This is a military ship. No civilians allowed."

"You could have kicked them off."

"We're short-handed."

She refused to accept thanks for her kind acts. Her hatred of his kind was well-documented; perhaps she didn't want to be caught showing mercy to the

Horde. Yet her demand that he and Bolivarr see the ship's physician and her giving three Drakken civilians what amounted to battlefield promotions fell under the definition of *compassion,* whether she was ready to admit it or not.

Her hands were behind her, clasped tightly and pressed to the small of her back, a sign of tension she might not think was obvious, but he did. Street rat turned pirate turned battleship captain Finn Rorkken missed little when it came to body language. He never would have survived this long if that hadn't been the case.

"Thank you for sharing your concerns, War-leader." Her voice was calm but definitely strained. She turned and walked toward the private lift they'd ride up to the bridge.

As they waited for the door to open, he pressed his point. "I'm your first officer, the second-in-command on this ship. Drakken I may be, but I intend to be more than a square-filler on some politician's postwar, we're-one-big-happy-family checklist. When we work together as one, the crew wins. If neither of us knows what the other is doing, the crew loses, and the running of this ship will be nothing less than chaos."

"Chaos…" She waved a hand at the room that was noisily emptying—noise that came from mostly his people. "You'll feel right at home, then, yes?"

Finn winced, his irritation now directed at the Drakken. "Aye."

"There's something that will require our working together—ship's discipline."

"I have a few ideas."

"Beyond threatening to kill or maim errant crew members?"

He sensed a shift in the mood. Was it her way of letting him know she'd deemed valid his concerns about joint decision making?

"Don't look so surprised, Warleader, former *Scourge of the Borderlands*. I well know pirate methods. Years back, I captured quite a few of them, trying to get to you."

He flattened his hand over his chest. "And now you got me without even trying."

"I'm still analyzing the irony," she said dryly.

"So, what will it be for me, Admiral? Brig or bridge?"

With a wry, sidelong glance, she warned, "Don't tempt me, Warleader."

Gods be. He'd actually gotten Stone-Heart to respond to his teasing. Perhaps there was hope yet.

They boarded the lift. A charged silence filled the small compartment. It was that way every time they were close, and alone. He knew it had to do with what had happened between them in Zaafran's office earlier. Again he wished he could take back that moment.

No, you don't, Rorkken. It haunted him. Maybe he'd get her a little drunk one night, and she'd tell him more. It was the way of the Drakken, that. Drink and tell. Drink and…

Gods, she's your commander. You can't bed her.

A man could dream, couldn't he?

Bandar burst out the door as soon as it opened. Personnel assigned to the bridge quietly prepared for the launch. The group consisted solely of experienced Coalition from large ships such as the *Vengeance*. The unexpected departure had left no room for anyone else to be trained for their new positions. Over time the new people—Earthling, Horde— would be sharing these jobs. In that, the terrorists had scored a small victory, Finn thought: the galaxy's newest ship had the greenest crew.

Bandar remained at the view window until the very moment of departure. "The crew's ready," Finn announced when it was time.

Without turning, she issued her command. "To the Borderlands."

"To the Borderlands!" Finn repeated to the crew.

A thundering vibrated beneath his boots as the great ship broke dock with the Ring. The *Unity* turned, slowly, gracefully, until it faced the stars. With a surge of awe-inspiring acceleration, it was off.

To the Borderlands, Finn thought. *Here we go.* Although he very well might live to regret it, he was glad to be going along for the ride.

CHAPTER SEVEN

BRIT TOOK SHELTER in the command office in the hours following the launch, busying herself with administrative details that didn't need to be addressed as of yet but that she did anyway. Any distractions from the dizzying events of this single, interminable day were welcome, no matter what form they took. From her desk in the luxuriously appointed room, she heard the various goings-on outside on the bridge but her relative isolation was assured.

She'd divided the crew duty day into thirds as it was done on all Coalition naval ships—one shift on, two off. Brit was technically off duty and Rorkken was on. Star-Major Vinnson Yarew, an intelligence officer, was third. She didn't know him, but his background was in the Ministry of Intelligence located in the palace on the planet Sakka. Since she steered clear of the palace and Yarew preferred ground to a deck beneath his boots, it was no surprise that they hadn't crossed paths. He seemed pleasant enough, a loyalist with a stable if dull career, and was a sensible addition to the crew. Unlike Rorkken.

Once more, she peered through the glass wall that offered a view of the bridge. Arms folded over his chest, Rorkken observed one of her senior pilots from the *Vengeance* instructing the Earthling, Major Barrientes, and the Drakken girl Cadet Pehzwan at the controls. He then walked over to a nav holo-vis, leaning his hands on a table as he studied the star routing. She supposed when confronted with a source of clean, running water and orders to use it, Drakken weren't so grubby after all. His hair was neatly combed, secured in its ponytail. He'd shaved. The glittering earrings were still of notice, but the tattoos were mostly out of view. She'd hoped the Triad uniform would diminish his good looks and blend him into the background along with the other males serving on the ship in the same way every male she'd served with over the years had done. Alas, it had not. He was as handsome in his Triad tri-colors as he'd been in his leathers. Although she had to say she missed the peeks of golden flesh.

Brit... She admonished herself, forcing her attention back to the personnel lists she was studying. It seemed a cruel game of the gods to make the first man she'd reacted to in all these years a Drakken. Little wonder she didn't believe!

It's only because he resembles Seff, she reminded herself.

Less and less, common sense argued.

But enough, her conscience shouted back, *needing* that reason, needing an explanation, any explanation, to desire this man. After that horrible day on Arrayar, she'd never again looked at another man, never responded to flirtations or sexual invitations. Rumors that she preferred women to men never lasted; she made it too plain that she wasn't interested in either gender. Human contact, the physical closeness she craved, had to be satisfied while on shore leave on distant planets with men who wouldn't demand that she give more than a few nights of sex. She couldn't give more.

And yet, she couldn't change who she really was, either. She was a sensual, sexual being and had always been that way—much to her devout parents' dismay—leading to her early marriage. But after Arrayar, her focus changed. *She'd* changed it, redirecting her passion to war. It had worked out quite well. She was the highest-ranking military female in the Coalition forces. *The Triad Alliance,* she corrected, watching that damned pirate Finnar Rorkken patrol the bridge of a ship that should have been transporting him to a prison planet rather than providing him with a uniform and a paycheck.

And purpose. Purpose, yes. He didn't want to be a square-filler, a figurehead, he said. He, a Drakken, wanted to be her second in the truest sense of the word.

And what had she gone and done? She gave it to

him! She hadn't refused his request to share in command decision making. What was she going to surrender to him next?

"Admiral."

Brit jumped at the sound of Hadley's voice in her PCD. "What is it?"

"I have the medical report you requested."

"Bring it here."

Brit swung her chair around to face the clear wall as Hadley crossed the expanse of the bridge, headed toward the office. The lieutenant's pace accelerated past the training pilots. The Earthling Barrientes swiveled in his seat to follow Hadley with narrowed, interested eyes. Hadley kept her chin in the air, but pink cheeks revealed she was as aware of the handsome officer as he was of her. She hurried through the open door. "Here are the reports, Admiral," she said breathlessly. "Dr. Kell says you are to call him if you have any questions."

Brit hid a small smile. "What do you think of the new Earthling pilot?"

"Ma'am?" More blushing. The lieutenant was going to have to learn to keep her face free of emotions if she was ever going to rise through the ranks. She had the smarts to do it. Perhaps not the hardness required, nor the experience. Brit made a mental note to wean Hadley off some of the administrative duties that ate up her time and assign the girl more demanding tasks as opportunities arose.

"The Earthling," Brit clarified. "He seems to be paying some attention to you. What do you think of him?"

"I think he's an ass." Hadley's blush deepened.

Ah. So, her lieutenant had indeed developed a soft spot for the pilot. Brit opened the data-vis that held the doctor's report. "I don't believe he sees you in quite the same light."

"Really?" The girl started to look over her shoulder and stopped. Then she frowned. "Do you require anything else, ma'am?"

"No, Hadley. You are dismissed."

So, the Earthling was an ass, was he? Unsuitable men did have that certain allure, Brit reasoned, her eyes returning to Warleader Rorkken. The Drakken scratched a hand over his chest, laughing at something his little imp of a pilot told him. He was far more than simply unsuitable. He was wrong on every level. He was Horde.

Frowning, she opened the report the ship's physician had sent to her and used her light pen to follow along. As ordered, Rorkken had visited the medical ward and submitted to tests. The findings were listed in several columns. Dr. Kell's text provided translation of the figures:

It is my personal observation that Warleader Finnar Rorkken is a male in good health.
Age: approximately 35 standard years.

Birth date: unknown.
Birthplace: unknown.
Father: unknown Mother: unknown.

Irritated, Brit scanned the data. She wanted answers, not more questions. Unknown, unknown, unknown! What, did he arise from the seas? Appear spontaneously in a birthing basket? It would seem that way. If Rorkken was to be believed, he'd had no formal schooling or medical care until he was twenty-seven, which corresponded to the approximate year he enlisted in the Drakken Imperial Navy. Preposterous! How could so many years be a blank?

She read on.

Warleader Rorkken reported to me several prior injuries and illnesses of note. At a young age, he contracted what he thinks was Harkoo Fever. It may have been; however, most often the virus is fatal in young children. The most common consequence of the virus is a damaged heart. However, the warleader's cardiovascular system is normal.

So, he'd survived a fever *and* without consequences. Twice lucky, she thought. The man had the luck and lives of a kir-cat.

Warleader Rorkken's body scans confirm he has suffered fractured ribs, broken bones in the arm, wrist and nose, as well as dislocations of the shoulders. Several body scars can be classified as significant. The warleader refuses cosmetic removal of the scars at this time. However, he consented to a transfusion of nanomeds. Blood count after one ship-hour showed normal acceptance and replication.

He'd consented to nanomeds because she'd asked him to. That pleased her. She couldn't have him running around with no way to self-repair.

Eyesight: above average.
Hearing: slight degradation of the left auditory nerve likely due to the high fever associated with Harkoo; otherwise within normal range.
Strength and endurance: well above average.
Intelligence, mental acuity: exceptional.

Exceptional, eh? She scowled. A smart Drakken was a dangerous Drakken.

Doctor's note: Bone and teeth analysis show signs of uneven enamel. The likely cause is extended periods of nutritional deficiency in infancy and childhood. Nanomeds will repair and rebuild the loss although not all damage will be repaired fully. I recommend a follow-up exam next month.

Nutritional deficiency in infancy? Brit blinked. Rorkken had starved as a baby?

In a miasma of shock and concern and disbelief, she read the text a second time to make sure she'd comprehended it. The words remained the same. Rorkken, the strapping warleader, had been a hungry orphan.

She threw down the report. Damn him! Damn him to the dark reaches. She made fists on the desk, her head throbbing. Of all the things she hadn't wanted the Drakken to become, human topped the list.

CHAPTER EIGHT

WELL INTO HIS FIRST SHIFT on the bridge, Finn went about his duties, cross-checking the route and star charts even though the shipboard computers did so much more than those he was used to on Imperial Navy vessels.

What about the computers in his body? Would they be as efficient? He turned over his hand and scrutinized the plump veins in his forearm. Already a few small scratches he'd gotten from unpacking his few possessions had shrunk. More changes were taking place throughout his body; he could feel them. All his life, he'd lived with a faint humming noise in his left ear. It had gone away. As much as the thought of foreign bodies in his bloodstream made his skin crawl, he realized the accelerated healing would come in useful in a battle situation.

If not, there was Dr. Kell. The man had poked and prodded, assuming Finn would give him a free pass into any orifice he chose. The doc soon found out otherwise. *"Don't bend over,"* Finn told Bolivarr, who'd been on his way in as Finn was leaving. His warning had left the former wraith looking uncharacteristically worried.

"That's it—you got it. Bring her in, yes, like that." One of the more experienced Coalition pilots was giving the Earthling Tango and Rakkelle the first of their official training on the flying of the *Unity*. Finn walked over to watch.

"This is cake," Tango told the instructor, completing a simulation of a docking and receiving with, from what Finn could tell, perfect scores. "Give me something hard."

"I know a few men on my crew who wouldn't mind helping you out," Rakkelle said saucily.

Tango snorted. "I don't blow that way, girl."

"That's what you say." Rakkelle took the controls for the identical docking simulation. "I'd have to see for myself before I'd know if you were telling the truth."

"Is that a dare?"

Rakkelle's eyes had that saucy spark Finn was well used to seeing. "In my world, men know the difference between a dare and an invitation." She winked and turned back to the flying simulation.

Tango's smile was one of self-congratulatory speculation. Rakkelle was flirting, and the pilot was eating it up. Aye, but the woman flirted with everyone, Finn included. He decided not to enlighten the Earthling. Let him figure it out for himself.

Rakkelle completed the docking maneuver with

praise and a few pointers from the instructor. Tango stood, leaning over to tell her, "Looks like you might be better off concentrating on your flying for a while, Cadet. Hooking up with me would be too distracting. For the sake of our mission, and your chances at becoming an officer someday, I wouldn't want to interfere with your instruction. And you'll need it if you're ever gonna be as good as me, Rocky."

Rocky? Finn choked on a laugh. Rakkelle looked shocked and amused, and maybe a touch annoyed. If he'd thought Rakkelle was cocky, she didn't come close to Tango. The Earthling was full of himself, as a soldier and as a male.

The pilot swaggered off, no doubt in the direction of the bar, which, at last report, was in full swing. Zurykk was keeping an eye on things, making sure no fights started that weren't Drakken-on-Drakken. If trouble erupted between factions, Finn didn't want anyone from the *Pride* listed as instigators. Although now that they were under way, if Bandar wanted to evict him or his crew, there would have to be some discussion involved.

Or so you hope, Rorkken.

Across the bridge in the office, Bandar sat at her desk, her hands in fists as she glared at data. Gods knew why. It wasn't her shift, it was his, yet she was still up. Combing the crew manifest for more civilians or wraiths? Judging by her expression, she might have found some. Gods, he hoped not.

They weren't that far from the Ring that she couldn't turn the ship around. Of course, there was the terror menace waiting if they returned. For once he was grateful for a death threat. It would likely keep him and his crew on this luxury vessel of a ship— for a little longer, anyway.

Or would it? He looked in Bandar's direction again, and not only because he liked looking at her. He worried about her. Anger had definitely replaced the signs of exhaustion he'd spied earlier, however. Aye, something she'd read had made her very unhappy.

A few hours' sleep would fix her right up, he decided. She needed to go on break. He'd told her twice already in as many hours, to her withering looks, naturally. It was clear she didn't like him addressing the issue of her crew rest. She probably wasn't used to it. She'd existed for so many years in an isolated world where she took care of others and few returned the favor. He'd say none did, but he sensed a good deal of affection for the admiral in Lieutenant Keyren. Still, it was clear that Bandar didn't like anyone looking out for her, especially him.

Too blasted bad.

Finn strode across the bridge and stopped in the doorway to the office. Arms folded, he leaned a shoulder against the door frame. "Once again I've come to ask you to go on break, Admiral. This time I'm going to have to insist. You need your rest." The observation came out gentler, more protective than he'd intended.

She glanced up, her eyes blazing with fury—anger that morphed into a startled softness before settling into something with which he was more familiar: aloof poise edged with intense dislike. "Worry about your duties, Warleader, not me."

Perhaps she considered his protective tendencies sexist. That wasn't it at all. He'd grown up with women, fought side by side with them. He knew well a female's strengths, and her weaknesses, but this woman, Brit Bandar, did something to him. She brought out a desire to look out for her, and more. *That is your problem, not hers.*

She returned her glare to the report she was reading.

Funny girl, thinking he'd be so easily dismissed. "What's there that's got you so concerned?" he asked. "Whose records are in question? Bolivarr? Gekken? Meer?"

Or perhaps it would be better not to volunteer information.

"Yours," she blurted.

He reared back. "Mine? But you know what my records contain."

"Not this." She shoved the data-vis toward him. He squinted at the contents. It was a medical report of some kind, filled with figures and readings. A flicker of dread went through him. "What did the good doctor find? A deadly disease that nanomeds can't cure?" He tried to joke. "How long do I have, Admiral? Weeks? Days?"

"As much as I'd like it, you're not going to die. The report shows evidence of childhood hunger in your bones and teeth."

The doctor had left no stone unturned, he thought. Or orifice unchecked. Finn ran his tongue along his teeth. Straight and white they were, although it was likely more from healthy genes than anything else. "I'm sure Dr. Kell can fix me if I go toothless." He flexed his arms. "And the bones seem to be holding up, when I don't go doing something stupid that breaks them."

"Blast it, Rorkken. Broken bones are one thing, but no child should go hungry. Dr. Kell thinks you went for long periods without adequate nutrition as a baby. Is it true?"

Finn hesitated until he'd shoved aside his personal distaste at revealing his beginnings, lest it generate pity, which he despised. "Aye. It is."

"Damn it. What's wrong with the Horde that they couldn't look after their own people? They poured money into their warships, yet you starved as a baby. That is unconscionable." Then compassion blunted her usual harsh tone. "You lost your parents. How?"

"I was orphaned as an infant in a Coalition attack. From what I learned, and it isn't fact, I was rescued from the site of the attack and brought off-planet."

"And what—abandoned there?" she demanded.

"Probably offered up for adoption, but few could care for their own kids let alone someone else's."

She turned her chair to face the blackness of space that filled the view window on the opposite wall. "You were left to die."

"Aye. Luckily, I was found and taken in by other children. My earliest memories are of the girls who raised me. We belonged to a pack of orphans and runaways, or throwaways, taking shelter in an abandoned building behind a refinery. It was easier to survive in numbers in some ways, harder in others." Like when there wasn't enough food to go around, or blankets or sweaters. "I grew, and I survived. And here I am." Enough talk of the past. It was the future that interested him. He aimed his attention at the reflection of Brit Bandar's face in the window. "And here you are, when you're supposed to be off duty."

She turned around. "I have more reports to go over."

"They can wait. Your shift is long over."

"I will remain here, Warleader."

In two strides he was at the desk. He bent forward and flattened his hands on the glossy surface. "I pledged to run a safe ship, even if that means making sure command of the bridge isn't handed over to her captain if she be exhausted. That's right. With all due respect, Admiral, if you come on duty in less-than-optimum condition thinking you'll be alert for an eight-hour shift, I'll make sure Star-Major Yarew sends you back to bed. I'll carry you there myself if I have to, and we both know how entirely inappropriate *that* will be."

The hunger always simmering between them boiled over, instantly doused as each pulled back from the attraction they weren't supposed to feel. Finn regretted the joke. The image of her in his arms as he lowered her into bed was slow to fade.

"Inappropriate indeed, Warleader." It wasn't his imagination that her voice sounded huskier, or that she pondered him with the same speculative consideration that Tango had given Rakkelle.

Finn aimed for a neutral, professional tone. "So what will it be?"

Her attention shifted to the bridge behind him. It was humming with efficiency. She wasn't needed. Her routine reports could wait. Yet, she seemed reluctant to leave.

Of course. He was Drakken. He was the Scourge of the Borderlands. How could one of the Coalition's greatest commanders leave him in charge of *her* ship, unattended? Oh, she'd vowed as much to her superiors, aye, but putting it into practice was not as easy as it sounded.

She didn't trust him.

"Permission to speak freely," he said.

"Not asking permission hasn't stopped you so far, Warleader, so why ask now?"

"To be able to speak freer."

She huffed. "I would expect any second of mine to speak freely and, more important, to think freely."

"Here it comes, then." He folded his hands so that

he supported his weight with his knuckles. "You don't like the idea of leaving a Drakken in command on the bridge."

When her lips compressed, just slightly, he knew he'd guessed right. "I know the same stories you do, Admiral. I know Horde often killed civilians on purpose. Blame it more on a lack of discipline and guidance from the higher levels and a lack of good example than any government orders. I'm no innocent, but I never killed for sport, Admiral. Nothing about killing ever appealed to me."

"But you stole, you hijacked ships, you bribed and kidnapped." She rattled off the charges against him, and even where many of the crimes occurred.

His mouth tipped in a crooked smile. "Is your memory that good, or did I alone of the Borderland pirates remain in your thoughts all these years?" As the memory of her had remained in his.

"So cocky, aren't you, Warleader? Well, it's not about you. I have a memory like a steel trap. I don't forget." Pain flickered in her eyes before she cast them downward.

She'd lost friends in battle. So had they all. Finn understood the pain of losing comrades. Aye, he'd spent one too many days trying to forget that pain— namely by drinking too much sweef. "In this business," he said quietly, "a good memory can be a curse."

"A curse indeed."

"And a bartender's blessing."

She let out a sound that might have been a laugh if it had contained any mirth at all. Then she jerked upright. It was as if she'd caught herself identifying with him and the idea repulsed her. She was cool and composed when she spoke again, but her hands were twisted together. "Is that all, Warleader?"

He sighed. He wasn't any closer to reassuring her of his presence on the bridge. He owed it to his crew, to the Drakken people who weren't murderers, who didn't slaughter for entertainment, to convince her to have some faith in him. "The war is over, Admiral. I intend to do my part to keep it that way. I want peace to work. You know my story now. I'm sure you have stories of your own. This war long ago ceased being good for either side. Horde and Coalition, we've all suffered."

Her hands were clamped together so tightly that her fingers were turning red and white. She sat there, perfectly still, as if she were carved of ice. Finn knew the woman was anything but. *Fire, not ice.* "You can sleep easy knowing this Drakken is on the bridge, Admiral," he assured her. "You can trust me."

She lifted her gaze then and studied him for the longest time, all while he watched her battle with her reservations—comparing what he'd said to what her experience told her. In the end the officer in Brit Bandar won out. Logically, she saw she couldn't stay on duty all hours of the day. Nor could Yarew. At some point, she had to let him take command.

She nodded, rose, stepped around the desk. Then, with her new Triad colors hugging her curves, she walked out of the office.

No good-night, no comment. She simply left.

Into that, he'd have to read the best: she trusted him, if for this night only.

IT WAS LATE, and Brit was alone. Surrounded by holo-cubes of her infrequent travels, she sipped Kin-Kan wine and stared out at the stars distorted by faster-than-light travel. For so many years, these solitary dinners had been her routine. Her solace. They reminded her of her mission, what she'd pledged to do three standard weeks shy of her nineteenth birthday. Hunt the murderers. Hunt the Horde.

Finnar Rorkken, she thought with a scowl, the Scourge of the Borderlands at the helm of *her* ship. He wanted her to trust him, because he wanted peace to succeed. She wanted peace to fail. That put them at permanent cross-purposes, didn't it?

She swallowed more wine, holding it in her mouth, savoring the taste. *You can trust me,* Rorkken told her. He'd observed her with those eyes so much like Seff's, and she knew he spoke the truth.

He's a good officer, Zaafran had said. Brit didn't want Rorkken to be a good officer; she wanted an excuse to see him and his fellow Horde off the ship. He'd revealed the hardships of his youth, but she didn't want to know him; she didn't want to see him as a human being. Didn't he know doing so turned her neatly ordered priorities upside-down? She despised "upside-down." She wanted life to go on as it always had. Shake her up and the past might come back. Shake her up and she might *feel*.

Damn you, Finnar Rorkken.

That was quickly becoming her mantra. She emptied her glass, grabbed the bottle and realized it was dry. Blast. She'd finished it already? Where was the needed blur of drunkenness?

She'd take the blur of pleasure.

She loosened her hair and shook it out. Then she slipped between the cool sheets. They adjusted instantly to her preferred temperature. She slid her hand over her belly, and lower, closing her eyes. She tried to picture Seff's face as she touched herself, as she always did. But as her body tightened, coming quickly to climax, it was Rorkken's face that she saw.

Brit cried out softly as she shook her head in denial. *No.* She rolled onto her belly, grasping the pillow with both hands as her body throbbed for the completion. It was her attraction to Rorkken, damn it. That's what had her so unsettled.

What was she going to do? It was clear she couldn't go on like this. To get rid of a craving, sometimes you had to have your fill of it. Maybe she should indulge in Finnar Rorkken. He'd fuck her good and hard, like the man-toys she bought on shore leave always did, and then she'd be immune to his charms from that point on. It wasn't the most pleasant of prospects, nauseating in fact, but what choice did she have? She needed her focus back, her drive. She needed the Drakken pirate out of her head. To do that, she needed him in her bed. Yes, it was no longer a matter of if she'd put her theory into practice—but when.

CHAPTER NINE

HADLEY SCURRIED after Admiral Bandar as the woman headed swiftly down the corridor toward the gym. She hoped the admiral planned an exhausting workout. Hadley had been run ragged by her commanding officer before, but not like this. The past two days had been a blur of orders. She'd not made any errors, but she was terrified she soon would. Not that the admiral had ever berated her, not once during their three-year tenure together, but it would pain Hadley immensely to disappoint her greatest hero.

A group of Drakken walked past them in the corridor. One was tall and lean, the one with the tortured dark eyes that some were whispering had been an Imperial Wraith. Bolivarr, his name was. He nodded at Hadley. His gaze was deep and searching. It didn't make her blush like Tango's did. It made her flush with heat and shiver at the same time. She swallowed and turned her eyes away as she gave a polite nod to the group.

"Good day, Admiral," the Drakken greeted the admiral.

She growled something in reply. At first the admiral had been cordial to the new crew members eager to gain her favor after her impromptu promotions—but she'd been in an ugly mood for two solid days. It seemed to intensify whenever Warleader Rorkken was around.

"Hadley," Admiral Bandar said as she walked swiftly toward the gym. "Do not wait for me. I'll return to my quarters on my own."

"Yes, ma'am."

"Have my room scented and the bedding turned down."

"Yes, ma'am."

They passed by the bar. It was crowded. Music vibrated. The scent wafting out was an acrid blend of alcohol and sweat. She craned her neck to see inside.

Tango was leaning against the bar as she hurried past. *Yes, ma'am,* he mimicked silently.

Hadley scowled. Whipping her head around, she ran to catch up with the admiral.

She followed her boss into the locker room. This was the time of day set aside for senior officers to exercise, but none were here. Everyone had already gotten wind that the admiral liked to use the gym at this time each day, and avoided the place.

Admiral Bandar stripped out of her uniform, handing it to Hadley, who replaced it with a towel.

She couldn't help sneaking a peek at the admiral's toned, flat stomach as the woman pulled on her workout pants. She thought of the tiny shoes, and tried to visualize Bandar pregnant. If she narrowed her eyes and tried really hard, she could definitely imagine a rounded belly on the admiral.

"Is there something wrong, Lieutenant?"

Hadley almost jumped out of her skin. "No. No, ma'am." Guilt swamped her for snooping into the admiral's private things. She prayed it didn't show on her face.

"It's been a busy few days for us, Hadley. Have you partaken in some of the recreation activities on board?"

"No, ma'am."

"You should. Officers need to be able to unwind from the day in order to best do their duty."

"Yes, ma'am. I'll do that, ma'am." At least Admiral Bandar wasn't angry. She had an amazing amount of patience with her. She merely shrugged in that stoic way of hers and snapped the waistband of her athletic pants around her trim hips. "No need to wait until I begin, Hadley. Have you been to the bar?"

That caught Hadley off-guard. She'd rarely gone to the bar on the *Vengeance.* It was boring, and few felt comfortable socializing with her due to her closeness to Bandar. "Why, no. I have not."

"Go. Have a drink. Or two."

Was it her imagination, or had the admiral just winked? The admiral turned on her heel and headed into the lightball court, leaving Hadley holding her uniform, heavy with a career's worth of decorations.

Hanging the uniform, Hadley thought of the bar. And of Tango. She wanted to see him. She didn't want to see him.

Her legs seemed to have a mind all their own as they pulled her toward the door and into the corridor. A drink, or two. Why not?

She wondered if Tango would still be there.

FINN WAS ON HIS usual midshift patrol. After his shift was over, Star-Major Yarew came on duty, who was then followed by Admiral Bandar. Finn didn't like to go right to bed; he enjoyed walking the corridors of the ship, getting to know her, getting a feel for her, like one would with a new lover.

He snorted at his comparison. What would he know of getting to know a lover? When had he last stayed around long enough to learn a woman? Or even to care to get to know her? He had no experience in the matter. He had the feeling in his gut that forming permanent relationships was in his blood, his makeup, but his career had never allowed it. He did not cross the line and sleep with subordinates, which ruled out all the females on his crew. When it came time to order someone into combat, he didn't want feelings mucking it up. Beyond that one rule, he had none. His romantic entanglements had always been brief flirtations and casual affairs with no promise, or even hope, of any long-term commitments. It was a space-hand's life.

Finn rounded the corner where the ship's bar was located. He stepped inside the noisy room. Out of instinct his hand went to his pistol. No need of that, he reminded himself, his eyes adjusting to the dark. It was civilized here.

Despite the best attempts of the unification committee, the members of the Triad sat separated into its three components, although Finn saw some mingling amongst the Earthling and Coalition.

"Good eve, Captain."

Finn tracked the quiet greeting to its source. "Good eve to you, Bolivarr." Preferring solitude, as was the preference of wraiths, the former assassin sat alone at a table, his hands curved around a glass of plain water. Several others from the *Pride* sat at tables nearby, concentrating on twisting small cubes made of multicolored squares. Their drinks were hardly touched. Bolivarr was one thing, but the rest of the crew not drinking?

"Is there something wrong with the liquor?" Finn grabbed a glass and brought it to his nose. "It smells good. A cut above our usual swill." A few cuts, he thought.

Markar slammed one of the colored cubes down on the table. "I give up. It's impossible."

"What is that?"

"The Earthling gave them out. He called it a Roob... I can't recall."

"A Rubik's Cube." Tango sauntered over to them. "Hello, Warleader." He took the cube from the table, gave it several methodical twists and then held it up for all to see. Each side was now a different solid color. "Not so impossible." He then twisted it back to multicolored and tossed it back to Markar.

The man tried to reform it. Bolivarr observed the man's struggles with a pitying glance.

"Can I try?" another crewman asked.

"Take the freepin' thing," Markar snarled. As soon as his hand was empty of the puzzle, he was sucking down his untouched drink.

Finn noted a strange object in the hands of another crew member—this time a Coalition officer, and ensign. It was a brown glass container with writing he couldn't decipher.

"Corona," Tango said. "It's beer. Earth beer from a country called Mexico, though in Texas, where I'm from, it's practically the state drink. The cargo bay's filled with cases of beer." He beamed a smug smile around the bar. "I feel it's my duty to spread the word—my planet's culture."

Gods help us all, Finn thought. "How are the flying lessons going?"

But the pilot was no longer listening. His attention

had fixed on the bar's entrance. Bandar's pretty assistant walked inside the bar. Clearly shy, but pretending not to be, Lieutenant Keyren held her head high and walked to the bar, where several Coalition officers she evidently knew huddled over drinks. She joined them, avoiding looking at Tango, who had eyes only for her.

Hadley alone? Where was Bandar?

Finn made his way over to her. "Off this eve, Lieutenant?"

"Oh, yes, sir. Admiral Bandar's in the gym."

"In the gym…" Hmm. "Thank you very much." He started to go and paused. "I think you have an admirer." He pointed to Tango. The lieutenant turned red as she scowled.

Finn chuckled and left the girl with her companions. Tango stopped him on the way out. "Buy you a drink, sir?" he asked Finn.

He shook his head and patted the Earthling on the back. "Buy one for the lady."

Leaving Tango behind, he continued on his walk. Bandar was in the gym, he thought. Doing what? Curiosity overtook him. He checked the time. It was the period reserved for senior-officer workouts. He flexed his arms, rubbing a bicep. He hadn't done much in the way of exercise since he'd arrived, having not yet settled into a routine, but he didn't want to go soft, did he? With a grin that felt almost feral, he turned in the direction of the gym.

TANGO CAUGHT Hadley's eye and winked. She turned away quickly. Didn't she know she'd end the evening in his quarters, cuddled close for a showing of *The Devil Wears Prada?* It was a chick flick, and Hadley was a chick, even though technically she was an alien. She'd love it. She'd love him.

He made his way through the crowded bar, her cute blond head centered in his sights, as he absorbed the sights and sounds, just a boy from Dallas far from home. Not so far in some ways. Advanced tech, light-years from Earth, it didn't matter: a bar was a bar. It didn't make a difference if you were in Texas or on a spaceship.

He sauntered over to Hadley and leaned an elbow on the bar. She sat perfectly erect in front of a tall, thin glass filled to the top with electric-blue liquid. "What the hell is that?"

"Poru punch."

"Punch," he scoffed. "Is it alcoholic?"

"Yes."

He lifted the glass and sniffed. "Barely. It's a girlie drink."

She grabbed the glass away from him. "I'm a girl."

"Hell yeah, you are that."

He loved that he could make her blush. How many women her age still blushed? "A Bud," he told the bartender. Then he dug in his pocket for the trinket he'd been carrying around. "Your hand, please."

"My hand?"

"Do you always answer all statements with questions?"

Her pretty little mouth twisted with displeasure. "When the statements make no sense, yes."

He snatched her right hand and pulled it toward him. She resisted, pulling back. He found her huge blue eyes and said, "Trust me," in his deepest, softest voice, the one he knew worked every time. She relaxed. He smiled. Ah, his sweet Hadley, his ripe little apple: fresh and juicy, and just a little bit tart. She was going to taste so good going down. "I have something to give you. A ring."

"A ring?"

"There you go again. More questions." He calculated the slender width of her fingers and slid the ring up her index finger. "There." He held up her hand so she could see. "Like it? It's called a mood ring." She didn't need to know they were Chinese imports that cost two bucks apiece and that he had a bag full of them as part of his "trinkets for the natives" collection like the Rubik's Cubes. He aimed to be the self-proclaimed Johnny Appleseed of Earth, planting Earth culture across the galaxy, from Coca-Cola to mood rings, to grow and flourish. So what if the mission was unsanctioned? Ol' Johnny didn't have official backing, either, when he went west a couple of centuries ago and started planting apple trees in the Ohio Valley.

Hadley pulled her hand away, turning it from side

to side to admire the ring. Her cheeks flooded with pink. "You brought this all the way from Earth?"

"Indeed, little lady. Just for you."

"Thank you. It's beautiful." She sighed. "As gray as a winter sky on my home world."

"Gray? Let me see." He'd been banking on deep purple—purple for passion.

She wriggled her fingers. Sure enough, the ring had changed to gray. It didn't bode well for his effect on her.

"Is something wrong?" she asked.

"The colors reveal your mood." He pulled out the tiny guides he had made up in her language and handed it to her.

"Gray," she read, scanning the page as if committing it to memory. "Anxious, very nervous, strained…"

"Beer, Earthling." The bartender slid a frosty longneck toward him. He popped the top with a louder-than-usual fizz. The pressure was slightly lower here on the ship than it was at home.

"Here, try this, Hadley." He offered her the bottle. She sniffed delicately, took a sip and grimaced. "It's bitter. And bubbly." She handed the bottle back. "I don't like it."

"Ah, man. I'll have to find a way to wean you off those fruity girlie drinks." He took a long, deep swig, suppressing a belch. "Ice-cold heaven. I just hope what we Earth folks loaded lasts a while, or I'm in trouble."

"You can always drink sweef," a deep voice said.

The tall, lean Drakken officer he'd seen observing him had appeared on the other side of Hadley. Bolivarr. Everyone seemed to know who he was, yet the guy said next to nothing. Rumors were flying. If they were to be believed, Bolivarr had done everything from eating small children to serving as a martial arts trainer to the dead warlord. Somewhere in between, Tango figured. "That hydraulic fluid that passes for alcohol?" he scoffed.

"Too strong for you, Earthling?"

"Dude, I don't see you drinking none."

Bolivarr pushed away from the bar. Tango started to follow, but Hadley grabbed his arm. "Major Barrientes, don't."

"It's Tango. You gonna come have some sweef with me and my Drakken friend?"

"Tango, sweef's really strong."

Her blue eyes were huge and worried. She didn't think he had what it took to keep up with the Drakken. Shit. All the more reason to take Bolivarr's challenge. So far, Tango had done nothing but un-impress Hadley. It was time to reverse the trend. He'd just gotten off duty, and didn't go on for another sixteen ship-hours. Plenty of time for sweef to metabolize through his body.

"Come on, girl. Keep me company." He took her warm, soft fingers in his. Again there were those few seconds of resistance before she gave in. Hand in hand, they made their way over to the Drakken table. The men were hunched over some kind of dice game.

The way they looked up, in unison, their expressions hard and suspicious, reminded him of a scene out of an old Western, the city-bred sheriff meeting the local gunslingers for the first time.

Tango had flown fighters for his entire career. He'd seen combat time in Iraq. Then he'd gotten on with the Thunderbirds. He'd always considered himself a soldier, but looking at the hard faces of these Drakken, he knew he hadn't seen the kind of war they had. The bloodshed. The despair. They were too young to look the way they did.

He let go of Hadley and tossed a Rubik's Cube onto the table. It skittered across the table and stopped. "Keep it. Payment for my drink."

They frowned at the cube and then at him. "What the freep is this?" one said.

"A Rubik's Cube." He demonstrated. "It's a puzzle. Exercises the brain."

"Children play with toys," someone muttered, downing a shot glass of sweef.

Tango let the comment roll off. The boys would have to warm up to him. Bolivarr said quietly, "The Earthling says he's never tried sweef."

"Major Barr— Tango." Hadley tried to caution him again.

One of the men pulled the stopper off a black bottle.

"Wait a second, baby. I gotta sample a little sweef."

Hadley made a small sound of dismay. A Drakken poured him a shot glass full of the liquid. It was mostly clear with a hint of amber. It did look disturbingly like hydraulic fluid. Tango lifted the little glass, aimed it all around the somber group and tossed back the contents.

He choked, sputtering. It felt as if someone had aimed a blowtorch on the back of his throat. Eyes tearing, he managed to choke the rest down.

The Drakken were watching him, their tattoos visible, their earrings glinting. *Wuss. Sissy. Girlie man. Weakling.* It didn't matter in what language or in what slang they were thinking, he'd just failed their test.

He tried for his best smile. "Ah, man. That hit the spot." Like napalm. Vertigo unsteadied him. He stared at a fixed spot on the table until it passed. "I'm a Texas boy, and one is never enough. I'll have another. Who'll join me?"

CHAPTER TEN

I'VE GOT TO GET HIM OUT of here, Hadley thought. Tango was irritating and arrogant, but he was also naive. He hadn't spent a lifetime at war like the Drakken had. They, too, saw him as naive. She could see it in their faces. Except for Bolivarr. She caught his attention, controlling the shivers those dark, soulful eyes conjured in her stomach to aim an accusing glare in his direction. *Why'd you encourage him to come over here?*

Hadley groaned silently when Tango sat down with the group. If he drank more sweef he'd regret it. Her only chance to help was to coax him to leave.

"Tango…" Hadley tapped him on the shoulder. "I want to watch that holo, the Lord of the Dark Reaches dons Prude."

"The Devil Wears Prada," he corrected, reaching for a fresh glass of sweef. "And not holos—movies. Baby, you will have that chance. I promise you that."

She tipped her head, canting her hip to one side as she tried her best to pout. She wasn't any good at this, but she had to get him away from the Drakken. They were bad news. "I would like to watch the moo-vee now."

"Now?" He blinked at her in surprise and dawning delight.

She tried to make her voice sound sultry. "Now you're the one answering statements with questions. Yes, now. You promised."

"And you just made my night, baby. A movie and a little private time upstairs."

Hadley smiled. She had a date.

And, maybe, later, a kiss. A daydream of tonight turning into more floated through her mind. She couldn't help spinning the clock ahead. It was the way of her homeworld, known for its romantic stories and ballads. She was a daughter of that world, no matter how far she'd run from it. Smiling, she let her thoughts take her and Tango into the future. Their first date would lead to another one, and another, and eventually to the night she'd give him her virginity.

Hadley released a happy sigh.

Tango put the glass down. "I'll catch you guys another time. I've got plans." He started to push away from the table when a shout rose up from the men. "Rakkelle!" they called out.

A skinny woman with shiny, jaw-length black hair had arrived. She wore earrings like the Drakken men did, but the jewelry wasn't confined to the lobe; it studded the entire rim. A tiny gem glinted on the side of her nose. Hadley remembered the pilot from the day Admiral Bandar commissioned her.

"That's *Cadet* Rakkelle to you—woo!" Rakkelle held up her hands, gyrating her hips as she walked over. She was dressed in only half a uniform, having substituted the upper half for a tight black tank top. Admiral Bandar would not be pleased. "You are either in uniform or out of it," she always said.

Someone handed Rakkelle a shot glass of sweef. She downed it as if it were plain water. Then she draped her thin body across Tango's lap and dragged a fingertip over his chin. "I don't care what you say, I'm a much better pilot than you, Earthling flyboy."

"Keep dreamin', Rocky."

Rocky? Hadley's mouth dropped.

"Better, better, better, mmm…" Rakkelle looped her arms over his shoulders and planted a kiss on his lips.

Hadley stood there, rooted to the spot, even though all she wanted to do was run out. It wasn't that he kissed the pilot cadet that hurt—it obviously wasn't of his initiation—but that he spent a few long seconds kissing her back.

The ring he'd given her had turned black. *Stressed, tense or feeling harried,* the guide claimed. How about murderous?

Hadley didn't stay for the rest of the show.

Humiliated, she found the exit and left. Her fantasy was over and done, vaporized into so much cosmic dust. If she lost her innocence before the end of this voyage, it would be with one of her own kind. Earthlings were too…too…

"It's just Rakkelle."

She spun around. Bolivarr stood there, tall, dark and intense. His black hair was short and glossy; a lock fell forward over his forehead. He had a way of appearing and disappearing like cloud shadows on a summer day, sliding silently in and out of sight. He'd come after her to make amends, apparently.

Good—he ought to feel guilty. What happened was all his fault, luring Tango over to the Drakken table and setting him in Rakkelle's path of destruction. "*Just* Rakkelle?" Hadley blurted out. "So she *usually* throws herself all over strange men?"

"And not-so-strange ones, too, like your Earthling. Rakkelle's an equal-opportunity lover."

"He's not *my* Earthling." She twisted the ring off her finger. The gem had turned a dark purplish blue. Goddess—she knew what the guide said about indigo. She had a photographic memory that never failed her. *Romantic, passionate, in love.*

With *Bolivarr?*

Stupid ring! It had already malfunctioned, just like the man who had given it to her. Turning on her boot heel, she walked away, her head held high,

Admiral Bandar–style. She kept up the aloof facade until she'd rounded the corner; then she broke into a run and left the bar far behind. Her love life was over before it had ever begun.

FINN HAD NEVER SEEN anyone play lightball, but he'd heard of the sport. Bandar whirled and lunged in a glassed-in court, the ball of light whooshing between her hand and the walls. She looked like a fire goddess. Her dark blue tank top bared her stomach, and clung to every curve, her short pants revealing legs that were as gods-be-damned long as he'd imagined.

He settled in to watch her play. Aye, why not? She might outrank him, but he felt no less a male in her presence.

With each slam of the lightball, she expelled a breath, her skin glowing with a light sheen of sweat. Her hair swung in a long ponytail as she spun, sending the ball of light on another arcing flight across the court. It came back at her fast, a shooting star.

While she was so in control in her job, down to every mannerism, here she seemed to hold nothing back. Finn couldn't help but wonder what else she threw herself into as heartily and completely. His cock gave a twitch.

"Ah, no!" she choked out, missing the ball. It rolled to the edge of the court. His fire goddess noticed him and stopped, her chest heaving. A dark lock of hair was stuck to her cheek and jaw. She peeled it out of the way. "Warleader," she greeted, breathless, seeming softer somehow here on this court.

Something about her out of uniform…

"Admiral." He nodded, the ball glowing on the floor between their feet. "I was admiring your skill with the game."

"Do you play?"

"We Drakken play with real balls."

She snorted. "It takes real balls to play lightball."

"I hope you're interested in playing doubles, because there is no way I'll back down from that challenge."

"Take off your uniform," she said.

Oh, how he'd dreamed of her telling him that. Grinning, he unbuttoned his Triad jacket, placing it on the floor. Underneath he wore a black T-shirt, part of his old Imperial Navy uniform.

"Your boots, Warleader."

She was barefoot. He glimpsed a pair of pretty feet as she walked away, arms raised as she tightened her ponytail. Loose, her hair would reach almost to that sexy ass.

His cock protested the direction of his thoughts. Protested, aye, because they both well knew thoughts alone wouldn't satisfy.

"The ball, Warleader," she said, impatient.

"Aye." He tossed his boots outside the court and scooped the ball of light into his hand, and almost let it fall. "Damn, it's *hot!*" He tossed it from hand to hand. So much for a warning.

Her half smile was smug. "I told you it takes balls to play." She walked around, waving a hand at the court. "All walls and the ceiling are fair impact points. A floor hit ends the round. The game is played taking turns. You can use any part of your body you choose. No double hits. One scores when the other misses." She pointed to a visual display outside the glass. "Points are shown there. The scoring system recognizes the differences in our bodies, via ball contact, and will keep score." She walked back to him. "Ready to play?"

"Aye, Admiral." He was tossing the ball, one-handed. "I'm ready."

"Serve."

He swung his arm, sending the lightball to the back wall. It came back fast, faster than he'd expected. Bandar returned, putting it in the corner. He had to dive to keep it from hitting the floor. He'd barely gotten his feet under him when the ball whooshed, hissing, at his face. He ducked like he'd dodged bullets and thrown knives in the past, but it passed close enough to feel searing heat across his scalp.

He danced backward, breathing heavily, as the ball skittered across the floor. A glowing circle appeared in her score column.

"You have to be faster." She'd retrieved the ball

and sent it speeding toward the left wall. It rico-cheted, but he was there. Again, the ball came at his head, hissing and hot.

Her eyes gleamed wickedly.

"You wouldn't be doing that on purpose, would you?"

"Of course the hells I am!"

"Hells? I thought you weren't a believer." He sent the ball across the court.

She volleyed back. "I'm not."

"You refer to the Dark Reaches yet not the gods?"

"You could say I'm better acquainted with the underside of our existence." She served and another volley was under way.

Another point went in her favor. She had the upper hand from practice and experience, just as he used to have when she'd chase him unsuccessfully across the Borderlands, his haunt, not hers. "This court is your domain," he acceded. "But not for long." He sent the ball screaming across the court.

"That's one thing I like about you, Warleader—your ability to delude yourself."

He threw back his head and laughed—cut off mid-chuckle when the ball sped from her hand to the left wall. He sent it back with a kick that caused her to miscalculate where it would land. It skittered across the floor. She stared at the fallen lightball as if she couldn't believe she'd missed.

"Ready to surrender?" he asked.

"You're—" she let the ball fly "—deluding yourself again."

"Do you know what this is beginning to remind me of?" he asked, swinging hard. "The days in the Borderlands, you trying to catch me."

"I would have caught you, given a little more time," she gasped, diving for the low hit. "You were far from my primary mission. Other duties called me away."

"Now who's being delusional?" He slammed the ball. She returned it, hard. He laughed with the exhilaration of the game. His desire for victory equaled hers. "Are you ready yet for duties to call you away again?" he teased.

"Why, have you had enough?"

"Not even close." He used his shoulder to send the ball across the court. "You almost caught me. On Mirkuu."

She stumbled. He thought for a moment she'd miss his volley. She didn't. "What do you mean?"

"I was there, on Mirkuu."

"No, you weren't. We knew everyone who was on Mirkuu."

"You thought you did."

The ball zipped back and forth at lightning speed.

"That merchant," she said on a burst of breath. "That merchant with half a brain who took our money and gave us faulty intel." She threw her whole self into the next hit and whirled on him. "That was you!"

"Aye. That was me."

He aimed the ball low and left. She missed the point.

Sucking in air, his fire goddess glared at him in disbelief. "You're only one point up now," he informed her.

With a growl, she scooped the ball off the floor and flung it across the court. She played hard, and he played even harder, anticipating her every move. He laughed with the joy of the game and his pirate's pride at fooling one of the greatest commanders the Coalition had ever seen. And the smartest. Bandar had come uncomfortably close to snaring him one too many times. His pretending to be a merchant on Mirkuu had been a rushed, last-ditch effort as the Coalition closed in on him. Even he'd thought his luck had finally run out. To this day, he couldn't believe that it had worked: the real merchant bound and gagged under the counter all while Finn gave Stone-Heart's hunting party false leads with a smile and a wave, picturing Bandar waiting for his disgraced arrival on the *Vengeance,* never dreaming her team would fail.

The volley was vicious, lasting longer than the ones preceding it. It ended with them colliding and the ball going wild. He caught her to keep her from falling. The ball bounced off the back wall, came around from behind and caught him in the ass.

"Point," she said. "My point!"

He coughed out a laugh of his own, unable to keep from staring as she laughed—a real laugh, husky and melodic. He thought she was gorgeous, aye, but with her face all soft with happiness, she was breathtakingly beautiful.

He doubted his thoughts were hard to read.

Her smile faded. She shook her head, her shoulders sagging, as if she'd given up on something. Before he realized what was happening, she pulled his head down to hers. "Damn you, Rorkken," she said and kissed him.

He almost staggered, shocked by the feel of her lips on his mouth. The delicious, exotically floral scent of her hit him next. His instinct as a naval officer was to pull away—by the gods, she was his commanding officer—but he was a pirate first and always would be, aye, and no fool. He'd admired this woman for too long, had desired her since he set foot on this ship and realized who she was—though in truth he'd desired her even before that. She could have been plain in looks, it wouldn't have mattered; he'd been half in love with her ever since their days of cat and mar-mouse in the Borderlands. Wrong it may be, but if she wanted him, he wanted her right back.

Gods, she tasted good. She felt even better, pressed against him like this. He slid his hand up her arm, up that long, smooth throat, and over her hair. Was that a sigh he heard? As if he required any more encouragement.

Grabbing her by the base of her ponytail, he held

her where he wanted her, and that was up close and personal, very personal, aye. He wasn't just merely hard; he was ready to explode. It was no secret what he thought of this kiss. The evidence was hers to keep or discard.

When at last they separated, it was only to draw in air. For another kiss like that, he'd happily asphyxiate, he thought.

Her hands had made their way to his shoulders during the kiss. They stayed that way, with his arms still looped around her waist. Her eyes were closed. He wasn't sure why, but he'd have thought she of all people would be an eyes-wide-open kisser—no fantasies, no bashfulness, nothing but clear reality. Brit Bandar never ceased to surprise him.

"I knew you felt the attraction, too," he murmured in her hair.

Blinking, she jolted away from him. Her expression matched the look in her eyes that fleeting moment in Zaafran's office. Her vulnerability, he thought. The hurt. It got to him every time. It was the kind of look that would send a man to the ends of the universe to make it better, if he could.

She seemed almost startled as she disentangled herself from him, and conflicted, as if waging an inner war. *A war against* you. Aye. He wanted to slap himself upside the head. *Damn you, Rorkken. Talking about it brought her back to her senses*. That was the last thing he wanted—for either of them. There were too few surprises of the pleasurable kind in life—his life, anyway. He didn't want to lose this one he'd found. Not yet.

She turned away to retrieve a towel, pressing it to her face and neck. When she glanced at him again, it was with an air of quiet determination. "I have to shower. Perhaps, afterward, you can come to my quarters to finish what we started."

"Perhaps," he repeated. "That's not an order."

"It should be obvious that this is private and outside protocol. If that makes you uncomfortable, then…"

He almost laughed. "I'm many things right now. Uncomfortable isn't one of them."

"Good." She ran the towel over her graceful neck.

She'd invited him to her quarters, after all, and, he assumed, into her bed. "Would you like to share dinner?" he offered lamely. He'd never have thought it possible, but Finnar Rorkken, Scourge of the Borderlands, was actually nervous. A meal would break the ice.

"If you're hungry, I will order dinner. It's not necessary, though." She walked away, hips undulating. "You, however, are."

Dropping her towel down a nanocleaner tube with an elegant flick of her wrist, she disappeared into the changing room.

Gods be. He was famished—and not, for once, for food.

CHAPTER ELEVEN

Finn walked across his room, dressed in nothing but his tattoos. He turned on the shower and stepped under the drenching stream, savoring the blessed downpour and the blessed cleanser before finally drying off using the blessedly soft towel—all done in the privacy of his own quarters. He'd lost count of how many showers he'd taken since coming on board the *Unity,* but having started out as a street urchin, he doubted he'd ever take such luxury for granted. The Drakken ship had been a step up from his pirate vessel, but this was light-years beyond even that. Since coming aboard, he'd been taking far longer showers than was necessary. Not tonight. Aye, tonight he had reason to be elsewhere.

He threw open the door to his wardrobe. He didn't plan to be in his clothes for long, but he wanted to look his best. He'd forgotten how little he now owned. There was his old Imperial Navy uniform, if one could call it that, a threadbare, mended collection of little more than rags and leather. Another pair of old leather pants hung next to a pair of cloth trousers, a vest and several faded shirts, none of which would impress a woman like Brit Bandar. She was a class above him—several classes. *You own nothing but rags, Rorkken!* Except, maybe, the Cloudan tunic.

He grasped a luxurious sleeve, examining the condition of the garment. It was silver and light blue, shot through with threads of pure karnelian. It was a fitted piece, allowing for the breadth of his shoulders. It was entirely handmade and hand-tailored, no advanced tech inside or outside. As a pirate, he'd had no need for a uniform, but for the times he had to make an appearance, or an impression, he'd wear this, his finest article of clothing. With the Cloudan belted over his leathers, a sword hanging from his belt and polished boots, he'd been able to maintain the image of prosperity even during the lean times between raids when the coffers ran low. It was during one of those lean times that he saved the life of the leader of a rogue encampment in the Cloudlands. In thanks, the man had gifted Finn and the crew with treasures, including this tunic, tailored specifically for him. Nothing lasted long in pirates' hands—valuable goods were sold and bartered—but Finn had never let go of the Cloudan. He was too freepin' sentimental. The day he'd received it, he was called a hero, selfless and honorable. That didn't happen often—not at all, in fact. The tunic was a way of hanging on to the memory. Aye, and he looked good in it, too.

The clothes of a pirate king.

Bandar will laugh her ass off if you show up at her door dressed in that.

Finn frowned as he shoved the tunic back in the wardrobe and slammed the door. He stalked naked across the room to where he'd left his Triad uniform hanging in the nanocleaner. He'd reached for it and a fresh, sleeveless undershirt when his PCD beeped. So, she was growing impatient for him, was she? He smiled wickedly as he answered, "Don't despair, I'm on my way."

"To the bar, sir?"

"Zurykk?" Finn swore. Damn tech. You couldn't see who was talking to you. He was glad he hadn't said anything more revealing. "No, I'm not coming to the bar."

"Captain, you might want to. There was a fight. I broke it up, but tempers are still hot. Security's here."

"Keep them there. Tell them I'm on my way, and that I'll take care of it."

"Already did."

Finn was shoving a leg in his uniform pants as he spoke. "Don't let them tell the admiral. I'll do that."

"Aye-aye, sir."

He sent a prayer heavenward just in case. The last thing he needed was Bandar's mood to sour. He didn't want her thoughts veering anywhere else but his taking her to bed.

STAR-MAJOR YAREW WAS outside the bar when Finn arrived. It was the man's watch. "You left the bridge for a bar brawl?" Finn asked.

"Quiet night," the intel officer explained. "Not so in there, though."

Inside the entrance to the bar, several Drakken stood, favoring limbs or bleeding faces. A Coalition officer was passed out on the floor, peaceful, as if he were sleeping—too much to drink, Finn thought. A few tables were overturned. Shattered glass glittered on the floor along with puddles of spilled liquor. It stank of sweat and alcohol.

It looked like a Drakken haunt. Finn winced. Thank the gods Bandar wasn't here to see it. "Zurykk," he bellowed.

His former second was at his side in seconds. Finn draped his arm over the man's shoulders and steered him away. "Before I start yelling, maybe you can tell me what happened here."

"We didn't keep the sweef to ourselves. Some Coalition started drinking it. An Earthling, too, but he left after two glasses. Smart enough to know his limits."

"His name wasn't Tango, was it?"

"The pilot giving out the little toys, aye."

Finn snorted. It wasn't his limits that stole the man away, it was a woman; he'd probably left with Lieutenant Keyren. "So the Coalition got drunk and picked a fight."

"Something like that, sir."

Finn stormed back to the bar. Medical personnel had arrived to attend to the out-cold ensign. "He'll be all right," Finn assured them. "Best that he sleep it off."

"Yes, Warleader." The medical techs had replied politely—Finn outranked them—but he didn't miss the glance they exchanged. Hoodlums, barbarians: he knew how they viewed him and the men. They were low-class Drakken, drinking their Horde brew and endangering the good people on the ship.

Finn jerked a finger at the remaining Drakken. "Out here, now." In answer to his snarled order, four suddenly pale men followed him down the corridor.

Finn said nothing until they'd turned the corner. Then he whirled on them. "What were you freepin' thinking, giving them sweef?"

No one wanted to answer. "You, Markar, speak."

"Captain—"

"I'm not this ship's captain!"

"Warleader." The newly commissioned space-hand apprentice cleared his throat. He, Finn noted, had taken the beads out of his hair and cut it shorter, Coalition-style. It seemed others in the crew besides Bolivarr sensed the importance of blending in.

And not causing trouble. "Speak, Markar," Finn demanded.

"They wanted to try some sweef. And we... We—"

"We thought it'd be funny to see them fall on their faces," Yerkksen volunteered. "Drinking sweef like it was their weak liquor."

One of the men chuckled; another snickered.

"Funny?" Finn snarled, rendering the men silent. "Just what I like to see, my people acting like fools." He wrapped his knuckles in the collar of the third man and jerked him off his feet. Nimmson was the least injured of the group but he still winced. In fear or in pain? Finn hoped it was both. He needed a lesson to be learned here. To teach a Hordish space-hand, fear and pain worked best.

"And how did the fight start?" Finn demanded. "Zurykk said it was us."

"Aye, sir."

"Help me to understand, then, how this went from sweef tasting to jaw punching."

The man was turning purple. Finn lowered him to his feet. No use killing anyone. "Tell me!"

"They got drunk and called us killer swine. They said we slaughter defenseless women and babies because we aren't brave enough to fight real soldiers."

Finn went still. He knew the humiliation of those words. Unfortunately, sometimes they were true. The Drakken had earned their shameful reputation by playing outside the rules of war. Not all crews or all ships, but enough to paint them all with the same broad brush. Unless a ship was commanded by a captain with a sense of right and wrong, there was no stopping them from killing noncombatants, or worse. On the *Unity,* he and his crew had been given the benefit of the doubt. They'd been treated as fellow human beings rather than as the animals many of their countrymen were. Finn knew how delighted the crew was to receive the promotions, a brilliant PR move on Bandar's part, and one for which Finn was eternally grateful. Little by little over the course of their first week aboard, they'd been starting to feel part of the team, part of something bigger and better than any of them. Now this.

Most of Finn's anger drained away in a tired sigh. "It's not going to be easy for us here—we knew that. But do we let a few cowardly barbs make us show what they think are our true colors?"

They shook their heads. "No, sir."

"Go to sick bay, all of you, and get some of their nano-ointment for those bruises." The men's expressions of distaste told him what they thought of that suggestion. "It's not showing weakness to use their medicine. Unlike most of ours, their drugs freepin' work. I want you in ship-shape tomorrow—that's an order. No limping around and swollen noses, eh? No reminding everyone what happened here tonight. We're better than this, right?"

"Aye, sir."

"If they want to act like arrogant assholes, let them. We've got better things to do than fall for their games."

"Aye, sir!"

With a swell of affection for his crew, he watched the men walk away in the direction of the sick bay. It was not going to be an easy transition for them—

or for anyone from the *Pride.* On a smaller scale, it reflected what the rest of the galaxy was going through, and would be for years to come. It was more difficult to get along than it was to fight.

He walked back to the bar where Zurykk waited. The med techs had already taken the fallen Coalition officer away. The bar had emptied with most looking to rest before their next shifts.

Brit.

Worriedly, Finn glanced at the time. If he waited much longer, she'd have to go on duty, and he'd miss the chance to be with her. With something that good within his reach, he damn well wasn't going to risk losing it.

He turned to Yarew, who waited with the security team. "Seeing that both sides shared the blame, I say we let it go. No one was killed. No need to disturb the admiral."

"Security was called, Warleader. I'll have to put this in my end-of-shift report. Ship's rules."

"Of course." Coalition and their blasted rules. "The admiral can then read it at her leisure tomorrow without interrupting her rest." Or anything else she might have planned, he thought with an inner grin. "Speaking of rest, I'm off to get my own. Good eve, gentlemen."

With visions of the hours to come in his mind, which resembled anything but rest, Finn left for Admiral Bandar's quarters.

BORED, BRIT HAD LONG SINCE grown impatient for
Rorkken's arrival. Well into her second glass of wine,
she fell onto her bed and stared at the ceiling. Her
silken robe fluttered and went still. Underneath, the
barely there negligee would be for no one's entertainment but her own, and her own wasn't what she
wanted tonight. Or needed.

*To get rid of a craving, sometimes you had to have
your fill of it.* Hard to do if he was a no-show.

Damn you, Rorkken. She wouldn't call him and
ask where he was. The last thing she wanted to
appear was needy. She wanted him for one purpose,
and that was to put out the fire he caused in her. One
long night of fornication, and she'd be over it. Over
him. Obsession was best ended when faced head-on.

He wasn't coming.

Quite frankly, it surprised her. She'd felt the hunger in his kiss, and felt that hunger pressed against
her belly, too. Had either physical sign left her with
any doubt of his desire, the lust in his eyes would
have burned it into so much ash.

What could he have found to do that was better than
her? She rolled onto her stomach and checked the time.
It had been over an hour since they'd parted company.
Yet, she ached with such anticipation that her breasts
tingled and the wetness between her thighs was hard
to ignore. Too bad he'd found something else to do; he
would have liked what she intended to offer him.

Or maybe the pirate was a stickler for protocol. Two top officers on a ship bedding each other *was* highly irregular. Maybe he'd had last-minute regrets.

His kiss had said otherwise. She licked her lips. He could kiss, no doubt about that. It was the first thing she usually checked out before purchasing a man for the night. She'd never put up with a lover who didn't kiss well. They had to be able to kiss so she could close her eyes and remember…

Her entry chimed. "Warleader Rorkken," the room-bot announced.

Brit jumped upright, swinging her legs off the bed. *Don't run to him, you foolish girl. You'll frighten him away.* With a tremble in her belly, she knew the odds of frightening Finnar Rorkken were low.

The door viewer showed the man standing outside in the corridor. He was in his Triad uniform. Smart Drakken indeed. This way they could say they were having a staff meeting and no one would be the wiser.

"Open," she told the room-bot, loosening the sash holding her robe closed. Crimson silk rustled. She let the sleeves slide off her shoulders and down her scented arms to her elbows. Her hair flowed shiny and clean, also smoothed and scented with the oil. She'd taken extra steps to ensure Finn Rorkken's seduction. She had to be sure. It was the first time since losing Seff that she hadn't paid a man for sexual favors. No financial promise would keep him here, only the promise of her. It had to be enough.

The door slid open. "Sorry about the delay. I had to…" Rorkken strode in—and stopped at the sight of her, his legs apart, his expression instantly sharp. The lust in his eyes, the desire, made her blood sing with nerves, with hunger, and her body ache for his touch. *Not much longer now. You'll have your time with him, and he'll vanish from your mind.*

"A goddess in the flesh," he murmured hoarsely as his gaze tracked down her body. The silk was so thin that her erect nipples jutted against the fabric. The slightest movement caused a whisper of abrasion that sent shock waves through her body.

She swallowed, nodding. "Warleader."

The door slid shut. He closed the distance in three strides, stopping close enough to feel his body heat, to smell his unique scent, spice, soap and man. His work-roughened thumb slipped under one strap of her gown, moving it off her shoulder. He brought his lips to the crook of her neck as he slipped off the other strap. She shivered. Only his hand pressed to her upper back kept the gown from sliding to the floor. "Not Warleader," he corrected. "Finn."

She sighed in answer, eyes closing as he kissed the side of her throat. He felt good. He felt *right*.

"There's a time and place for rank and rules," he breathed in her ear. "One's bed is not one of them."

"We're not in bed yet."

"No?" He let go and her gown whooshed into a

puddle of silk around her ankles. Then he swept her off her feet so fast that she gasped, a breath interrupted when he sealed his lips over hers.

A second later, her back hit the mattress. The solid weight of Rorkken's body followed. She was nude; he was fully clothed, boots and all. "We are now," he said gruffly, crushing his mouth to hers all over again.

The kiss wasn't meant to tease or to coax; it was raw and hungry, making no secret of what he wanted of her.

Good, it matched what she wanted from him.

She wanted his touch all over, and he seemed to know it. Hot and callused, his hands smoothed over her bare flesh, sending her into a frenzy of need—of *now*.

The unending kiss broke only when she helped him struggle out of his uniform jacket and undertank. A glimpse of broad shoulders, ripped abs, a hard chest and just the right amount of chest hair tempted her before he returned for more kissing. He looked and felt like a man; he smelled like a man under the fresh soapy smell of cleanser. He didn't douse himself in exotic oils like the man-toys did, something she'd always found unnecessary and often a turnoff. When she was in a man's arms, she wanted to know it.

"I'm still wearing too many clothes," he said a short, breathless while later. He reached for the waistband of his pants, unfastening it with one hand. Rolling off her body, he shoved off his boots.

Her lips tingled, missing his mouth already. She

curled up on her side to watch him undress. His pants came off next, treating her to a view of a muscled back and tight buttocks. It seemed the Scourge of the Borderlands had a very nice backside. He was, however, nothing like her past lovers. The man-toys were physical perfection. Rorkken, on the other hand, wore his life's history on his skin.

A scar, waxy and lumpy, sliced across his rib cage. Another on his thigh looked like a healed-over puncture wound. He'd been stabbed with a knife or sword. As a pirate, a Drakken combatant…or as a hungry, desperate orphan?

Sympathy swelled in her heart for the tragedy of his upbringing. She blocked the emotion immediately. If she felt anything for this man, it was to be lust. Nothing more. Yet, her gaze was drawn to his body even though every glimpse of that golden, imperfect flesh reminded her of what she had done— and what she was about to do. Whitish slashes laced his chest and stomach, most of them lost in the tattooing that covered his shoulders and swirled onto his pecs, all of it created with black ink, not by painless imprinting with nano-dye, she was certain. He'd gotten that body art the hard way.

The savage way.

Don't look at him. She forced her eyes away for the last time. She didn't want to see the scars, the tattoos. She didn't want to see a Drakken.

With a feral twinkle in his eye, he climbed back

into bed, taking her by the shoulder and rolling her onto her back. "Mmm," she purred. Finally.

Leaning over her, he braced his upper body with extended arms. His erection seared the flesh of her inner thigh as he straddled her. He should be inside her already. What was taking so long?

"Come here." She tried to pull him closer.

He resisted, locking his arms. "In a moment." His mouth formed a mischievous smile. A rugged, wicked boy, that's what he reminded her of when he smiled like that.

A very grown-up boy, she thought, acutely conscious of the feel of him against her thigh. As if he'd guessed the direction of her thoughts, he moved his hips, sliding between her legs, intimately, but not penetrating. Damn him. She made a strangled moan of frustration, which only intensified his look of satisfaction. "Why are you waiting?" she asked, impatient.

"I'm soaking it all in."

"Soaking in what?"

"This—me, here with a beautiful woman." His voice was huskier now. "Me, in bed with you."

Unfortunately, she didn't want to be reminded that they actually knew each other. She didn't want his sentimentality, either. It was just sex. It wasn't supposed to mean anything. "Take me, Rorkken. Take me now."

"Finn."

She groaned. "Finn."

"All in good time." He sifted his fingers through her hair, watching in awe as it rippled down. "Gods, you're beautiful, Brit. I know I said as much before, but you truly are."

The sound of her given name on his lips wasn't something she'd given him permission to use, but of course he would. The bed was no place for rank he'd said, and he was right.

"Thank you," she murmured, suddenly shy. She'd been paid similar compliments by many men over the years, men she'd paid to say such pretty words. Yet none displayed the frankness in their eyes that Rorkken did now. None had actually made her *feel* beautiful with one look, like he did.

Finally, he lowered his head. Thank the stars that he'd stopped talking and started exploring. He took one nipple into his mouth, hot and wet, suckling. A sigh slipped out of her, her back arching with the gentle, erotic tugs of his lips, the rasping of his tongue. Yes... Her eyes closed as his touch took her away to another place, another time. Then he moved lower, kissing his way to her navel and below.

She choked back a moan when he started pleasuring her between her legs. What was he doing? Hadn't she been clear enough regarding her desires? If he kept this up, she was going to come apart. That was not the way she wanted it done. She wanted intercourse. She wanted it over and done with.

She tried to sit up, but he pushed her back down

with a firm, flattened hand on her stomach. "Enough foreplay," she protested. She had not the patience for it. "I want you inside me."

His grin was smug, his eyes dark and hooded. "All in good time."

"No. Not in good time. *Now.*"

He chuckled, slipping two fingers inside her. "Is that an order?" His voice was husky, sounding as if it had come from far away.

Against her will she made a strangled moan as those wicked, determined fingers explored her. Her thighs fell open, hiding nothing from his view. He found her clit and she gasped. Damn him to the Dark Reaches. He wasn't as practiced with his touch as the man-toys were, but it was that lack of bought-and-paid-for finesse that pushed her to an unexpected and far-too-fast climax.

She cried out as her body convulsed. "Damn it!" He'd made her come. He'd taken over the entire act, right down to her premature orgasm. How dare he?

He withdrew those magic fingers, leaving her throbbing with little aftershocks of pleasure. Eyes squeezed shut, she felt rather than saw that damned boyish grin as he returned to kiss her, murmuring smugly against her lips, "All that swearing, Brit. Why? You seemed to like it very much."

"I wanted you to be inside me when it happened."

"I plan to be, when you come the next time. And come again, you will. All in good—"

"No, damn it. Not in good time. Now." She found his mouth for a scorching kiss. There was no time for teasing, no time for talk. He was here for one reason, and it was this.

She threw her leg over his buttocks to keep him from escaping. He caught the fever; his kiss was hard, burning. The weight of his strong body pressed her into the sheets. His movements were less controlled now. His scent was sharp. Soon, she thought. Soon he wouldn't be able to hold back, no matter what his damned timeline was.

As she'd guessed, he moved between her legs. Closing his hands in her hair, he lifted his hips and thrust oh, so deep. *Yes…* Her entire body sang out in pleasure, welcoming him.

He slid a hand under her thigh, gripping her backside to keep her pressed close. She swayed with him, letting him take charge of their rhythm.

Ah, yes…

His touch was firm, possessive. His breaths were harsh, his skin damp with exertion. Brit savored the sounds and scents, letting the sex sweep her back to the past, a time before pain, before the grinding loneliness. Eyes closed, she escaped into her mind.

Seff… She imagined their small, narrow bed, and the window above open to Arrayar's dry night breezes. She was so young then; Seff, too. Afterward, they'd cuddle and giggle, careful to keep their voices low.

"Brit," he said on a groan. "Ah, Brit."

Why, oh why was he compelled to talk? His voice was nothing like Seff's. Every time he opened his mouth to speak, it threatened to spoil the mood. Yet even in the silences, even when there was nothing but breathing and sighs, Rorkken kept jolting her out of the past, reminding her quite vividly with every heated caress, every kiss, every thrust of his hips, that she was in bed with him: a man, not a long-dead boy. Even with her eyes closed and the past filling her mind, she felt the scrape of his shaved beard, something Seff didn't yet have. Those rough whiskers contrasted with soft lips, grazing down her throat, her shoulder, her breasts. No, Rorkken didn't feel like Seff and yet, damn it, he felt so *good*.

Worse, the longer he made love to her, the more difficult it became to block out his unique scent, the feel of his scarred body, the tinkle of the jewelry piercing his ear. Every time she felt a scar under the palm of her hand, every time she felt his powerful body move, she was reminded of who he wasn't. Yet it was his frank desire for her, and the obvious and genuine pleasure he took in making love to her—*to her*—that pushed her closer to the edge. The man-toys could fake passion so well that sometimes she would almost believe they were overcome with it. Rorkken's desire, however, was genuine.

With that realization, she convulsed with pleasure, bringing her precipitously close to climax. Crying out softly, she tried to hold back. She wouldn't let go with Rorkken in her mind's eye.

It needs to be Seff.

"Come for me, sweetheart," a deep, raspy voice urged. "Let go."

She almost exploded with that gentle command, as if she were Rorkken's puppet, climaxing on order. Holding back, she gritted her teeth, moaning.

Where was Seff?

"Brit," he whispered in her ear. "Look at me...."

She squeezed her eyes shut even tighter and buried her face in the warm, scented hollow between his shoulder and neck. Skin that tasted and smelled like Finn Rorkken. His powerful pulse rapped against her cheek.

He rolled onto his back, pulling her with him. No! Her head hung low. She didn't want him to see her face, to see her eyes closed. To invade her fantasy— or to prevent it altogether.

He remained hard, seated deep inside her, but his touch was warm and tender as he touched her cheek. "I want you to see me when you come, Brit. Me. I want you to know who's making love to you."

That was the thing: she didn't want to know who was making love to her.

He pushed upward to get her attention, grinding against her so that she couldn't ignore him any longer. She moaned. "Please."

Rorkken made a deep, satisfied sound. Her body

was so taut, so ready. One more push like that and she'd...

"Sweetheart. Look at me."

Sweetheart. She didn't like that he called her that. She loved that he called her that.

Gasping, she opened her eyes to his hard-featured face and the eyes that didn't look quite so much like Seff's anymore. His gaze was less boyish, less playful, darker and more intense. "That's it, sweetheart. That's it. Look at me. Feel me."

She did feel him. Gods, she did. She brought her head down to kiss him, a spontaneous move. He held her there, stroking her back as he kissed her, sweetly, hotly, and with feeling, feeling that she, incredibly, returned.

One more thrust, and she was gone, shattering with pleasure. It so blinded her to anything else that she was only vaguely aware of Rorkken's fingers pressing into the flesh of her upper arms, and the violence of his last plunges, as he, too, peaked at last.

He tore his mouth from hers, growling her name, shuddering as heat spurted into her. And then it was quiet.

Dazed, she sagged atop him, blinking, trying to collect her wits. Somewhere in the midst of her passion, she'd closed her eyes again—not to block out sensation this time, but to hold it in.

Gradually, her mind cleared of fog. Below her,

Rorkken wore a soft expression as he threaded his fingers through her dangling tresses, bringing her hair to his lips as he inhaled then twisting the strands around one thick finger. The way he lay there, sated and drowsy as he played with her hair, seemed almost more intimate than the sex. She shivered, enjoying that affectionate touch, hungrier for it than she ever would have guessed.

He'd wedged his left hand between his head and the pillow. On the underside of that raised arm, just to the inside of his rounded bicep was a single tattoo. Her gaze stopped there as if tripping over a road-block. It was separate from the other tattoos as if in a place of honor: a black bird of prey clutching two crossed sabers in its talons.

Sudden recognition sent a chill racing down her spine. That raptor had visited her in nightmares more times than she could count; it had haunted her ever since the day it swooped heartlessly down from the sky to steal what she loved most. It was the centuries-old symbol of the Drakken Empire, and her lover wore it on the arm closest to his heart.

Drakken...

Her ears began to ring, and it suddenly became hard to breathe.

What have you done?

A small sound of pain escaped her lips as the full impact of her actions slammed into her. She'd taken a Hordish soldier to bed. She'd fucked the enemy.

What have you done!

She'd abandoned everything she stood for.

She'd disgraced the memory of those she'd loved.

Slut, she called herself. *Traitor.* She struggled out of bed. With a hand pressed to her stomach, she fled to the bathroom and slammed the door.

CHAPTER TWELVE

FINN SAT UP as Brit leaped out of bed. The bathroom door crashed shut. Was she off to fetch birth control of some sort? No, advanced tech prevented pregnancy as well as disease. She was safe *from* him, if not *with* him.

Aye, not safe at all. Chuckling, he laced his fingers behind his head and waited for her return.

The door remained closed. He wished she'd hurry and get her sexy ass back in bed. He wanted to hold her for a bit before he fell asleep and recharged for round two. And round three, if there was enough time before she had to be back on duty.

From inside the bathroom came the sound of water. She was running the water. And running it and running it. No one ran water longer than he did, but that was in the shower, not the sink.

He hopped out of bed and walked to the door. The water didn't quite drown out a soft, unhappy groan.

He folded his arms and leaned against the door. "It was good for me," he teased. "Was it good for you, too?"

She groaned out a curse, sounding even more pained. A flicker of worry invaded, then. "Brit, open the door."

"Please go."

"Not until you tell me what's wrong."

"I'm…not feeling well." The water turned off and a cup clattered.

"Do you think it's something you ate?"

"What do you mean?"

Of course she wouldn't know what he meant. Nanomeds took care of food poisoning or viruses. No one had been sick since they'd come on this ship, thanks to Dr. Kell. "Never mind. Come out and I'll give you a back rub. That'll make you feel better."

She groaned.

"Perhaps it's what you haven't eaten. You skipped dinner. You expended a lot of energy just now on an empty stomach." He chuckled. The water came back on. Then he heard splashing, as if she were throwing it on her face. "Tell me what suits your fancy, and I'll order. I for one have worked up an appetite."

"I'd rather you go."

"You want me to leave…."

"Yes. Please."

You always did have a way with the ladies, Rorkken. Exhaling, he picked his scattered clothes off the floor and dressed. "I'll wear my PCD to bed," he told her, pulling on his boots. "I don't do that for just anyone, but I'll do it for you. I want you to call me if you feel any worse. I'll make sure you get to the sick bay." What was he talking about? She was the commander. "No, Dr. Kell will come *to you*— even if I have to carry him from his bed to here."

"Don't do that." Her disapproval of that idea gave strength to her voice. "I'll be fine. Just leave."

The sound of splashing started all over again.

Sighing, he shrugged. Never had such great sex ended so badly. Finn rolled his eyes to the heavens. "Are you laughing now?" he muttered to the gods. Someone up there must have a sense of humor.

He trudged away from the bathroom and let himself out, waiting until he'd heard the security lock in her door move in place before he walked down the corridor to his quarters.

Once inside, Finn stripped out of his clothes and walked directly into the shower. He stood there for long moments with deliberately cold water drumming down on his head. It wasn't enough to keep him from reacting physically to an image of Brit writhing under him as he'd made love to her. Gods, he was hard again. He fisted his hands to keep from grabbing his cock and finishing the job. Doing so would somehow cheapen what he'd experienced with her. Instead, he forced his thoughts to the way she'd embraced him right before she climaxed, pouring her soul into that kiss. The memory blazed in his mind.

He didn't understand why she'd fought so hard to avoid looking at him before that point. For him, it was the emotional connection that he craved during love-making. He didn't get to experience it much, but when he sensed it was there to some degree, it added exponentially to his physical pleasure. He hadn't wanted his time with Brit to be "just sex." He'd wanted it to be different from his past encounters. It *had* been in the end, gods, far better than those other times, but not without some work. She was so blasted stubborn!

It was almost as if she'd wanted to avoid interacting with him. It wasn't shyness. He didn't know what it was.

The first reason that came to mind was her possible awkwardness with their being shipmates. He himself had violated his golden rule of no fraternization with a crew member. What about her? Yet, they'd assured each other before he'd ever stepped into her quarters that whatever they did in private would happen outside protocol.

Then another reason surfaced. He wasn't of her class. Aye, that was more likely it. He was raised an urchin, and she, if he made an educated guess, hailed from high-born origins. To become the equivalent of an admiral in the Drakken world, a Battle-Lord, you needed a wealthy, powerful family backing you, like Brit probably had.

She was the kind of woman he'd thought out of his reach in his old life, and for good reason. She was powerful, smart and rich, and he was a former starving pickpocket. She likely saw him as an object of lust. No chitchat, nothing extraneous—just sex, nothing more.

He cracked a smile as water sluiced over his body. An object of lust—him? When it came to men and women, didn't the female usually have such doubts? Well, he liked to help out others when he had the chance; if sex was all Brit Bandar wanted from him, he'd be happy to accommodate her. Very happy. But he'd be no whore, no indeed.

He thought better of himself. Aye, were he in the position to be a mate to a woman above his station— or below it—he'd be a worthy one. That he knew.

She wants to keep you at arm's length.

So be it. He'd chase Brit Bandar's true affections the way she'd chased him through the Borderlands. Only she'd not escape him like he'd escaped her. If she made the task of winning her over difficult, all the better. Finn Rorkken had never been able to resist a challenge.

WHEN SHE WAS SURE the warleader had left, Brit emerged unsteadily out of the bathroom. She found the box on the shelf above her desk. Her sacred box. She hadn't opened it in so very long. Good girl, Hadley, putting it in the same relative place as in her old quarters on the *Vengeance*.

Her hands shook as she lifted the lid. It hurt too much to look at the precious things inside, and so it was rarely that she did. Her throat closed at the sight of the soft pink blanket. Tears were already tracking down her cheeks by the time she dug out the *Agran Sakkara* from under it. She pressed both keepsakes to her cheek. They were all she had left of her children. She'd had them both such a very short time. All too briefly they'd blessed her life. "My babies. My precious babies." She wept because it hurt so much, the missing them, the pain never dimming after all these years.

Sometime later, drained, she placed the blanket and bible on her lap and found Seff's gift at the bottom of the box. Reverently, she slipped the bracelet on her wrist. "I'll never forget the day you gave me this." She smiled wanly. "We'd just found out I was pregnant for the second time. Remember? You wanted me to know that no matter how big our family grew, you'd always be my true love." *Me and you forever. Seff.* Her chest convulsed with a sob. She pressed her fist to her stomach, fearing she'd be ill all over again. "I'm sorry, husband. I'm so sorry...."

It was as if Seff were there in the room with her, forever young and watching her with his perpetually smiling eyes as she confessed her betrayal. "It was a weak moment," she whispered when she could speak again. "You know I don't have those often. I needed him. I needed him to hold me the way you used to hold me." Weeping, she fingered the bracelet. She remembered it covered in Seff's blood. She'd never seen so much blood, then and since. She had been bathed in it, clutching his broken body to hers. "He's one of them, the Horde, and yet he's not. He's not a murderer. I made sure. He's…different."

She grabbed her forehead, inhaling on a sob. It had been nothing but sex with Finn Rorkken. At first. Then…then something had changed. What started as the slaking of physical need ended suspiciously like lovemaking.

No! You feel nothing for this man.

This Drakken. "Seff," she cried out in the silent room. "Help me. Keep me strong. Don't let me repeat tonight's mistake. I miss you so much that I don't know what to do anymore. I'm so horribly lonely. I'm tired of being alone. Forgive me my weakness."

Her dead husband offered neither absolution nor advice. Weary and sick at heart, Brit took the blanket to bed. Wrapping it around her shoulders, she cried herself to sleep.

THE NEXT MORNING, the telltale signs of weeping and passionate kisses—puffy eyelids and lips—had vanished, thanks to an application of derma-cream. Happy to dive back into her work, Brit led a virtual journalist on a tour of the ship. She knew by the news streams courtesy of the palace that the *Unity* and its mission were of interest across the galaxy. In the past, she'd avoided dealing with the press. As a hunter-warrior, she didn't often have to; there was too much potential of upsetting the public with her seemingly coldhearted focus on exterminating Drakken. She never understood that. War wasn't pretty, it wasn't fun, yet the military's public affairs machine insisted on it being reduced to a form benign enough for mass public consumption.

Hands clasped behind her back, her Triad uniform perfectly crisp, she led the journalist onto the bridge. "Here is where I command the ship. On our Triad Alliance bridge you will find service members from Earth, from the former Coalition, as well as from the former Drakken Empire."

For a panicky moment, she feared Rorkken would be there, smiling his wicked smile, pumped up with the knowledge of what they'd done last night and the memory of her coming apart in his arms. She needn't have worried if she hadn't revealed so much of herself to him, but she had, and now she'd have to suffer the consequences, awkward as they were. She knew she'd have to see him, only she hoped not yet, and not unexpectedly. She needed a little extra time to fortify the wall she'd built around her.

At Brit's direction, Lieutenant Berkko described the various stations of the bridge as the virtual journalist nodded—a flickering image of a real woman, pretty, reddish-haired, and light-years away, recording the data as it streamed in. When Hadley reached the pilot's chair, even though the Earthling wasn't in it, her frown deepened and her eyes flashed with hurt. Brit sighed to herself and made a mental note to start hardening the girl, beginning with more tasks that challenged her. Leading a virtual journalist around the ship didn't come close.

"Come," Brit told the journalist. The ghostly image followed her to where Vinnson Yarew sat in the command chair.

"Admiral." He rose, offering a snappy fist-to-his-chest salute at her arrival, acting his part for the show.

"This is Star-Major Yarew, overseeing command of the ship while I am on break. We work a tri-shift day. Warleader Finnar Rorkken—" she hoped no one detected the slight change in her tone "—is the other senior officer as well as the next-highest-ranking officer here after me. Now that I am on duty for my shift, I will relieve Star-Major Yarew of his command. But first we exchange information from the previous hours in our change briefing."

As Yarew rattled off the mundane details of course and track, Brit paged through the records logged on the star charts. How dull, she thought, not having any Drakken ships to pursue this morn. She'd hoped some of the rogue vessels talked about would have surfaced by now. Zaafran's intelligence people would be calling in shortly as they did each day at the beginning of her shift. Maybe they would have better news. Peace bored her.

Discreetly, Yarew slid his data-vis under her eyes.

He'd typed a message. NEED 2 TALK IN PRIVATE
ABOUT LAST NIGHT.

To her horror, she blushed deeply. It spread before
she could do anything about it. Luckily, he'd turned
away, and Hadley wasn't looking. Dry-mouthed, Brit
swallowed and cleared her throat. "Lieutenant Keyren, escort our journalist to the engineer's station
and discuss some of the duties performed there."

"Yes, ma'am."

The two walked away. Brit turned to Yarew, her wall
firmly in place once more. "What is it, Star-Major?"

"There was a fight last night in the crew bar. An
ensign was injured—one of ours. The Drakken were
drunk on sweef and got out of hand. Warleader
Rorkken came down and took care of it. He advised
me not to say anything to you. He said he'd brief you
on the incident himself."

"I see."

"He didn't inform you?"

"No."

"That's what I was afraid of. I wrote up a full
report per ship's rules since security had been called.
It's loaded in your data-vis."

On one hand, she was delirious with relief that "last
night" hadn't meant, well, *last night.* On the other,
however, it infuriated her that there had been a fight
before Rorkken showed up in her quarters, and this
was the first she'd heard of it. He'd said nothing. Why,
because he wanted her focus on him and not shipboard

matters? Probably. All he'd cared about was getting laid, apparently, and to hells with everything else.

"Thank you, Star-Major Yarew. I'll look at the report during my shift. Good work. Is there anything else?"

"No, Admiral. Other than that, it was dead around here."

"You are dismissed."

"Yes, ma'am. Have a good shift."

"I intend to." Anger simmering, she smoothed her uniform and returned to the journalist, making sure she wore a good face for the camera.

THAT MORNING, *his* morning—time of day was relative on a tri-shift ship—Finn took a quicker than usual shower at the end of his sleep period. A colder than usual shower, too. Since he'd left Brit last night, she'd invaded his thoughts and his body. When he wasn't worried about how she was feeling, he was thinking of what they'd done, *feeling it* as he hobbled around in an almost constant state of semihardness last night and now. Sex with Brit Bandar had been erotic, hotter than the deepest hells, and over too soon.

He wanted more. Yet, he mustn't forget he had a job to do, and that had to come first. He was second-in-command of this ship. The responsibility and all that entailed needed to be forefront in his mind.

"Water—off," he told the water-bot and grabbed a towel, scrubbing it over his chilled flesh. The water temperature had been brisk, to say the least.

The PCD he'd left on his bed was beeping, and had been for some time, he suspected. He recognized the distinctive chime—two short pips and a longer tone. It was an urgent message from the bridge.

His heart lurched. Something had happened to Brit. She was in the sick bay in grave condition because instead of staying last night to make sure she was well, he'd taken himself and his disappointed cock back to his bedroom to sulk. He never should have left her. He should have seen her first with his own eyes and made sure everything was okay. He grabbed his PCD, hooking it on his ear. "Rorkken," he said.

"Warleader, this is Lieutenant Berkko, first-shift watch officer. Admiral Bandar requests that you report to the bridge immediately."

So, she was recovered and back to work. He shrugged on his uniform and boots, wasting no time trekking through the corridors to the bridge.

There he found her peering at a navigational holovis. Her hands were clasped lightly behind her back. Her posture was impeccable. He tried not to gape at the curve of her back, or the swell of her sweet bottom. It mattered not if her breasts were covered with war medals or red silk; he found it equally difficult to ignore her body. If they were somewhere private now, he'd… *Gods be.* He thanked the heavens that his uniform jacket extended below the belt line.

"Attempt contact on all channels," she ordered the comm officer.

"Yes, Admiral."

"And, Hadley—" she turned to her assistant "—call up the past year's history on anomalies in the W-285 sector and transfer it to my data-vis."

"Yes, ma'am." Lieutenant Keyren wore a perfect uniform and shadowed eyes. She hadn't been drinking last night like some of her cohorts, but it appeared she hadn't gotten much sleep, either.

Finn nodded at her and halted, hands on his hips as he turned to her superior. "Good morn, Admiral."

At the sound of his voice, Brit glanced over at him, barely acknowledging him, barely civil. Cold anger frosted her gaze. He'd expected some awkwardness, aye, perhaps a quick, private smile, but not this. The admiral was freepin' furo, as the space-hands liked to say. *Furious,* he'd translate to an officer. Not explosive fury; hers was frigid and still, like a polar morning after a storm front had passed, just as he'd expect.

She'd taken cover behind her Stone-Heart facade. She'd taken cover *from him.*

Finn didn't react. No spurned-lover sullenness from him. He knew better. His body language would appear as unaffected as hers was to the casual observer. Aye, he'd not give the crew anything to gossip about. He had too much respect for Brit to do anything less.

In her usual clipped, elegant tone, she told Finn, "It appears contact has been lost with the Cupezikan outpost. As ordered by Triad Alliance Command, we're to aid and assist as necessary in getting their deep-space comm back online."

He followed her eyes to a blinking light depicting the settlement on the holo-vis. He rubbed his chin, trying to remember what he knew of the region. He got his bearings quickly. W-285 sector straddled the border between Coalition and Hordish territory, a line considered arbitrary during the war.

Star-Major Yarew joined them. "Population—seventeen adult males. They've had comm outages before. Historical data shows sporadic instances of signal disruption when the system passes through its asteroid belt. Cupezikan is a science outpost."

It was a long way to come to study science, Finn thought. "What do they research—asteroids?"

"Sea life. In reality, though, not much. It's quite obviously a land grab under the guise of research."

"Aye." Finn was familiar with the practice of land grabbing. To maintain presence and continuously push the boundaries of the border, the Coalition had offered land and often employment to those civilians too naive or maybe too desperate to realize all the dangers of living so close to Hordish territory. Or perhaps to the settlers the risks were worth the reward of land and freedom. Most of the land-grabbers were force-evacuated or destroyed during the warlord's last offensive, but peace had brought the settlers back, apparently, including these seventeen men under the pretext of scientific study.

"It matters not why they are there, or how they got there. If the cessation of regular communications is enough to generate a go-see order, then we shall go see," Brit said, sounding vaguely annoyed at having to respond to such a lowly directive. "It is not as if we have any other pressing, relevant business." She tugged on the hem of her uniform jacket as if it wasn't already immaculate. "Set course for Cupezi-kan. Ninety percent full acceleration."

A pair of former Coalition pilots on duty responded. There were no wormholes through space to speed up their journey. It would be more than a ship-day before they got there.

Everyone on the bridge went immediately to work on matters relating to their first official mission. No one complained about how mundane a mission it was, helping an outpost with a tech issue. They were soldiers glad to have something to prepare for.

"Warleader."

"Yes, Admiral."

"We'll need a standard expeditionary crew to go down to the settlement tomorrow. Gather one."

"Aye-aye, Admiral." Brit fairly crackled with suppressed anger, most of it cloaked behind her chilly professionalism. She was all business. He wasn't sure what he'd expected to change after last night, but he'd expected something a hair warmer than this.

She's freepin' furo with you. Aye. How could sex that good make someone so angry? Or ill, for that matter? Before the day was over, he'd have his answers. For now he'd do her bidding. She was, after all, his commander, and he'd vowed to serve her. He'd give his life to fulfill that pledge.

He walked to a comm panel to assemble his team and sat down. The smart chair sank almost to the floor before rising to the height he'd programmed. Blast the damned thing! "Do that again, and out the airlock you go," he muttered. Was it his imagination, or did the chair give an extra jolt?

Only a few amused glances veered in his direction. He altered the settings—again. No matter what he adjusted, the so-called smart chairs did something else.

Not so different from Brit Bandar, eh?

Wary, he took his hand off the controls. The chair seemed to be holding steady now—that was, behaving like a normal chair, and he got down to business.

A peacetime minimum expedition team consisted of a shuttle craft, a pilot, a mechanic, an observer-liaison and a leader. That was a little too minimum for him. He'd throw on a couple of guards. He drummed his fingers on the console as he pondered who would make up his team. Automatically, he thought of Rakkelle to fly the shuttle. He changed his mind before he rang her quarters. He'd use the Earth-ling Tango instead this time, and her the next. Both pilots were well-trained in shuttle operations, but he aimed to put together a balanced team. With him along as leader, and Bolivarr as one of the guards, he needed to pick outside his own people to ensure a balanced team.

Within minutes, he'd spoken to Tango and Ensign Odin, a Coalition mechanic, a small, quiet woman who was rumored to be a genius with machinery. Next, he roused Bolivarr and another Earthling, Commander "Dice" Rothberg, formerly a type of soldier known as a SEAL. Both would provide the protection he didn't want to go planet-side without.

A familiar, almost irresistible scent drew his attention from the data-vis.

"Admiral," he said, turning. Brit stood behind him observing over his shoulder with Lieutenant Keyren in her shadow, as always.

"Warleader," Brit said. Her slightly husky voice did something to him. He wanted to snatch her hands and tug her arms around his shoulders. He wanted to drag her onto his lap and kiss her until she sighed and begged him to peel off her clothes. Begged him to be inside her, just as she had last night.

Growing warm, he ran a finger around his collar. The chair bobbed suspiciously as he shifted his weight to hide any possibly visible reaction to his thoughts. With interest, Brit scanned the data-vis for the names of the team so far. "Lieutenant Keyren will serve as observer-liaison," she said.

"Me?" Hadley gasped. At Brit's frown, she cleared her throat and seemed to get hold of herself. "Yes, ma'am!"

"You," Finn said, crooking a finger at the fair-haired lieutenant. "Meet me and the others in briefing room three on deck four."

"Yes, sir." Crisply, she turned on her heel and hurried off the bridge. Finn shook his head. Tango, Rothberg, Odin, Bolivarr and now Keyren—it was the kind of motley crew he was used to, but on a much smaller scale.

"Lieutenant Keyren?" he queried Brit after the woman had gone. "I like her, but she acts inexperienced."

"She is. I'm to blame. I never wanted to try her out on a combat mission, and that's all there was on the *Vengeance.*"

"I can see why. She's your assistant. An admin specialist."

"And I was a gunnery ensign for my first assignment. What were you when you first got on the pirate ship?"

"A deckhand," he admitted. "I moved up."

"And so will Hadley. She's a Royal Galactic Military Academy graduate—with honors—with a specialty in political leadership. She has the ability to command a ship of her own someday, but she has a long way to go before she gets there and won't get any closer following me around all day. As for you, Warleader, I need to see you in my office. There are other things that need to be addressed." As cold as ever, Brit walked off the bridge.

Other things. Here it comes, he thought. The brush-off.

He followed as Brit led the way, her hands clasped behind her back in her classic admiral's stride. She sat at her desk, but he stood, avoiding the smart chair on his side. It didn't matter that he'd updated the program only a few moments ago with his apparent preferences, the blasted things somehow continued to defy him.

"Door, close," she commanded the room-bot. "Sit," she commanded him.

"I'll stand."

She leaned back in her chair, her blue eyes glinting with cold fire. He had the feeling he was about to get his ass chewed. They were behind soundproof walls, although still in plain sight of the bridge. "Why didn't you tell me about the bar fight?"

Blast it. He'd meant to. *After.* Then she had gotten sick, and there was no after. Finn scrubbed a hand over his face. "I forgot."

"Conveniently. It might have spoiled the mood, hmm?"

"Damn right it might have. I happen to have liked that mood we were in. I didn't want to see it spoiled. Did you?"

That damned dark brow lifted. She said nothing and waited for him to speak.

She's hurt. Of course! He was a fool not to have seen it before. It wounded her that he'd come to her quarters with secrets that might have affected the turnout of the evening. If he had to hazard a guess, she felt used. He'd withheld information in order to get something he wanted: her. "I take full blame for not informing you immediately. Yarew said he'd write it up. I knew you'd see the report when you came on duty. It was no secret."

"They were your people, Rorkken. You said you'd take responsibility for them."

"And I did. I took care of the situation." He couldn't believe they were back to arguing after being with each other so intimately. It was like last night had never happened. Not so. His aching cock and the charged atmosphere between them attested that something had indeed happened, and changed things between them whether she wanted to see it or not.

He'd be a professional, though; he'd not risk his job or his crew's future to get back in her bed. He wanted her, gods he did, in and out of bed, but if he were forced to choose one or the other, it had to be his people. They were his responsibility, the reason he was here. By the heavens above, he hoped he was not forced to make that choice. "I spoke to the men. They won't be doing it again."

"I want sweef off my ship."

"Now wait a minute, Admiral. That's going too far."

"Is it? It's known galaxy-wide as a poison. It takes very little to make a person drunk. Overdosing causes irreversible brain damage."

"And so does drinking too much of your pretty Kin-Kan wine. Anything abused is dangerous. Especially sweef," he admitted. "My crew knows the dangers. It's your people who don't." He dragged his hand over his face again, pacing away and then back. "What are we saying? They're *our* people. Drakken, Coalition, Earthling."

"Yours, mine, ours," she said dismissively. "The ship's club is a public-use crew recreational facility, not a Borderlands drinking hole. Some on this ship don't seem to know the difference. Like the group of Drakken who drank too much last night and injured a Coalition officer without provocation."

Finn stopped, flabbergasted, his hands hanging at his sides. "Is that what it says in the report?"

She slid the data-vis across the desk. By the time he scanned to the end, he was damn well pissed off. "The information here is inaccurate."

"Star-Major Yarew is an intelligence officer, War-leader. A highly experienced one at that. We can trust his ability to construct and record an accurate summary of events."

"Not in this case. The blame for what happened last night was shared. There was some tension between the Drakken and the Coalition groups in the bar. No surprise, right? Drinking sweef degenerated into a contest to see who could tolerate the most. Insults were thrown." He decided to keep the actual accusations of murdering civilians private for fear she might agree. "The men reacted. And people were hurt."

Brit tapped her light pen on the desk, a slight frown tugging on that luscious mouth. If he had to hazard a guess, he'd say the discrepancies between his version of events and Yarew's troubled her.

"I've talked to the four Drakken involved. They'll know what to do the next time. I'll work with Dr. Kell. We'll make sure everyone understands the precautions to take when drinking sweef. But you can't ban it outright. It will make things worse."

"How so?"

He liked that she asked for his say—more evidence of her comfort with command. She listened to input before making a decision. She could even be talked down from a decision after making one. A Hordish battle-lord, on the other hand, would likely have lopped Finn's head right off—or his balls, whatever was more convenient. Although he suspected he wasn't out of danger yet.

It wouldn't stop him from looking out for his crew, though, even if they were no longer technically his. He'd give her the sleeping skins, aye, but he'd not give her the sweef. "It's all they have left. We already took the skins. Many have reported trouble adjusting to beds. I already took the liberty of banning grabble on board—it's a Hordish dice game. Losers pay up by being on the receiving end of punches."

"Nice," she muttered.

He rubbed his jaw, remembering more than one game of grabble gone bad in his younger days, usually played in dark, dank, smoky bars with much too much alcohol in the belly. "If you take away their sweef, too, it will be too much, too soon. It will demoralize them. They're still Drakken in Triad clothing. Give me a little more time to help them adjust. They're trying hard. Truly they are."

She sat back in her chair, tenting her elegant fingers on the desk as she pondered him. Something wasn't quite so hard about her anymore, yet he couldn't discern what had changed in those few moments. "All right," she said. "The sweef can stay."

There was not a single note of surrender in her voice. Only respect. Somehow, that meant the world to him.

"However, if there is any further trouble, it goes."

"Aye, Admiral. You have my word on that."

Her anger had faded some, but the aloofness remained. "That will be all, Warleader." She went back to reviewing data on the vis.

Disbelief grabbed at his gut. She was dismissing him like an annoying space-hand. He knew they needed to maintain the appearance of propriety in public, but no one could hear them in here. It amazed him that she hadn't acknowledged the previous night, not even in a small way. He knew damn well that he hadn't been the only one enjoying it. Talk about feeling used.

After a few moments she glanced up. Seeing that

he was still there, she frowned. "Officially, you're off duty, Warleader. Go rest."

"I have rested since last night." He walked to the desk, leaned his hands on it. He intended to remind them of the one thing they had in common and couldn't ignore. The heat. "I've taken my share of cold showers, too. How about you?"

Her cheeks flushed ever so slightly.

"I thought so. Now, I'm left wondering about your miracle recovery."

"There was nothing miraculous about it."

"You sounded mighty debilitated last night in the bathroom. Or faking it damn good. I'm ready to award you with acting honors. What else did you pretend last night?"

"Out," Brit said, bristling.

He pushed up from the desk. "That's what you said last night, too. What is it, Admiral? If it gets too close for comfort, you kick out the trespasser? If you wanted me to leave last night that's all you had to say. I'd probably have tried to convince you of the folly of your ways, but I'd have listened."

"My…condition was real. What happened in bed between us was real, too," she added, softer, even though no one could hear them. "If it hadn't been, I certainly wouldn't have reacted as poorly as I did afterward."

He responded with a classic double-take. "Was I just insulted, or…?"

"It's 'or.'"

"Or *what?* Guilt? Regret?"

More like shame, loneliness and overwhelming, all-consuming need, Brit thought. She stood, making sure her posture was perfect, and walked to the sideboard to pour a glass of water. She stood there, drinking, trying to gather her composure. "Nothing you saw in bed was staged. That is the truth." And far more than she'd revealed to any man since Seff died. "Ask me no more questions about what happened afterward. I can't talk about it. Accept what I've told you at face value." Her voice lost its harsh edge. "And that the woman you saw in bed was not pretending…anything."

"I'm glad, because last night was nice…very nice." He coughed out a laugh. "What am I saying? It was freepin' amazing, hot as hells. Sorry for my lack of finesse, but I want to do it all over again."

Damn him to the Dark Reaches, so did she. Like a fuel flash-fire, the heat came on so fast that it seemed to take all the air out of the room. It threatened to vaporize any lingering resistance.

Forgive me my weakness, Seff. Shame burned hot, almost as hot as her desire for Finn Rorkken. He was Drakken, yet it wasn't enough to keep her from thinking about him, from dreaming about him. From wanting him so badly that she was willing to risk the disgrace of her dead family to have him.

You'll burn in hells for this.

You're no longer a believer, she argued back, taking

shelter behind her utter lack of faith. She'd stopped believing the day the gods saw it necessary to take Seff and her babies. Innocents! She'd cut herself off from her devout parents so they'd stop trying to make her see the error of her ways. She'd spent the years since insulating herself from futile, silly pursuits such as wishes and fairy tales and religion. Even if she were still a believer, she probably wouldn't care at this point if she burned in hell. The past and the future had faded in the blaze of the present.

In the blaze that was Finnar Rorkken.

To get rid of a craving, sometimes you had to have your fill of it. Yes, she'd indulge in him once more. Tonight. Obviously, it was going to take several tries to get the blasted man out of her system. Then she'd be immune and her life would return to normal.

She feigned calm. "What are you doing after your shift, Warleader?"

"Now that's a loaded question if I ever heard one. What am I doing?"

"Improving your game of lightball. It needs work. Meet me on the courts after your shift later today. I'll be rested and ready to whup your sorry pirate's ass."

Rorkken threw his head back and laughed. "Thank you, Goddess," he said to the heavens. "The woman's come to her senses."

Smart Drakken. He already knew what she had in mind for after the game. A game of a different sort. "This is crazy, you know that," she said. "Highly

irregular, the two senior command officers…"
Fucking each other was the most fitting term but she couldn't bring herself to use such a coarse description in front of him. She never had any trouble doing so with the man-toys. What was wrong with her?

"I don't disagree," he said.

"If the crew ever found out…"

"They won't."

She thought of the black raptor tattooed on his arm. She'd avoid looking at it, or any other Hordish reminders. And if she couldn't? Her hand hovered over her stomach.

"Don't worry—I don't think you'll be taking refuge in the bathroom this time. I'll be keeping your focus elsewhere." His smile sent shivers to her toes. *Her rugged, wicked boy.* Then, with a mischievous wink, he was gone.

CHAPTER THIRTEEN

HADLEY HURRIED to make the briefing on time. Tango leaned against the wall of the corridor outside the room, twirling a nano-pic between his fingers as he held it between his lips. The set of lips she was supposed to have kissed by now. Grr. She stared straight ahead, hoping that by not making eye contact, the Earthling would not say anything as she passed by.

"I heard you were on this team," he said.

She slowed, wincing. Why did he have to talk to her? She didn't want to talk.

"That's not a happy face."

She groaned, exasperated. "Is there something you need, Earthling?"

"Your forgiveness. I'm sorry about what happened last night in the bar."

She felt heat rush to her cheeks. Damn her blushing. How could she stop doing it?

"I really wanted to be with you."

"You had a funny way of showing it."

"I know." He didn't try to defend his actions with

Rakkelle. His expression was sincere, yet her gut told her not to believe it.

"I'd like to make it up to you, Hadley." Those white teeth flashed. "Come up to my quarters for a drink."

"I can't do that—you can't do that. We've got a mission coming up."

"We don't go anywhere until the morning. And we're not at war, baby. It's a repair call, okay? We'll send in the mechanic and wipe our hands of it. Besides, you don't have to drink anything. Just come over to my place and relax. You do know how to relax, don't you?"

"Why, of course I do." Didn't she?

"We'll watch some movies, and I'll prove I'm not that bad of a guy. Let me make it up to you. Come on, Hadley. What do you say? Don't make me get down on my knees and beg."

He started to crouch, but she squeaked, stopping him by grabbing his arm. "Don't." His eager-to-please charm was winning her over by the second. Men never chased her, never flirted with her.

Never begged her to be with them.

She squashed the lingering warnings of her gut with the high hopes of her heart. "I'll come," she said softly. She'd give him a second chance.

"Cool. Meet me in the officer mess. Eighth hour, ship-time. We'll eat then go up to my place after, unless you want to get a drink in the bar first."

"No. No bar." No Rakkelle.

"We'll have drinks in my place then. Or you can watch me have one. Tango won't make you do anything you don't want to do."

Did he have any idea what she hoped for? An image of a serious, loving relationship surfaced again but she squashed it. Kisses first. The rest would follow. After all, they had an entire voyage to get to know one another.

He started walking backward, grinning as he did. Then he bumped into another Earthling, Rothberg— tall, lanky, short and spiky dark brown hair—who draped his arm over Tango's shoulder, telling him something in their language. They both looked at Hadley and smiled. She smiled back. Then Rothberg pulled Tango away, whispering words in his ear that made him laugh.

Tango winked at her over his shoulder and slapped the other man on the back. Then, together, the men walked into the briefing room, laughing and conversing in their strange language. Hadley wished she knew what they were saying.

She dug the mood ring out of her pocket where it had been since the night before and pushed it on her finger, holding out her hand to admire it. It immediately turned a brownish black. Not again! She frowned at it, tapping the stone.

"Trouble with your ring?"

Hadley went still. Bolivarr was standing next to her, but she hadn't heard him approach. As smooth and silent as cloud shadows, she thought. How did he do that? He wasn't small, or thin. He wasn't bulky with muscles like Tango, but he was well-built and tall, way too tall to slip in and out without notice. Yet he did. It was probably part of his training to be a wraith. She tried not to dwell on what else he was trained to do.

Standing there next to her, he seemed relaxed, almost sweet-looking with those tragic eyes and that lock of black hair falling over his forehead, but she sensed that inside he was on guard, ready to react to any threat. She shook her head, freeing it of the crazy thoughts. Even as a little child, one knew of the legendary wraiths. She never dreamed she'd ever see one up close unless she was about to take her last breath.

She swallowed and showed him the ring. "It's supposed to reveal my mood, but it keeps turning black or brown when it shouldn't." Like whenever she spoke to Tango. "Black means stressed or tense. Brown means nervous, harassed or overworked. It's showing both."

"Hmm. It looks purple to me."

"No, it's not…." She glanced down. *Goddess.* He was right. "It changed." The ring's stone now glowed a rich indigo hue. Startled, she glanced from the ring to Bolivarr and back again.

"What does it mean?"

Passion. Love. Romance. "It means the ring is broken." She twisted it off her finger and shoved it back in her pocket.

THE LIGHTBALL MATCH went on for far longer than Brit expected. It left her exhilarated, exhausted and one point in trail of Rorkken. Every time she tied the score, he'd pull ahead.

She wanted the sex, yes, but her competitive nature kept her on this court. She was drenched with sweat, and so was Rorkken. It felt odd and rather pleasant to be doing something extracurricular with a lover. She never saw them outside of bed—or wanted to. What was different about Rorkken?

Nothing! Drakken or not, he was to be used for sex like she had all the others.

Rorkken sauntered up to her, tossing the lightball in his palm. "How much longer are you going to fight me for that point?"

"You can't possibly call this match yours. It's only your second time. I've been playing for years. I always win."

His eyes glittered wickedly, tossing the damn ball as he walked closer. "It's obvious you haven't been playing with the right men."

"If I play with you then I will lose? Is that what you are telling me?"

"If you play with me tonight…" He bent forward, his mouth close to her ear, and she shivered. "You will feel like you have won."

Her body tightened. She felt his deep, rumbling purr of a voice down to her toes. She turned her head, wanting to kiss him, and remembering they were in a public place. She didn't want to repeat the risk she'd taken last night, kissing him in this glass-walled court. "I accept your offer," she said, hearing the breathless anticipation in her own voice.

"That will require a change in location. Your quarters."

"I have to shower."

"I'll help you."

There. He'd voiced what they both were thinking. No wasting precious time showering separately. The sooner they'd peeled their clothing off, the sooner they would be pressed flesh to flesh. She swallowed. "All right."

How quickly she'd agreed. *To get rid of a craving, indulge it, indulge until you can no longer stand it.* Yes, that was it. She'd see this affair, this dalliance, this *obsession* through to its conclusion, whether it took one more night or several. She looked forward to the day when she could see him and not feel as though she were losing her mind.

TANGO'S QUARTERS WERE smaller than hers, Hadley observed as he let her precede him through the doorway. Her roomier living space was a privilege afforded her thanks to her position as Admiral Bandar's assistant. She didn't often think of the benefits of her job until she saw how an officer of equivalent rank lived on the ship. Then again, her job was all day, every day. At the admiral's whim, she could be roused from deep sleep and asked to assist in one way or another. She didn't mind. She loved serving her hero. It was a rare honor to have the chance to work with and learn from a legend.

"Welcome to Ground Zero," Tango inexplicably said. Not all he did or said translated properly. It kept her a little bit off balance every moment she was with him, leaving her with a nervous but giddy feeling she both loved and hated.

"Ground Zero," she repeated, turning in a full circle to marvel at how he'd transformed his quarters. It looked like none she'd ever seen on a ship. It felt as if she'd stepped onto Earth. She knew little of the protected shrine world, but if she were to set foot on the planet, she fancied that this was just how it would appear.

A large flag hung on one wall. One third each blue, white and red, with a big white star on the blue portion. "God bless Texas," he explained, placing his hand over his heart in obvious reverence. Clearly, the flag represented an Earth-based religion with which she wasn't familiar.

There was a large, two-dimensional image showing Tango with a group of men and a woman dressed in blue jumpsuits standing next to a primitive, fossil-fuel-burning air vehicle. "That's called an F-15. I was a Thunderbird pilot before this assignment— number six, solo. I tell you, girl, a chance to serve on the *Unity* was the only thing that could have pulled me away from that gig. This is a dream come true even more than that was."

Hadley continued to gape at the wondrous artifacts and objects in the room. A large, glittering sphere hanging from the ceiling slowly rotated in the ventilation breeze. "What is that?"

"That, baby girl, is a disco ball."

"What does it do?"

"Nothing. It's only a decoration. Vintage seventies—the last century—in Earth years. Disco is a type of dancing." He grabbed her hands, lifting an arm over her head and twirling her, before bending her over backward, supporting her lower back with one big hand.

She squeaked with surprise, her heart beating hard, her fingers squeezing his hand. "Disco doesn't come close to tango," he said, his voice softer, more seductive. "And, yes, it's a dance I aim to teach you." His gaze drifted to her mouth before he let her back to her feet.

Breathless and a bit dizzy, she swayed on her feet. His hand was slow to leave hers. Nothing like this had ever happened to her.

Nothing like him.

"I think we need something to drink." He opened the door to a small, humming black box.

"What's that?" It seemed she had only two words left: *what's* and *that*.

"It's a refrigerator. I like to keep my own. Stocked.

This ship doesn't have electricity like we have on Earth. I had to rewire the thing and reroute it to ship's power to get it running."

That was irregular. She hoped the chief engineer didn't find out. Or the safety officer.

Shyly, she gazed around his quarters. Her focus zeroed in on the bed. When they were finally together, that's where they would be. That's where she would finally lose her damned virginity.

"What's your pleasure?" he asked.

She jumped. "I beg your pardon?"

"What would you like to drink?"

She bent over to peer inside the cold black box. "It's so marvelously primitive!"

He laughed. "We cavemen like our beer." He handed her a bottle, but she wrinkled her nose, remembering the bitter taste. "How about a Coke instead?" He poured the contents of a red-and-silver metal container into a glass. Here you go."

Unlike beer, it was brown and fizzy and sweet. "I like it!"

Grinning, he tipped his head and seemed to drink in the sight of her. "So, I don't see the ring I gave you."

"Oh. I have it. It's in my pocket."

"Why? You don't like it?"

She stammered as she dug it out. "I wasn't sure if it was broken or not. The colors…"

"It's not broken. The stone in a mood ring is made of thermotropic crystals covered by glass. Heat makes the crystals twist and reflect different wavelengths of light, which changes the color of the ring. You have to wear it and let it react to your body heat first. Otherwise it won't work."

Hadley bit her lip. The ring *was* changing color. Just not to the color she wanted to see.

Maybe it's the color you need to see.

Hadley gave her head a shake.

Tango took the ring and slid it on her finger. "It's beautiful," she said. "And…gray." *Anxious, very nervous, strained.* But not black or brown, thank the gods. It was an improvement.

"You need to relax, that's why. Here." He patted a strange-looking place to sit. The chairs were nothing like she'd ever seen. They reminded her of sacks of grain with white velvety covers.

"They're beanbag chairs," he explained, using his language.

"Ah." She was relieved and disappointed at the same time to see that the chairs were separate. It would have been nice to get cozy on a couch. Then, as she got braver, she could slide closer. If she got braver.

As she tried to get comfortable on the cushions that felt as if they were filled with pebbles, Tango fiddled with another antiquated device into which he inserted a silvery disc. Music and a moving image came on a screen.

She clapped her hands together. "Finally—the moo-vee." The actors in the movie spoke his language, but she could read text in the Queen's tongue. "The god of the Dark Reaches wears Pra-dah!"

"You bet, baby. Just like I promised." He laughed, swigging the last of the beer in the bottle. He opened a new bottle. Hadley had barely touched her beverage.

Sucking down more beer, he dimmed the lights and put on music—music during a movie?—and walked back to her. "Scoot over."

Wasn't the chair too small for two? He aimed his rear at a spot next to her hip, and she rolled to the side. His heavy body crushed the chair. "Put your legs—" he lifted her thighs over his "—right here."

Hadley pretended Tango wasn't so close, and that she wasn't sitting on his lap. Onscreen, the "Prada" movie unfolded. A humorless woman and her curt behavior toward her assistant made Hadley uncomfortable. It was clear that Tango thought the woman acted similar to Admiral Bandar.

After all the admiral had done for her, she felt guilty watching, especially in light of the contents of the white box. If Admiral Bandar came across as faultlessly professional, or cold to people who didn't know her well, she undoubtedly had good reason to be. Hadley was sure of it.

Tango's hand now rested on her thigh. Her heart raced. Her skin pricked. She hadn't sat on a man's lap since perching on her father's knee to listen to stories when she was a child. She wasn't sure what Father would think of her sitting on Tango, hardly knowing him. She decided not to think of that. She decided she wanted a real kiss.

Tango's hand inched over her knee as he sensed her looking at him. He'd finished the second bottle of beer and put it aside. The sweetish scent of alcohol scented his breath. "Ah, you smell so good. What are you thinking about, pretty girl?"

Laps. Kisses. Things like that. Blushing, she looked down at her Coke.

"You are so sweet." He took the glass from her hands then leaned over her. She wondered if he could hear her heart beating. It was pounding that hard. "That mouth of yours looks so delicious, I'm gonna have to taste it."

She gulped as his face loomed closer. She gulped again as he reached behind her head and undid her chignon. Her hair spilled around her jaw. "I've wanted to kiss you since the first day I saw you," he said.

She let out a sigh. Hearing his confession, she couldn't help it.

"So sweet… Come here, my little apple."

Warm, dry lips brushed over hers. She felt the answering thrill in her belly. They touched mouths again, tasting each other. The tip of his tongue ran along the seam of her lips, parting them, allowing his tongue to push inside. Her hands closed over his shoulders in surprise. This was what she'd read about but missed experiencing for herself. Reading about love and sex was one thing; feeling it was another.

Tango pressed her into the crunchy cushions. Oh, to have a smart couch supporting her back. He was making soft groans as he kissed her. The tongue digging in her mouth was supposed to feel good, wasn't it? Except she remained all too conscious of it—that it was a *tongue,* and that it belonged to Tango—to enjoy the sensation as she suspected she was supposed to.

She wasn't quite sure what to do while he was kissing her other than keep her mouth open. He came up on an elbow. His other hand slid up her left thigh to her hip, hesitated, then traveled up her rib cage. He groaned again, and his thumb brushed over her breast. A flicker of sensation radiated outward from her nipple.

Her eyes were wide-open now. Now she was conscious of both sensations—that of his tongue, and that of his hand kneading her left breast. He'd clearly forgotten about the movie, she thought as she glanced back at the glowing screen.

Her attention snapped to Tango the instant he settled himself between her thighs. She clearly felt the length of his erection outlined under the fabric of his trousers. He was aroused. *She'd* aroused him. An oddly exhilarating sense of power came over her that she conjured this reaction in him.

He felt for her what she felt for him! He pulled his mouth from hers. "Baby," he breathed on her neck. "Sweet girl." His hand fumbled with her collar. Her hands were flat on his shoulders; she wasn't sure what to do with them. In the shadows, the mood ring glinted.

It was as black-brown as burned toast.

He unfastened the seam at her collar and tugged it open all the way to her navel. Hadley sucked in a shocked breath as cool air hit her bare skin. It was like getting doused with ice water; it woke her from her stupor. "Excuse me." She shoved on his shoulders, moving him to the side, and squeezed out from under his body.

Gathering her uniform closed, she got her feet under her. "I'm not ready for that." *Coward!* Now that she finally had her chance—her chance at everything—fear had overtaken her.

Tango came up on his elbow. His lips looked reddened, puffier. "Aw, baby. That's okay." His brown eyes were intent on her. Despite his gentle, slightly amused tone, she felt as if she were in the sights of a weapon. "We don't have to do anything you don't want to." He patted the cushion. The pebbles inside rattled. "I'm so lonely. Come back. We'll just cuddle."

Cuddling was fine, she decided. She smiled, and snuggled close. She liked the way his arms felt around her. He kissed her hair so sweetly as his hand circled over her back, her hip, her thigh. And then her rear end. "You've got the sweetest little butt, you know that?" Before she realized what was happening, he'd rolled her onto her back and was kissing her again—with more force and intent than before. She squeezed her eyes shut and concentrated, waiting to be swept away. How else would you feel comfortable enough about stripping naked and having someone look at you with no clothes on? To have them touching you…everywhere? Swept away was definitely a prerequisite, and all she detected was the faintest of undertows.

"Ooh, baby." Tango swayed his hips, grinding himself against her as they kissed. His movements had increased in intensity. He lifted his head, his handsome face so close to hers. "Girl, have mercy. You're torturing me here. You gotta let me out of my misery. I'm your slave. Your love slave. Set me free."

She giggled, and he slipped his hand inside her uniform, yanking down her bra and exposing her breasts. His mouth locked on one of them before she had a chance to protest. A suckling sensation on her tender nipple made her gasp; his mouth was warm and wet. She wasn't sure what she thought of the sensation, but she wasn't staying around long enough to process it. Everything was happening too fast.

She wriggled out from under him and bounded away. Pulling up her bra, she closed her uniform seam. "It was great, Tango. I had a good time. Thanks for the Coke. It's better than beer. But I've got to go."

She started for the door.

"Hadley. Wait." He was there in an instant. He loomed over her, his hair messy, his eyes dark and almost scary. She felt a flicker of fear. He might be a crew member, but she didn't really know him.

He shook his head at her, his hand sliding over her cheek so tenderly that it released a wave of relief. His voice was so gentle it made her heart ache. "Baby, you haven't done this before, have you?"

"Done this?"

He chuckled softly. "Miss Answer-a-Question-With-a-Question. *Made love,*" he murmured, kissing her on the side of her throat.

It was that obvious she was a virgin? Mortified, she blushed deeply. "Oh, that. I've done it lots of times."

"Yeah? What did those lucky gentlemen have that I don't?"

No words came to her.

He nibbled her ear. "You sure you want to leave?"

"Yes," she said quietly. She wanted to run back to her quarters and hide.

"Let me leave you with this for now." His hands landed on both sides of her red-hot face. "May I?"

She nodded, her heart racing again. He lowered his head and kissed her. This time, it was sweet, tender-sweet, and gentle. She trembled. He sighed in approval as he pulled away. "When we're together, it will be like that, Hadley. I promise."

Gentle and sweet. That wouldn't be so frightening.

"Okay," she said.

He took her hand, tipping his head toward the bed. "So, would you like to try again?"

The urgency was back in his demeanor again. He thought he'd hidden it under his amiable nature, but she saw it and lost her courage. "Maybe next time."

"Yeah? Don't be teasing me like that, girl."

"No, I mean it." *Do you, Hadley?* Yes, her virginity had to go. The sooner the better!

She pressed the door release. She flashed what she hoped was a flirtatious smile, flipping her hair around her neck as she stepped outside. "All good things are worth the wait." Where did *that* come from?

The door closed, ending the moment. She leaned against the wall to catch her breath. Gods. She was in over her head. It was frightening and wonderful. And yet it was relief that swamped her now, not disappointment, not unrequited lust. She was probably still too inexperienced for lust. For *passion.* That would come later when she knew what she was doing.

She took a deep and trembling breath and hurried back to her quarters, feeling older but not at all wiser.

FINN WOKE, alone. The lighting in Brit's quarters was set to a dim, amber glow, something she must have adjusted after he'd fallen asleep. The last thing he remembered after making love was her head resting on his chest, her arm and leg thrown over his body to hold him close.

Now, that was the way to settle into slumber, he thought: Brit clinging to his body as if she never wanted to let him go. Sighing heartily, he grinned. Now where was she?

He lifted his head and found her sitting in a chair facing the window. Her bare feet were propped on the window frame, her expression melancholy as she sipped from a glass of wine. The bottle on the table was half-empty. It was clear she'd been up for some time. How could someone who seemed to enjoy the sex as much as she did feel so low afterward?

Someone had hurt her in the past, and badly. Any heart that took this long to heal must have been broken beyond recognition. He'd like to find the bastard who did this to her. Aye, and flay him alive. In the meantime, Finn intended to do everything in his power to make her forget the grains-for-brains idiot who didn't realize the value of what he'd had. Maybe it was because Finn had started out with nothing, but he never took anything for granted.

He swung his feet off the bed and went to her. Brit's silk robe, cinched around her waist, split where her long legs emerged. His cock twitched at the thought of running his lips from her knee up the warm length of her inner thigh, and not stopping there. No, not stopping there. She liked it when he pleasured her, which made him want to do it all the more. The reward was always rich.

She barely glanced up as he crouched down by the chair. "You've graduated from hiding in the bathroom to being pensive and drinking," he said. "We're making progress, sweetheart."

He smoothed his hand up her thigh, parting the robe even more. Her flesh was blazing hot but he held back from a more intimate caress. Her eyelids dipped a fraction, telling him his touch aroused her, and that she craved more. Aye, he'd learned to read his Brit well in their hours together. He slid his hand the rest of the way, cupping her, possessing her.

"Finn…" she protested, a tremble running through her graceful body.

"Fire goddess," he whispered in her ear.

"Damn it," she said, and blushed. *Blushed!* She seemed an odd mix of embarrassment, desire and surrender.

On one knee, he took the wineglass from her hand and set it on the table. "Come back to bed, sweetheart. There's a little more time, and I aim to maximize our use of it. That is, if you're willin'…."

She turned in the chair and reached across the short distance between them, holding his cheek in her warm, soft hand. She didn't have to speak. Her expression was gentle, almost relieved, and told him everything he needed to know.

He scooped her out of the chair and carried her to bed. Before they even fell to the mattress, they were pressed together in the kind of feverish, scorching kiss that made him crazy for wanting her.

CHAPTER FOURTEEN

THE BRIDGE BUSTLED with activity as the *Unity* prepared to exit light-speed at the outskirts of the region of space where the outpost of Cupezikan lay in silence.

Hadley's blood sang with adrenaline as she entered the shuttle airlock dressed in expeditionary gear: a black, all-condition one-piece suit, and thick boots. She carried her gloves and a data-vis in her arms. The weight of the weapons on her belt was unfamiliar—a light, a variety of tools and a pistol. It had been one blur of a crazy day since yesterday: her first real kiss and her first real mission.

Tango, Odin, Rothberg and Bolivarr joined her. "Come on, my motley crew," Warleader Rorkken sang out. "We've places to be."

The Drakken acted positively buoyant this morning. What put Rorkken in such a good mood? He must love the idea of getting off the ship as much as she did.

"Move, move!" he ordered, though Hadley saw he

was clearly having fun. Yep, he must have had a really good day.

Or a really good night.

Tango brought his mouth close to her ear. "He sounds like my old drill instructor. Talk about an ass-leap initiator. He always had his boxers in a twist."

Finn grabbed the pilot out of ranks and pushed him up against the wall. "You got something to say about me, Major, you say it *to me*. Got that?"

Tango's dark brown eyes flashed with humiliation and anger. He looked as if he were about to strike back. Did he not respect the Drakken? The war-leader's leadership style contrasted sharply with Admiral Bandar's but it was no less effective. He'd long since won Hadley's respect.

"Go ahead, I dare you," Rorkken snarled softly.

Hadley held her breath during the charged silence as everyone looked on. Then Tango mellowed, his shoulders sagging. "Sorry. Sorry, *sir*. My bad."

Rorkken let him go but kept one hand flat on the wall to the side of Tango's head. His voice was steady, quiet. "As routine as it may seem, this is a mission, Barrientes. This is real. People have gotten killed on missions no different from this one. If you feel the need to show off in front of a girl, do so back on the ship."

Suddenly, Hadley shivered, as if a shadow had passed over her on a sunny day. Cloud shadows, she thought, shifting her attention to Bolivarr. Decked out

in black expeditionary gear, very much resembling
the assassin he used to be, he watched her quietly,
keenly, as if he could see all the way through her—
including (and maybe especially) her awkwardness
at not knowing as much as she should about men at
this stage in her life. Bolivarr didn't need to kiss her
to figure out her utter lack of experience. She wore
it like a badge. No wonder none of the men on the
Vengeance had ever sought her out for sex. Forcing
her eyes from his, she wanted to melt into a puddle
of embarrassment.

"Or I'll replace you with Rakkelle," Warleader
Rorkken threatened. "Got that, Major? Say the word
and I'll call her down here. She'll be happy to take
your spot."

And flirt with every man aboard the shuttle?
Hadley narrowed her eyes.

"Hell, don't do that," Tango said. At least they
were on the same page where Rakkelle was concerned. Maybe not for the same reasons, though.

"All right, then." Rorkken slapped the pilot on the
shoulder and pushed him on ahead. "Fly us down
there, and do me proud."

"Yes, sir."

Seeming meeker now, Tango didn't make eye
contact with her. She, on the other hand, didn't make
further eye contact with Bolivarr. No one was
looking at anyone. It was going to be an interesting
expedition.

The interior of the shuttle was snug and brand-new. "New shuttle smell," Tango said as he strapped in.

The Earthling said the strangest things.

Warleader Rorkken secured himself into a forward seat near Tango. "Initiate separation sequence," he ordered.

Tango ran through a checklist. "Auxiliary boosters. Check. Weapons systems…"

"Online," Rorkken confirmed.

"Life support systems," Tango finished.

"Check," the entire crew chorused.

"Tell them we're ready, Major."

"Shuttle One's good to go," Tango commed to a space controller sitting at the bridge.

"Cleared to launch," the controller replied.

"Separation initiated." The shuttle broke free of the enormous battleship. "Separation complete."

As they fell away into the silence of space, Hadley could see Admiral Bandar watching them, framed in the forward windows on the bridge of the huge ship. A proud, lonely shadow in Triad uniform, hands behind her back.

Who owned a box with a pair of baby shoes hidden inside. There was so much more to her hero than Hadley knew, so many layers hidden beneath that calm, capable exterior. If only there was a way to learn more. Hadley's curiosity was driven by compassion more than anything else, although she suspected that showing concern regarding anything remotely emotional would not sit well with the admiral.

When Hadley brought her attention back to the interior of the shuttle, she found the warleader watching Admiral Bandar, too, with the oddest mix of confusion, yearning and tenderness. What was this? Her breath caught in her throat. She might not have much hands-on experience with men, but she knew what a man looked like when he had feelings for a woman. Powerful feelings. *Moonstruck,* the people on her homeworld, Talo, would have called it. Much was told and sung about the magic of such a glance.

Which isn't at all how Tango looks at you.

Yet, she thought.

Her attention shifted back to the warleader. No, she wasn't mistaken. He was moonstruck. She expected to be horrified on Admiral Bandar's behalf but as a true Taloan she found herself wishing crazily and probably futilely that there was something romantic brewing between the pair. The admiral deserved to have someone look at her that way, even if he was a Drakken.

Hadley let out a silent sigh and settled in for the ride down to the surface.

"READY, SIR? I'm going to juice it," Tango said, dragging Finn's attention from Brit's silhouette to the mission at hand. Try as he might, he couldn't get last night—or her—off his mind, but he had to. Duty first.

Finn double-checked his safety straps, a reminder that he had more reason than ever to want to return to the ship in one piece. *Someone to come home to.* Aye, he liked the sound of that. Plans had already been made for a lightball match later. As much as he enjoyed the game, he liked her more. He'd use his pirate wiles to convince her to skip the match and play with him instead.

His mouth slid into a smile he directed to his team. "Ready for some fresh air, my motley crew? Wantin' to stretch yer legs planetside?"

A roar of enthusiastic "ayes" came in response. Finn chuckled. A pirate's crew they weren't, but they sounded damn convincing. "Aye, juice it, Major."

Lowering his black visor over his face, Tango gave Finn a thumbs-up. "Course heading, Captain?" he asked.

"Are you blind? The planet's right there."

"You're supposed to say, 'Second star to the right and straight on 'til morning.'"

It grew silent in the shuttle as everyone stared at the Earthling. Only Rothberg snickered. "You're an f-ing idiot, Tango."

The shuttle flipped over on a stubby wing and soared down to the mist-swathed planet below.

Within moments, they'd hit the atmosphere. The air was rough. Anything not tied down bounced around. Tango had his hands full with the flying. Rothberg and Odin looked a bit green. Keyren glowed with excitement. Bolivarr, ever watchful, sat so still and silent that he almost blended into the shadows of the instrument panels above his head— everything but his black, intense eyes, that was. If the former wraith remembered anything yet about the five-year gap in his memory, he'd made no indication of it. The man rarely spoke, and only when necessary. No wasted words, unlike the Earthling.

Tango maneuvered the shuttle to within touching distance of enormous towering cloud formations. They soared over an immense sparkling sea in clear skies, searching for a massive, finger-shaped island, the only land on the planet, and where the settlement was located. Finn had a repeat of what Tango saw on his nav-display on his data-vis. He studied the general layout of the encampment. "It will be on the western shore…between the hillside and the beach."

He squinted in the sunshine, looking for arrays of antennae and equipment and habitation domes. Nothing yet. They were too far out to acquire anything visually. "Attempt comm contact." While their deepspace comm might be out, local comm would be working.

"Cupezikan, this is Shuttle One," Tango tried. "Do you read?"

They'd made similar attempts all through the night and when entering orbit.

"Still no reply, sir."

Below, the landscape was idyllic: turquoise water,

wide beaches and lush trees. With peace having taken away the dangers of living so close to the Horde-lands, this planet would be an ideal location to start a new life. Not that the dangers had often mattered during the war; land-grabbers were fiercely indepen-dent, and were known to ignore warnings when it came to their safety if it meant abandoning their land.

Lieutenant Keyren was half out of her chair, using eye-tubes to scan manually through the window while Tango continued trying comm contact. As they flew over the northern tip of the island, the habita-tion domes, a few roads and some cultivated areas came into view. The mechanic, Odin, scanned for heat signatures. "I've got the amplification at max. It's weird, sir. No one's around. There's nothing here but the creatures in the forest."

The scientists should be showing up as heat sigs, too. Faint unease washed over Finn. He knew never to discount his gut. Silver domes were scattered like pebbles along the beach, and not one human to be seen, inside or out. Where were they?

The back of his neck prickled as he commed the *Unity.* "Rorkken to Admiral Bandar."

After a moment, he heard Brit's reply, and some-thing shifted inside him, something soft and out of place in the middle of a mission. He tamped it down and focused. There was a reason you didn't sleep with someone on the crew, and this was it. Somehow he had to keep what he had with Brit special and separate. He didn't want to give her up. Gods, not yet. He knew how to hold on to something good, the rare times something good came his way. "The outpost appears to be empty. Are we in the right location?"

"Stand by," she said curtly.

The *Unity* streamed new coordinates to the shuttle. Tango downloaded the data to his nav-display. "We're in the right place, Warleader," the pilot said. He snap-rolled the shuttle up on a wingtip, circling hard as they descended to allow a better look. Odin made a strangled noise. A few seconds later, she was puking into a sick-sac.

Land-folk, Finn thought. That's what his crew would call her. Rothberg didn't look too good, either, but he was a man used to the sea, a different domain from the air.

Lower now, they blazed over the hillside. Hadley twisted around in her seat. "Look at that. There's debris on the beach."

Finn cursed and tossed aside the damned data-vis. Useless thing. The lieutenant had seen with eye-tubes and human eyes what hi-tech means could not. He threw off his straps to peer alongside her out her window, glad he'd brought Keyren along. She'd more than filled her role as observer.

An antenna array was down, most of it washed back up on the beach. "That explains the lack of comm," he said.

"A killer wave?" Rothberg suggested.

"Hmm. Possible, but the sand's not washed away…and the tree line is intact."

"Goddess…" Keyren's voice had changed tone. "Bodies, Warleader."

"Are you sure they're…?" *Dead,* he was about to ask. One glance eliminated the question. Quite clearly dead, all seventeen scientists were sprawled facedown in the sand, unmoving, some with their limbs at awkward angles.

"Freepin' hells," he snarled. No wonder no one had answered their calls. The entire population of Cupezikan had been wiped out.

BRIT CIRCLED the holo-vis, pacing incessantly. To her annoyance, the virtual journalist trailed her, asking too many questions: "Do you expect more search-and-rescue missions like this?" "Will there be more land-grab opportunities in the Borderlands now that the war is over?" "What does that light indicate, and that one over there?" "Do you miss your old post?"

Brit summoned patience, formulating and dispensing safe answers while she waited anxiously to hear back from Rorkken. She hated the silences between his reports. She hated that she hated the silences.

Damn him. Damn Rorkken for making her give a care whether he lived or died. She wanted him out of her skin, out of her head. She didn't want him getting near her heart.

Last night had made that a little more difficult.

What was happening to her? Her entire body reacted to thoughts of him—not just the sex, but the feel of his arms holding her. She'd felt utterly safe. Happy. She'd fled the sensation, yes, even tried using wine to numb her reaction to him; but he'd dragged her back into the refuge that was his embrace. She'd gone willingly, too! He was an addiction. A drug.

Forgive me my weakness.

She closed one fist. Time spent with him wasn't making her obsession better; it was making it worse. Her extracurricular activities were to blame. He was supposed to be a sexual partner, not a friend.

No lightball later; they were going directly to bed. Their only interaction outside work from now on would be of a sexual nature. She'd get him out of her system no matter how long it took. Then once more she'd be able to focus on meting out the justice denied her family on Arrayar. The war may have ended but her crusade had not.

Smiling softly, she turned to the journalist. "Yes, I do think of my old posting from time to time. I miss it. However, I am honored and proud to be serving the Triad Alliance in a diplomatic capacity so critical to advancing peace."

Propaganda, she thought. Utter crap.

Her PCD beeped. Her hand flew to her ear. "Bandar."

"Admiral, we've got a problem down here—"

"What, what is it?" She winced, detesting the

anxiety in her voice, making it sound as if she cared about the warleader's welfare. *Damn him.* And Hadley…The girl was with him, also in harm's way. It was dangerous, caring about others. Why did she continue to form attachments? Hadn't she learned? "Report."

"All seventeen inhabitants are dead."

Brit's pulse may have doubled but her outward appearance remained unchanged. "Noted." She waved to Berkko, the chief watch officer. *Get her off the bridge,* she mouthed, jerking her chin at the virtual journalist who was now perusing a grid map of the settlement and probably cooking up more questions.

"I'm sorry," she told the woman. "I must attend to the team down on the planet. We'll finish this up later, yes?"

Berkko hit the signal disconnect. The journalist vanished before she could utter another annoying syllable. Then Brit turned away to take Rorkken's incoming comm.

ON THE SHUTTLE, Finn finished briefing Brit. "It's not clear what killed them. The antenna array is down, and there's debris. We're going down to find out more."

There was a prolonged hiss before he heard her voice again. It was controlled but softer. "Use caution, Finn."

Finn. She'd actually called him by his given

name outside bed, and without him wheedling her into doing so.

That one, simple acknowledgment of their secret relationship turned him to putty in her hands. He'd walk to the ends of the universe for her if she asked. On the other hand, he was all too aware of the many ears listening to his end of the conversation. "Aye. I'll resume contact planetside."

Finn told Tango, "Put us down beyond the hillside."

"Yes, sir."

The shuttle's vertical engines whined in the thick atmosphere—humid air, if the vegetation was an accurate indication. "Atmosphere still at safe levels," Odin said.

"Confirmed," Finn said, checking his readouts.

With a gentle thump, the shuttle touched down and went silent. "Shuttle secure, checklist complete," Tango reported.

They took extra care donning their gloves and checking their weapons and comm systems before Finn shoved open the hatch. Pistol drawn, he started to step outside.

"Sir," Rothberg called out at the same time Bolivarr warned, "Warleader."

"What?" he said, anxious to take a look around.

"We go first. Me and Bolivarr. It's why you brought us along."

Bolivarr said nothing. He didn't have to; the man's dark, enigmatic gaze radiated both resolve and concern. Finn grunted his displeasure. Since when did his crew have to worry about him?

Since you got them real jobs on a real ship with real procedures. On the *Unity,* blast it, the boss didn't stick his head up first.

"No" almost slipped out of his mouth. Outside, the beach was deserted, but there was no telling what had happened to the men. If he got himself killed in the first seconds, the team would lose their leader, and Brit her second-in-command.

Use caution, Finn. Aye, he would, but not at the expense of his team's safety. Still, he needed to use the team members for what he'd brought them here to do.

"Go on, then," he grumbled. It took everything he had to let the two men go out ahead of him; he liked being on-scene first, not last.

"Be careful," Hadley told Bolivarr, her voice barely audible. Bolivarr's attention lingered on her a few seconds longer than what Finn would consider normal for the man. Interesting. Until this point, the wraith hadn't seemed to take much notice of anyone of either gender on either the *Pride* or the *Unity.* He'd noticed Hadley Keyren, however.

The wraith gave the lieutenant a nod before slipping silently and gracefully out the hatch behind Rothberg.

Nothing stirred on the beach but the breeze.

Before long, the men signaled it was safe to emerge. Damn embarrassing, Finn thought, having to wait for someone to tell him it was safe to stick his neck out. He strapped on his weapons and double-checked the fittings on his suit. "Let's go," he told the remaining crew. "Grab your equipment. Odin, you've got the medical kit."

"Yes, sir."

They took off in the direction of the bodies. It was the smaller items scattered along the beach that captured Finn's attention: a hat, a light pen, a shoe. Wind and rain had erased most footprints, but a few gashes in the sand pointed to a fight. "There was a struggle," Rothberg said, scooping up the pen to study it.

"Aye." A piece of metal poked out of the sand. Finn picked it up. It was round, metal, silver in color.

"Found something?"

"It looks like a utility clip for a rifle, probably a plasma rifle by the shape of it. Not a model I recognize."

"Coalition?"

"It must be. It's not Drakken." Finn turned the part over in his hand, studying it as he walked. It seemed unusual to find evidence of advanced weaponry on a backwater outpost, unless the Coalition had started arming scientist-settlers before the war ended. Having come from the other side, he wouldn't know. "I'll have Yarew analyze it back on the ship." It paid to have an intelligence officer on board sometimes. He dropped the piece in his pocket.

Where the corpses lay, the stink was powerful. Insects buzzed around the putrefying flesh.

"Ah shit, that's bad," Rothberg groaned as Tango made what appeared to be a religious sign over his chest. Odin was back to filling a sick-sac.

"Goddess…" Lieutenant Keyren covered her mouth. At her side, Bolivarr observed the scene without a trace of distress. Like Finn, the wraith had seen his share of death and destruction, as had the rest of the Drakken on the *Unity*. This was an unpleasant discovery, aye, but nothing compared to the scenes of carnage he'd encountered in the past. Yet, to someone not accustomed to a massacre, it would be disturbing. Take these seventeen corpses and times it by a hundred or more. That's when it started getting bad, when the bodies tangled together, and when the heads and limbs were no longer attached. Not that all Drakken were immune; their tolerance was simply higher.

Everyone had their limit. Some who witnessed the aftermath of atrocities never recovered. When the emotional damage was too severe, unable to be numbed by drinking and sex, suicide was sometimes the last, best escape. He'd seen it a number of times over his two careers.

"Put on your nose-breathers," Finn ordered the team. "I don't want anyone puking on the bodies." He left his breather in his pocket—he'd long ago figured out how to tune out the worst of what life presented him without any help—and crouched by the first body.

At the base of the man's skull was a blackened entry wound. He didn't need to see the other side to know what the face looked like. Traces of gore on the sand told him it was gone.

He shoved to his feet and walked to the next body, and the next, until he'd seen every last one of them. The scientists had been shot, each one, execution-style.

Skulled, he thought, dread filling him.

Finn stood, pushing his hand through his hair. Drakken battle-lords had long encouraged the use of mass execution-style killings to enrage and demoralize the Coalition. "Skulling," it was called in Hordish slang used by both sides. Was that what had happened here? *After* the war's end?

Millions had expired this way. The lucky ones were killed before anything else was done to them. Usually, though, something else was done to them first. The "something else" was the stuff of nightmares in the Coalition psyche, and Finn could understand why.

Yet, these were only seventeen men. Intelligence reports that Yarew had briefed already confirmed there were rogue ships plying these remote regions of space. Any passing raider could have done this.

Why use the methods of old, though, if not to incite terror? If only these men had died any other way but this.

It is what it is, Finn told himself. It had happened, it was done, a senseless act that would serve only to perpetuate the centuries-old prejudices toward his people, making it more difficult for those born under the flag of the Drakken Empire to assimilate into the new Triad Alliance. He and his crew were so much more than their dark reputation. They weren't the monsters their shipmates assumed they were.

That Admiral Stone-Heart thought they were.

In a twist of fate and circumstance—and dumb good luck—he was now the highest-ranking former-Drakken Triad officer. It gave him an opportunity to prove that the Drakken as a whole wanted peace—and a future that held infinitely more promise than the one they'd left behind. The skulling threatened to erase all the progress they'd made in the days since boarding the *Unity*.

And the progress you've made with Brit.

Finn rubbed a tired hand across his face. The battle-weary soldier in him wanted the galaxy to hold on to peace. The man in him wanted to hold on to her.

By avoiding war, he'd be able to do both, and he'd avoid war by not letting the skulling bring out the worst in those who hated the Drakken. Banked hatred existed throughout the Realm of the Goddess. It wouldn't take much for a few brazen terror attacks to fan it into flame. Fire didn't care who you were, or to what government you gave allegiance; it didn't care if you were Drakken or Coalition or from the Shrine of Earth. Once started, the fire of hatred would consume them all.

"ADMIRAL, the shuttle has docked."

"Have Warleader Rorkken report to the bridge immediately after decon," Brit said in answer to Star-

Major Yarew's statement. She kept her face pointed to the holo-vis where she'd been overseeing the team's progress back from the planet below. Her hands gripped the edge of the table. Pretending to read the data scrolling past, it was composure she was after. Hers.

"He said Drakken 'attack,' not 'raid,'" she thought aloud. Why? Unwilling or unable to elaborate, Rorkken had ended the call in the next instant, citing the need to upload the bodies to the shuttle before sunset.

"Rorkken chooses his words deliberately," Yarew said. "If he said 'attack,' he meant it."

"'Attack' means a military action."

"Did we ever believe they'd actually obey the treaty, Admiral? Come now, Horde is Horde. They'll never change. Their capacity for humanity is not what ours is. They're animalistic, prone to violence, incapable of the most sophisticated human emotions and certainly not capable of love."

As the officer rattled off characteristics of the Drakken mind that she'd always taken for granted were true, she thought of Finn's seemingly tender kisses, and his gentle caresses. When it came to expressing emotion, compared to Finn, she was the one lesser evolved: she was so closed up and closed off, and he was so very open. Not sophisticated? Finn's capacity for patience and warmth were undeniable, and certainly exceeded her own.

Was he not Horde?

Yes, yes he was! And yet…she wanted him. With the force of a plasma blast shock wave, it hit her that she wanted him as much for the affection he offered as for the sex—all while despising her weakness. Her betrayal.

A horrible sound of shame and confusion threatened to well up inside her throat. It took real effort to tamp it down. It was one thing having a meltdown in the privacy of her quarters. No matter how ill-advised her actions in her personal life, no one would ever detect her weakness on this bridge.

She pushed away from the holo-vis table, clasping her hands behind her back as she awaited Rorkken's presence. Perhaps his news of the attack would drive the wedge between them that she'd need if she were ever going to escape his spell.

FINN MARCHED OUT of the shuttle as soon as it docked with the *Unity*. A medical team led by Dr. Kell met the craft to attend to the bodies stored in the cargo bay.

Rorkken tore open the collar of his expedition suit and stormed down the corridor to take the lift up to the bridge. Zurykk fell in step with him. "Word around the ship says it was an attack, Captain. A Drakken attack."

"How in the freepin' hells did that get around the ship already?"

"It's Rakkelle's shift. She's on the bridge—pilot duty. She overheard Stone-Heart and Yarew speculating."

"I can only imagine what was said. Anything in Yarew's view is slanted against us."

"Aye, I hear ya, Captain. Blaming the bar fight on us, almost getting sweef banned."

"You know about that, too?" Finn could swear that conversation with Brit had been private.

The man shrugged. "Rumors. And a few good guesses."

Finn groaned. Serving on the *Unity* hadn't diminished his crew's ability to spread news and gossip at light-speed.

"It was more than the work of rogue Drakken space pirates down there. They skulled them, Zūrykk, the entire outpost."

His former second-in-command swore. "Does *she* know about the skulling?"

"The admiral? No. Not yet. She will soon. I'm trying to think of a good way to break it to her." *There is no good way.* He suspected that scene would be almost as ugly as the one on the beach.

The moment Finn stepped onto the bridge, he made damn sure that he stood tall and proud in his Triad colors. He wanted to send the right message to Rakkelle and the others. Whatever reasons the rogues had for skulling the settlers, Finn didn't want her or any of the Drakken he'd brought aboard to feel shame for it. He'd bear that burden for them.

Rakkelle's curious gaze followed him as he strode past. Rumors spread fast on a ship, but they were just that: rumors. She, like the other Drakken, was hungry to know what he really thought and saw while on Cupezikan. With all the speculation, the sweef would be flowing in the bar tonight.

Finn dropped the weapon fitting he'd found on the beach in Yarew's hands. "This was near the bodies. If it didn't belong there, I want to know."

Next he reported to his commanding officer, the woman he'd spent half of last night pleasuring, the woman who this morning advised in his PCD, *"Use caution, Finn."* That woman wasn't in sight. She was hidden behind the rock-hard facade of Admiral Bandar. Aye, but she was there.

"You called the killings the result of an attack," she stated, one dark flare of a brow lifting.

"Aye, I did." He decided to tell her straight up what happened on the surface: trying to sugarcoat or put off what his entire team had witnessed would only make it worse. Rumors were already spreading. He might as well end them here. "They were skulled, Admiral. All seventeen men."

A flash of pain and hatred came and went so fast in her face that it was gone before it truly registered in Finn's mind. The hatred he could understand. Why the pain?

"Skulled," she said. "You're certain."

"Aye. Burns at the base of the neck, nothing left inside the skulls, faces gone."

Her steely facade wavered again, her mouth tightening at his description. Battle-veteran Brit Bandar should be used to hearing of skulling after all the years she'd spent at war with the Horde. Yet, the subject affected her more than she let on.

"I see." She turned, took a breath and seemed to make an inner decision. Then, coming to life before his eyes, every last bit of distress vanishing, she addressed the bridge crew. "All hands, prepare for pursuit!"

A flurry of "Yes, Admiral"s met her order.

"Search for ion echoes," she directed the engineer next. "I don't care how faint. If their ship has left the barest trace of a wake, we will find it and follow it."

"Yes, ma'am!"

"I intend to track down every last one of those skulling bastards if it takes us from one end of the Borderlands to the other." Her hand closed into a fist as if she'd grabbed one of the rogues by the throat. "Justice will be served. Justice will be swift."

"Admiral," the engineer called. "I've found possible echo traces. Analyzing now."

"No. Download them to the pilot station. We'll analyze later. I'd rather head off on a hunch than sit here doing nothing. Cadet Pehzwan—follow those echoes."

"Aye, aye, Admiral!" Rakkelle called out and the mighty battleship shuddered as it turned to a new course, accelerating as it did so.

Brit circled the bridge, looking over shoulders, offering comments or encouragement and checking new data. She acted with a focus that was almost frightening in intensity. This was the Stone-Heart of legend, he thought. The transformation from a moment ago was amazing. Whatever he'd glimpsed that looked like anguish at the idea of skulling was nowhere to be seen. Who was that woman he glimpsed from time to time, and why such misery? By the gods above, he needed to know.

"Warleader, Star-Major, join me in my office." Coldly, she summoned both her senior officers.

Finn exhaled through his nose. Here comes the ugly part, he thought—so ugly that she wanted to do it in private. Rakkelle cast him a pitying glance as he followed Brit.

Finn remained standing before her desk. Like Brit, Yarew settled into a smart chair that actually seemed to act smart. With both officers seated, though, it would appear odd if he didn't sit.

Finn aimed his ass at the nearest seat and dropped into it. It sank below the level of Brit's desk before dampening its movement, leaving him at a lower point than either officer. He pushed down with his feet, released, and the chair sank again. "Freepin' thing," he muttered under his breath, making sure his palm was pressed firmly to the ID reader to make doubly sure genetic identity was visible to the computer inside. It was. The "smart" chair had simply decided on its own that he was to be seated below the others. "This is done purposely at the factory, isn't it, lest we Drakken get too uppity?"

Neither of the officers' facial expressions changed. Brit's was as stony as ever. Finn swallowed a sigh.

"We will treat this as a wartime situation," she began. "Warleader, I would like you to organize regular combat drills and ship-wide simulation exercises. Levels of experience vary on this crew. They must learn to work together."

"Aye, we must." Work together: it was good to hear her thinking in those terms. "I'll hammer them into fighting shape." If there was one thing he knew how to do, it was taking a fractured, motley crew and teaching them to work as one. Teaching them to be soldiers.

"Star-Major, you will communicate with the Intelligence Ministry and debrief them thoroughly on what we found at the settlement."

"Permission to make a suggestion," Finn interrupted.

"Speak," Brit said.

"Be careful how we share what we know. Here's why." Finn leaned forward to rest his laced fingers on her desk. It was an odd angle with his lowered chair, but he needed his body language to convey a desire to confide. "There's a world of difference between the rogues who massacred the scientists and the deserters running scared and hungry. The raiders we were sent here to coax into the Triad are acting out of desperation to fill their bellies. On the other hand, the skullers I am quite sure acted out of malice. They chose the one method *they knew* would strike fear into the hearts of the Coalition. We don't yet know if it's an isolated act or the beginning of a terror campaign by those with designs on resurrecting the Drakken Empire's former glory."

"Never," Brit murmured as Yarew glowered.

"Believe it or not, most Drakken feel as you do, even though we lost the war. Peace is the best thing that's happened to my people in centuries."

"Centuries of fighting a war that the Horde started," Yarew pointed out.

"And finished. We killed our warlord and declared allegiance to the goddess."

The officer knew that; he merely wanted to bait him, laying the blame for hundreds of years of war on Finn's shoulders. He set his jaw, refusing to give in to anger, especially with Brit sitting close, watching his reaction. "We have to look past blame to hold on to peace. You've seen the tension in our own crew, for gods' sake. The wounds are still raw. It won't take much to get them bleeding again. An incident like Cupezikan is just the excuse needed to keep fighting until every last Drakken is exterminated."

"What do you suggest we do, Warleader?" Brit asked.

"We treat the skulling as an isolated incident."

"And if it isn't?" Yarew asked.

"We reassess if that comes to pass. And pray to the gods that it doesn't."

"The gods," Brit muttered in a barely audible snarl as she rolled her eyes. Clearly the woman didn't put much stock in divine help. It was another piece of the puzzle that he wanted badly to assemble.

Picking up her light pen, she rolled it between two fingers as she pondered what he'd told her. Then, finally, she nodded. "Star-Major, tell the ministry what we have discovered. Tell them…" Thinking, she tapped the pen on the desk. "Tell them that a group of fanatics attacked a small settlement in the Borderlands. Call it a brazen attack on innocent settlers, and tell them that the entire, multinational Triad crew serving aboard the *Unity* looks forward to bringing the terrorists to justice."

"Thank you, Admiral," Finn said.

"Gratitude is irrelevant to this discussion, War-leader," she said coolly, rising to her feet. "I simply want to buy us some time to hunt down the amoral beasts. If Zaafran sends the fleet after them, I may not have that pleasure." Her eyes darkened as they narrowed. "And trust me, I do want that pleasure. Now then—" she seemed to return to normal "—let us return to the bridge."

Lieutenant Keyren had finally showed up. Back in uniform, she took her place at Brit's side.

"Update," Brit called to the engineer.

"Still working on that echo, Admiral."

"Good, good. Fools to think they can terrorize the innocent and get away with it. Let's see how arrogant they are in smart-cuffs down in the brig—that is, if they live that long." The idea of wreaking vengeance on the Cupezikan murderers clearly energized Brit.

It was contagious. The bridge was abuzz as everyone bent to their specific tasks. Even Rakkelle seemed caught up in the excitement—her first time on a real ship with a real mission.

Brit seemed to take in the sight of the busy bridge with satisfaction. Then she nodded at Finn and Yarew in turn. "Warleader, Star-Major, your presence is no longer needed on the bridge." Turning on a polished heel, she returned to her office.

"But it's my shift," Yarew protested, appearing confused as he watched her go. "She's not even officially on duty."

"Aye, she tends to forget she doesn't live on the bridge," Finn remarked, turning to follow her. "I'll see what I can do to help her remember that she doesn't."

CHAPTER FIFTEEN

BRIT SHUT THE OFFICE DOOR, sealing herself off from the bridge, and sank, drained, into her desk chair. The smart seat caught her, dampening out the sudden movement.

She turned to gaze at the stars, putting the bridge and the bustling activity there behind her. Finally, she had a mission again. She had purpose in her life once more, a reason to wake up each day as opposed to diplomacy—bah, such a ridiculous notion, especially in light of the events on Cupezikan.

The settlers had been skulled.... In her long years at the helm of a battleship, she'd received worse news, had seen worse with her own eyes. It was a tragedy, yes, but what was a mere seventeen dead when she'd seen thousands? She'd built up a certain tolerance to horror, a consequence of a long military career. This shouldn't have affected her the way it had.

There had been no warning when Finn broke the news. She'd let her guard down. For a sickening moment the doors to the past had threatened to fly open. Focusing on exacting vengeance held those nightmarish memories at bay, but barely.

Control had always come so easily. It helped her survive when she'd wanted to die. Perhaps now with her mission once again clear, doing what she had for the past two decades, she'd be able to reclaim her old self and regroup.

She wanted life to stay as it always was, and had been ever since she walked away from Arrayar, dry-eyed and determined to make a difference.

Determined to exterminate Drakken.

Now what had she gone and done? She'd taken a Hordish lover, all because he had Seff's eyes.

Liar. You've long ago stopped seeing Seff's eyes when you look into Finn's. And still you let him in your bed. You like it with him, too, admit it. You like the way he makes you feel.

Hell, she more than liked it. The Drakken war-leader, the pirate captain, was the best lay she'd ever had in a long string of men, including her late husband.

May the gods punish you for soiling Seff's memory with such sordid comparisons, Britasha, her mother would have cried. Life was punishing enough without having punishing gods around to make it worse. There were many reasons Brit no longer believed, and that was one of them.

Brit winced. She should be thinking of rogue ships, not what she did in bed last night! What was happening to her?

In the meeting with Yarew, Rorkken had had her eating out of his hand, telling her what to do and say, and she'd agreed like a little, mindless puppet! Yes, she agreed somewhat with his view on not inciting unrest, but still, he was Rorkken. He was *Drakken*. She was not to give him any real power…over her ship, or over her.

Good in bed or not, Rorkken threatened her focus like nothing else ever had. She needed to start weaning herself from him. Now. She needed to show some discipline about bedding him. Maybe tomorrow she'd take that step. Tonight would be the last of him. She grew warm, aroused, conjuring the feel of his warm lips on her—

The door to her office opened and closed as Finn barged in, ending any question of her sleeping alone anytime soon. He waited until the door sealed shut before he opened his mouth to speak—and stopped midbreath to take a closer look at her face. "Aye, I know how it feels," he said, gentler. "You think you have no right to go on with your life when others have died in such a fashion."

She stiffened. "I'm fine."

He studied her with those too-perceptive eyes. "Are *we?*"

"I don't know what you mean."

"You and me. Tonight. We have plans." He leaned on her desk, supporting his weight with spread hands. "In light of what happened today, I suggest canceling our lightball match in favor of a quiet dinner. Your quarters or mine?"

"Yours?" She recoiled in irritation. "And risk making our affair the subject of gossip? There are a hundred excuses for you coming to my suite and none for my going to yours."

"No excuses? I think not. I know for one you're hungering for one of those kisses you've come to love—" his voice deepened with a hint of huskiness "—and wanting me deep, deep inside you while we're sharin' one of those kisses. That's two reasons right there."

She swallowed, feeling her face grow hot—hells, her face and everywhere else. "Damn you, Rorkken."

"Tell me more sweet words over dinner. Come—up, up. Time's a-wasting. Yarew's anxious to get in your chair. It is, after all, his shift."

Surprised, Brit glanced at the ship-time readout. "It is, isn't it?" She brushed a tired hand over her face. "I'll need a shower."

"I'll help you."

She considered his offer. Getting drenched with Finn Rorkken would be a perfect distraction to the day's jarring events. "All right."

He gave her one of his grins that she felt clear to her toes. One look at those smiling eyes and she was helpless.

With as much pride as she could muster, she pushed to her feet.

On her way out of the office, she told Hadley, "I'm calling it a night. I'll have no further need of you until the morning. Disturb me for emergencies only."

The girl's curious gaze flicked to Finn and back again. Brit froze. Did Hadley suspect something between them?

It served as a warning to be extra careful in the future. Her secret affair with her Hordish second-in-command must remain exactly that, or she risked compromising everything she stood for to her crew, and her people.

THE MOMENT THE DOOR to Brit's quarters slid shut, she was in Rorkken's arms. She shook off her identity as Admiral Bandar as swiftly as she shook out her hair, letting it fly soft and loose over her shoulders. Alone with Finn, miraculously, she could be someone else. Someone she hardly remembered.

He hoisted her off her feet, hiking her thighs up and over his hips, walking her to the nearest wall where he kissed her to within an inch of her life.

"I've waited all day to do that, Brit. Through everything that happened, I waited, thinking of this…of you," he said and kissed her again.

"I thought we were going to take a shower…."

"A little foreplay first…." He lowered her to her feet to strip off her uniform and the filmy undergarments she wore underneath. "Gods, woman. Now that I know what you're wearin' under your Triad colors, it's going to be damn-blasted difficult not thinking about it at inopportune times."

"What would you consider inopportune?" She knew, but she wanted to hear him say it. The day had been long and awful. This was her reward. She wanted the distraction of his sexy words.

"Inopportune would be…" He lifted her again, his big hands supporting her rear end as he spread her thighs wide. The fabric of his expedition outfit set up a dizzying abrasion as he walked her to her desk and sat her on it, easing her fall to her back as his upper body followed. "Throwing you onto the holo-vis table in the middle of the bridge and doing this—" he yanked open his trousers and filled her with an astonishingly hard, blazing-hot erection.

She sucked in a startled breath with the explosion of sensation. "I think…I like…inopportune," he said tightly, affected by the sudden joining as much as she was.

He withdrew nearly all the way only to plunge deep all over again. She couldn't contain her pleasure. Crying out, she arched her back to press even closer. The rough feel of his uniform contrasted with the velvety heat of his groin was erotic beyond belief. "So much for foreplay, or a shower before sex," she gasped, clinging to his heaving shoulders.

"I obey your orders on the bridge, sweetheart." He thrust oh, so deep. "This is not the bridge." He lowered his mouth to her throat, kissing her moist skin.

"And this is not sex. In fact, we haven't had sex a single time."

She half laughed, half moaned. "I must have been dreaming it then, as I'm dreaming this."

"Now, we've *made love* about six or seven times."

"Call it what you will, but it's been eight times we've coupled in one fashion or another."

"Eight, then." Chuckling, he returned to her lips to kiss her. He always took time to kiss her. To kiss her until she sighed.

As he moved deep inside her, the rough fabric of his trousers set up an erotic abrasion. Each wave of pleasure brought her closer to the edge. She seemed to have no self-control with him; none.

Then he stopped, going absolutely still. Only the sound of their harsh breaths filled the silent room. "Are you still insisting this is mere sex?" he murmured against her mouth. "Or will you admit we're making love?"

"There's a difference?" she gasped.

"Aye, there's a difference. I'm going to teach you what it is, too, no matter how many times it takes. As long as you're a willing student."

"Move," she urged him. "Please."

"Like this?" he said on a deep chuckle, swaying slowly before turning more aggressive. "Or like this?" Even he sounded breathless now.

"That…" Letting her eyes fall shut in pleasure, she hung on as he took her to the verge of climax all too quickly. "Finn," she whispered. He needn't wonder any longer who she saw behind her closed eyes. It was him, all him. "Ah, Finn."

The sound of his name proved his undoing. He made a guttural sound, his body jerking once, twice, as he unsuccessfully tried to hold back from orgasm. It didn't matter; she was already coming apart in his arms, her teeth sinking into his uniform-covered shoulder and holding him close with her legs. Clutching each other, they shuddered as one then finally went limp, exhausted and, for the moment, satisfied.

It had been fast and furious and what they'd both obviously needed after the long day. She couldn't move a finger. Who knew where he found the strength to lift her off the desk, but the next thing she realized, he was carrying her into the shower.

She sighed against his epaulet-clad shoulder as he set her on still-shaky legs and turned on the drenching stream. Spray glittered in his hair. Sometime during his tenure on the *Unity,* he'd ceased wearing his pirate beads and braids—she couldn't recall when—but his hair was still shaggy and long when not gathered in a neat, leather-wrapped tail at the base of his neck. Dark brown with burnished highlights, his hair hung clean and thick around his shoulders. It swung around his boyishly handsome face as he stripped naked and stepped into the enclosure with her. Finally, a shower.

"I knew you'd obey me in the end, Rorkken."

"Are you sure about that?" His gaze was dark and wicked as he sank slowly to his knees, sliding his big hands down the sides of her body until he knelt before her and placed his mouth where she needed it most. Her head fell back against the shower wall as he began to pleasure her with the eagerness of a pirate claiming his treasure. His impassioned attention to detail ensured her immunity from the past, forming a barrier to the nightmares clamoring to be set free in the far reaches of her mind.

Sex as medicine? She'd take it. Surely it wasn't more than just sex, no matter what he claimed. Surely he wasn't coming to mean more to her than...*this*.

Trembling, burying her fingers in his silky hair, she let him take her to the place where she felt safe, where no memories could intrude, not even those of Seff. All that mattered was *now*.

A GOOD WHILE LATER, they sat across from each other at a table, sharing a delicious hot meal and the usual bottle of Brit's beloved Kin-Kan wine. He hadn't been familiar with the vintage before coming aboard this ship. He wouldn't have been able to afford it even if he had. They'd lived in different spheres, he and Brit.

He'd pulled on his undertank to cover himself, and she wore a silk robe. Her hair flowed long and loose. "Tell me about your family," he said, savoring a tender piece of something avian—he didn't care what species, only that it was delicious. "Where are you from?"

Brit's fork froze in midair before resuming its path back to her plate, where it sat.

"Ah, come now. We've shared physically about all there is to share, and you can't even tell me where you were born?" he teased. "Are there brothers, sisters? Are you in touch with them much on the voyages?"

She picked up her fork again. "No," she said, pushing food around on her plate. "I am not."

"Sometimes I'd try to imagine what it would be like to have a family. Then I'd watch my crew and get to thinking it was easier without one. You've got no one to miss."

"No, you wouldn't...." Something infinitely sad flickered in her eyes before she averted her gaze, abandoning her food in favor of a long sip of wine. Did she miss the bastard who broke her heart? He hoped to gods she soon forgot the beast. She sure didn't act as if she missed the idiot in the throes of passion. That, he decided, was a very good sign. "I have no siblings. I haven't spoken to my parents in years, not since I left to attend the academy. I don't even know if they're still alive."

She would have been a teenager when they last had contact. "Were they not in favor of your becoming an officer?"

"You could say that. They were very religious. Pilgrims, actually. I never understood the draw of that kind of life, even then."

"Ah." He ate more of the savory fowl. "That explains your lack of faith. You rebelled."

Her mouth tightened suddenly. She lifted the wineglass to her lips to hide her reaction, but he'd caught it all the same. She didn't like revealing much about herself. Aye, but he'd find out more, bit by bit. He was a patient man. When good things crossed his path, he reached out and grabbed them. He was willing to wait until they grabbed him back.

"How did you come by the name of Finnar Rorkken?" she asked, clearly wanting to shift the focus from her to him. "It's a fine name, strong and uncomplicated. Did the children who rescued you think of it?"

"Believe it or not, it's my real name. It's all I have that's all mine. It's why I've never failed to keep it honorable."

"So that's why you let yourself be known as the Scourge of the Borderlands?"

"I thank the Coalition for that one." He grinned. "I kept it because I liked it."

"You *were* a scourge. A plague. A curse!"

"You're just upset because you never caught me."

"I've got you now." She observed him over her glass of wine. "Haven't I?"

"You have indeed, sweetheart."

At the tender name, she glanced away.

"Do you not like that I call you that?"

Her smile was soft, and somehow sad. "I do like it. Therein lies the problem."

She liked it. She liked him. Progress was being made rapidly. He reached across the table, taking a long lock of silken hair and tucking it behind her ear. "Problem? I don't see any problem. I also like to call you fire goddess. Is that better?"

Her expression had turned almost bashful. "Goddess, bah."

"Now it's time to think up a pet name for me. Something besides scourge, plague or curse, although I've been known to answer to all three."

She laughed at that, actually laughed. A throaty, genuine laugh. Charmed, delighted and more than half in love with her, he grinned back. "So how about…darling?"

She shook her head. "It doesn't fit you."

"My lovely, then?"

"Please. You're anything but." She laughed again, almost a girlish giggle. Was it the wine, or was he breaking through to the woman known to the galaxy as the legendary Admiral Bandar?

"Swee-bear," he suggested.

"No."

"Beast."

"Hmm, at times."

"Tootie, then."

Her eyes shone. "Absolutely not."

He was holding her hand now, rubbing his thumb over her knuckles. "I'm out of ideas. You'll have to help me out."

"Is it necessary that I call you by a pet name?"

"Very."

Her gaze turned decidedly mischievous. "I have it."

"I'm afraid to ask."

"My wicked boy. That's what I call you in my head."

In surprise, he sat back in his chair. "Really…"

"Yes. Although you're not, of course, a boy." She was definitely acting bashful now as her explanation tumbled out. "It's…that you have this twinkle of mischief in your eyes—when you smile, especially—and it makes me think that." Her voice turned soft. "My rugged, wicked boy…"

That's when he saw it, a flash of something more— more than sex-related passion, more than carnal heat. She'd developed feelings for him, too. In the next instant, all hints of that revelation had vanished, but he saw it. Aye, he did. It gave him the resolve he needed to finish the relentless drive to her heart.

LIKE SHE DID EVERY DAY, Hadley ate her off-duty meal in the officer's club as opposed to the larger ship's open-dining hall. There was peace here away from the noise of the space-hands and Rakkelle's swagger. She had more time than ever to eat these days, off duty or on. The admiral seemed to need her less and less, especially in the evenings. At one time, Hadley was on the go, running errands for Admiral Bandar, late into the night. Now the woman almost never called Hadley anymore.

The admiral might not think so, but the looks she gave the warleader explained her sudden independence. The time she used to fill with business was now being filled with Warleader Rorkken. While Hadley had never caught them acting untoward, there were fleeting looks when they thought no one was watching. Full-time romantic, born-and-bred-on-Planet-Talo Hadley Keyren was *always* watching.

She went through the buffet line and carried her tray to a quiet table with a view of the stars so she could eat and read or sometimes stare outside and dream. Her mood ring's green hue accurately reflected her mood: average, active, not under great stress.

She slipped a bite of dessert in her mouth—she always loved dessert first—and opened a data-vis containing a translation of Earth magazines Tango had brought along from Earth. She found them fascinating. Not only because of her interest in Tango, but because the articles were so outrageous and wonderful! The citizens of Talo would have loved such literature—and blushed reading the content. Was nothing sacred on the shrine world of Earth? *Cosmopolitan* magazine was her favorite publication. *How to Tell if He's Great in Bed Before You Waste Your Time,* blared the current issue. It sounded like something Rakkelle would write. Eagerly, she scrolled to the article in question.

"I'll take that, young lady." Rothberg lifted the tray from her table.

She grabbed hold of it. "That's mine."

"Mine now." They entered a little game of tug-of-war. "Stop fighting me."

"Well. It's my food," she argued, pulling on the tray. "Do you fight for each other's dinners on Earth like a pack of hounds?"

"Ruff, ruff!" He laughed and wrenched the tray away from her. The plate of dessert slid precariously to the edge. His face had clean lines and a square chin. He was focused when training but when off duty, he was Tango's sidekick. Speaking of which, where was Tango? Her heart pitter-pattered at a faster rate. She'd lost her awkwardness around him, but it had been days since the kiss and he hadn't made any other attempts to get her alone. She was beginning to think he'd lost interest, and she couldn't blame him a bit.

Rothberg walked away with her dinner. He set the tray down in the middle of a group of Coalition ensigns who immediately dug in.

"Why did you do that?" Hadley protested. "I'm hungry."

"You'll dine with me."

Tango entered the room dressed in what she recognized as Earth clothes: a tailored suit with no decorations of any kind, and a slim piece of silken fabric that he'd tied and left hanging around his neck. How quaint. "You look nice," she said shyly.

"And you look gorgeous, as always."

She felt giddy and a little breathless having this

exotic man flatter her with his attention. No one usually paid attention to shy Hadley Keyren. Unless they wanted something, like Admiral Bandar's ear, or for Hadley to put in a good word for them with their leader.

Tango joined her at the table. "What are you doing?" she asked.

"*We* are going on a date."

"A date?"

"Yes. It's the basic form of Earth courtship."

Her blush deepened. "Courtship…"

"Yes, I'm wooing you. I figure it's the only way I'm going to get you to pay any attention to me."

But I do pay attention to you, she wanted to argue. All the time. She daydreamed about him day and night. She'd named their children and their grandchildren. "Oh" was all she could say. She winced. *Lame.*

"Waiter." He snapped his fingers. Rothberg reappeared dressed in a white apron. He unfurled a white tablecloth from the days of old, before self-cleaning nano surfaces made such cloths obsolete, and snapped it open, letting it billow and settle over the table. Hadley laughed, clapping her hands together in delight. Next, Rothberg plunked down a candle.

The ensigns and quite a few of the other officers nearby gaped at the scene. Hadley whispered, "We're not supposed to have open fire in the—"

Tango pressed a finger to her lips. She tingled at his touch. "Shush," he said. "Our secret."

"But…"

He sighed. "If we're told to, we'll blow it out."

Rothberg lit the candle. The light flickered festively. "Menu, ma'am?" He handed her an old-fashioned paper card. She unfolded it. The lettering was blocky and unreadable. "English," she said, disappointed.

"She'll have the cheeseburger-and-fry meal," Tango told Rothberg. "And we'll share a bottle of your best champagne."

"Certainly." Rothberg bowed deeply and walked off.

"It's the only meal on the menu he can make," Tango explained.

Hadley laughed. "Earth food. I look forward to sampling it."

Acting as if he looked forward to sampling *her,* Tango reached across the table, despite the curious stares directed at them, and twined her fingers in his, casually, as if they'd been together for many years. "Tonight is yours, baby. It's all about you. Your wish is my command."

His fingers slid between hers.

Her mood ring, she noticed, wasn't green anymore. It wasn't black, either, but amber. *A little nervous, emotions mixed, unsettled.* So far so good.

He lifted the data-vis while keeping a grip on her one hand. She yelped, trying to snatch the viewer back. "How to tell if he's great in bed before you waste your time…" He smiled over the screen at her. "Ah, Hadley." His thumb moved to the soft underside of her hand, circling, circling, stroking. "You never need to worry with me, baby doll. No one's better than Tango."

His finger commanded all her focus. He made no secret of the fact he'd like to rub that finger on other, more intimate locations on her body. She'd all but stopped breathing. Rothberg returned and joyfully presented a green glass bottle and two tall, narrow glasses. "Champagne, sir." He placed the bottle between them and turned to go.

"Uh, waiter."

Rothberg halted. "Yeah?"

Tango waved at the bottle.

"You open it. I'm in the middle of frying the—" He exhaled. "Fine, but if anything gets too crispy, don't blame me—"

"Ahem."

Rothberg cut off his complaint and resumed his role.

Hadley laughed at all the body language and glances going back and forth between the two men. She decided she quite liked Earthlings. They were soldiers in their Earth forces, yes, but there was still a freshness about them.

Pop! Hadley jumped. A sweet, alcoholic-smelling foam came boiling out of the bottle. Rothberg filled both glasses and jogged away. Tango filled her glass the rest of the way, then his own, lifting it. "A toast."

They touched glasses. Some things were universal. "To…?"

"To a girl as sweet as an apple. May you fall as hard as I have fallen for you."

Hadley sighed; she couldn't help it. They sat there holding hands on the table, immune to the stares of the officers who came and went. It was the most romantic thing that had ever happened to her. She could have sat there forever.

"Dinner is served." Rothberg brought two plates of food out and stood by proudly as she stared in awe. She picked up a stick that seemed to be a vegetable. It had a savory, almost nutty smell.

"It's a French fry." Tango took one and dragged it through a puddle of thick red sauce. Then he held it to her mouth. "Try."

She nibbled it. "Oh my, that's good."

She grabbed the rest from his fingers and ate it. She took some more fries, devouring them as delicately as she could manage.

"One thing about fries, you gotta be careful," he warned. "Eat too many and they'll go right to your hips."

Suddenly self-conscious, she looked down. "You think I am fat?"

"No, baby, I think you're perfect." He brought her hand to his lips and kissed it. "I just want to help you stay that way."

"Oh." Would his feelings change if she didn't always look as she did now? Being with Tango, she'd want to always make sure she looked her best. She'd want to if she had him! What about when she was with child someday, though? Would he think her less beautiful because she was filled with their baby?

The ring was darkening, turning browner. *Don't look at it.*

Outside, the corridor had become noisy. Shift change, but not hers. She was off duty for one more cycle. She had all the time in the world to go back to Tango's room. He was being so sweet, going through the trouble of this "date," and it took some of her nerves away.

Suddenly, he stood. "Where are you going?"

"Alas, it's time for work."

"You have this shift?"

"Afraid so, baby." He flattened his hands on the table and leaned forward, bending all the way down until his lips brushed her ear. "Wait for me, Hadley. Don't go away again." His lips brushed her ear. "I need you, baby. I want to be with you. Later. Will you come to my quarters when I'm off duty? Say you will, baby. Give me something to look forward to."

She nodded. He straightened, leaving her dizzy.

"Think about me until then?"

"Yes."

He winked at her and sauntered off.

The moment he was gone, she blew out a stream of air and fell back in her seat. If he'd set out to woo her, it had worked.

THE FEEL OF BRIT shooting upright in bed dragged Finn from a deep sleep. Years of pirating had him instantly awake and without a trace of grogginess as he took in his surroundings. He'd left his PCD on the night table but Brit's was in her ear. She pressed her hand to it now, her breasts bouncing as she hopped out of bed and walked away. The glorious view of her bare, swaying ass got him hard all over again. "I understand the distress call is verified, Star-Major?" Brit said, ending thoughts of some good-morning lovemaking.

Finn shoved his PCD in his ear to listen. He could not speak lest his voice be overheard on her unit. "The signal is emanating from a settlement called Goddess Reach," Yarew said. "Population—fifty-six men, women and children."

"On my way."

"Admiral, I have not been able to reach Warleader Rorkken. He's not answering PCD calls."

Brit cast Finn a look. "I'll make sure to fetch him on my way to the bridge." She ended the call. Her hand gave a shake, which she immediately tried to cover up by making a fist. "Damn it," she snapped at him before he had a chance to speak. "We've received a distress call from the Goddess Reach settlement. Damn it all. What is it with you people? There are children in jeopardy this time. Children!" He knew she was thinking of the skullers and how impartially they dispensed their brand of horror; everyone was treated the same way, from infants to the elderly.

Her hooded glare didn't quite hide her anguish as she stalked away to the shower. Either he was getting better at seeing her pain, or she was getting less careful about showing it.

He followed her. She aimed her back at him to find some soap as the water sprayed down. His hand landed on her shoulder, forcing her around. She recoiled from the sight of his scars and tattoos, spinning her gaze away to avoid looking at his bare torso. "So, I disgust you now, do I? You quite liked this body last night."

"Finn." Her warning held a pleading note that made his heart wrench. "Don't." She'd gone white.

He backed off, touching his hand to her pale cheek to convey he was sorry. "We don't know what we've got at Goddess Reach. It might be terrorists, or a simple raid by starving pirates."

"If you're looking for my sympathy for pirates and raiders, you won't find it." She sneered, scrubbing clean—clean of any trace of him, it seemed like.

"Be wary of painting all rogues with the same broad brush."

"Skullers, murderers—not 'your people,' right?"

She dried off and pulled on her uniform while he stood there, dripping wet. She was baiting him. It was as if she was trying to make him angry. *To make you show your true colors, Rorkken.*

A Drakken's colors.

He wouldn't let her do it. Not all Horde were monsters; he'd prove it even if it meant choking down his pride. "Your typical Drakken isn't behind this. To insinuate they are is downright irresponsible for someone in your position. There are those on both sides who'd return to war over it."

"If peace is that fragile, then we should have finished the war."

"We did finish the war!"

"The politicians finished it. Not the command-ers." *Not me,* she left unspoken.

"It sounds like someone has unfinished business with the Horde."

"Who doesn't?" She fastened her gleaming collar as he buckled his belt.

"Consider your counterparts on the other side who feel the same. Chances are they're behind the terror crimes on Cupezikan and, I hope to gods not, God-dess Reach."

"Open," she told the room-bot. The door slid open, allowing her out before they'd finished the discussion.

This was why you didn't sleep with someone on your crew, he thought for the hundredth time.

Because when they frustrated the living hells out of you, you didn't have to fight the urge to strip them naked to get them to pay attention!

Growling, he took off after her. Their boots thundered down the deserted corridor. It was 'tween shifts. Everyone who lived in this part of the ship was either working, sleeping, eating or in the bar drinking.

"A long war makes for a fragile peace, aye. It wouldn't take much to break it. But who are we to make that decision for an entire galaxy? That's what we'd be doing if we jump to blame too fast, trying and convicting an entire people for the acts of a fanatical few."

They stepped into the lift. The door closed, sealing them in tense silence that seemed to last an eternity.

Brit's fists opened and closed behind her back. Quietly, and with some effort, she said, "I accused you of being capable of unspeakable things for no other reason than that you are Drakken." She hesitated as she stared straight ahead at the sealed doors, seeming to search for words. "I'm sorry. I'm angry. I'm scared," she added in an almost-whisper.

Something deep inside him wrenched with her pain. She'd exposed her true self, and it cost her, he sensed. If ever there was a time he wanted to draw her into his arms and hold her close, this was it. "Ah, Brit…"

"No." Her hand shot up. "Don't say anything." It was as if she was trying hard not to break down, knowing that if he offered tender words, she would. "What I said…isn't how I really feel about you. You're not like the skullers. I know that."

That came from the heart, bringing him one step closer to capturing it. "I do know, sweetheart." How oddly liberating to utter the tender pet name outside her bedroom, he thought, even if they'd likely never have the freedom to reveal their relationship in public. A pang of grief grabbed at his chest, and regret for what they'd never have.

The lift stopped at bridge level. "Door—remain closed," she told the lift-bot then turned to him. Her expression was confused, uncertain. "Why do you put up with me?"

"When I've found something good, I hold on to it."

"Good… Me?" She let out a weary laugh absent of any trace of happiness. "You're mistaken, War-leader. I'm not good. Not even close."

With that, she changed back to Admiral Bandar and released the door, walking out of the lift and onto the bridge.

CHAPTER SIXTEEN

"STATUS," BRIT CALLED out as she took command of the bridge.

"Distress call verified," the comm officer reported. "It's a data signal only. It shows voice, but we haven't been able to get it yet."

"In light of what we found on Cupezikan, we will respond immediately nonetheless. Time remaining to Goddess Reach at ninety percent speed," she demanded of Tango, the Earthling pilot.

"Five-point-seven ship-hours, Admiral," he said.

"Set course to Goddess Reach."

"Yes, Admiral."

In his hand was a multicolored cube. Curious, she walked over to his station and took it from him. "What is this?"

He started to rise to his feet. "Remain seated, Major. You're on duty. Any other time, yes, you would stand when I address you."

"Yes, ma'am." His throat moved. She made him nervous. She cast a glance at Hadley, who was pretending to look anywhere but at the Earthling. "It's called a Rubik's Cube," he said. "It's a puzzle."

"I see." Brit looked it over. "A toy. You've brought a toy to the bridge. Do I assume all this is a game to you, Major?"

"No, ma'am." He acted more like a frightened grass-bunny than a military officer. Cadet Pehzwan had more composure about her than he did. She returned the puzzle cube and made a mental note to start putting the Earthling to the test as she had Hadley. The officer-children on this ship needed to grow up. She helped them not at all by sheltering them; more than ever if the galaxy once again was leaning toward war. There would be no more deaths on her conscience. There were enough of them as it was. "Put it away, and don't bring it here again."

"Yes, ma'am. I mean, no, ma'am." Flustered, he corrected, "I understand."

Greener than pond scum, she thought and walked away. At Tango's age, she'd already had countless battles under her belt.

The comm officer called out urgently, "We've got a voice signal now, Admiral."

"Put it on."

The sounds of chaos exploded on the bridge. "They're here! They're coming! Oh, my gods…"

Everyone on the bridge went silent, riveted by the sound of screaming in the background and…was that the sound of plasma fire? Brit exchanged an alarmed glance with Finn. "It's the Horde!" the person shouted.

Horde. Everyone in the sector who cared to listen had heard that transmission. Finn's fears of mass retaliation toward the Drakken had just moved a step closer to reality.

"Oh, gods save us. Someone help us—*please.*" The communication ended with the sound of a baby crying.

Inside, Brit crystallized with purpose. "To Goddess Reach—maximum speed," she ordered, hoping they weren't already too late.

AT THREE-POINT-ONE HOURS into the journey to Goddess Reach, a proximity alarm blasted. "Drakken cruiser in range, Admiral," the bridge officer informed Brit.

A surge of excitement washed away the cold dread lying in her belly since Cupezikan. Were these the skulling bastards she was after? Were they foolish enough to cross her path? Did they not know who was tracking them? Vengeance was always sweet.

"Give me a holo," she directed.

An image of a smallish Drakken vessel appeared on the holo-vis. The ship was armed, but nowhere near the size it would need to be to take on a battleship the size of the *Unity.*

"Do you think it's them?" Hadley asked.

"Tell me what you think."

"Well…"

Brit waited for the girl to have the courage to advocate her own opinion. It was, after all, what she was training her to do.

"It's a small ship, Admiral. It looks rather banged up, too. I don't think it's the same raiders who killed the scientists."

"Small, banged-up ships can house monsters capable of committing atrocities as well as larger, sleeker models can."

"True...." Hadley thought some more, then said, "My gut tells me they're not the ones we're looking for."

"It is wise not to discount one's gut, Hadley. It is also wise, however, to never give a Drakken the benefit of the doubt." Brit stopped, realizing what she'd said. Realizing that she might be wrong, and yet not being able to fully commit to a sea-change of thinking she blamed on taking Finn as a lover. To her, Drakken were guilty until proven innocent. To her, they were all of the same mold—monsters in human form. That was, until Finn Rorkken showed up and turned her life upside down, forcing her to see him as a man, not Horde.

Her relationship with Finn was inappropriate on so many levels. Most troubling, it caused her doubt within herself as a military commander. He'd given her cause to think twice when before she would have acted without hesitation. Black and white, right and wrong, it used to be so clear.

It was no longer.

"More of an issue here, Hadley, is whether intercepting the raider vessel is justified. Likely you are correct, these are not our skullers and stopping to bother with them will delay our arrival at Goddess Reach. This is when a commander's own feelings on a matter will come into play, as mine will in this instance. I for one could not stomach knowing that I let murderers slip through my fingers. Thus we will intercept, board and remove the crew. I'll give them the chance to prove their innocence, of course." A swift chance, but a chance all the same.

And if they were the skullers? It was over for them. Her hand closed into a fist. She'd punish them for their sins and savor every moment of doing so, she thought, as bitterness filled her, a bitterness that felt at once more comfortable in its familiarity than the tolerance Finn advocated.

"Moreover, the distress signal from the imperiled settlement has stopped," Brit continued, in an attempt to justify what she never before felt compelled to justify: capturing a rogue vessel. "Unfortunately, it likely means the settlers are dead." *Skulled.* Children included, she thought, grateful that her position of command would keep her on the bridge and away from the actual scene of the massacre. For even the most experienced soldier, it would be a gruesome encounter. For her, however, every glimpse of bodies and blood brought her back to that day on Arrayar. The nightmarish visions were kept carefully at bay.

Even as a young officer, she'd been able to mask her reaction to such scenes. However, it was a situation she preferred to avoid now that the privilege of her position allowed her to do so. Draining it was, having to pretend it didn't affect her so deeply.

You told Finn you were scared.

Yes, she had. Yet, he didn't know the reason for her fear. Fear she'd mastered by transforming it into aggression, making a career of it. Oh, Prime-Admiral Zaafran knew about what happened on Arrayar; it was part of her official military records. But no one, not even Zaafran, knew the true events of that day.

She turned back to the bridge crew who awaited her orders: a command to intercept the rogue vessel, or dismiss it as an innocuous threat and proceed to Goddess Reach.

"Intercept the rogue," she ordered. If it delayed their arrival at Goddess Reach by an hour or two, so be it. All that awaited them there was death. "Pilot, time to intercept."

"Point-seven hours, ma'am."

Not much time. Finn was asleep, knowing he'd need rest before arriving at the settlement. She brought her hand to her PCD. "Warleader."

A pause—she counted one, two, three, and he answered. "Aye," he said, his voice gentle hearing hers.

"Rogue ship. Small, armed, no military ID. I've ordered an intercept. Less than an hour to capture."

"On my way." His capacity to turn alert amazed her.

"We need a boarding team," she told him when he arrived only moments later.

"Already done. Myself to command, Pehzwan to fly, Rothberg and Bolivarr for security."

"No Coalition," she noted.

"The rogues are desperate and scared. To lure them in, you've got to use the right bait. I have a Drakken crew, save one Earthling to show we're Triad Alliance and Rakkelle as extra enticement."

"Clever." However, not necessary. The raiders were coming aboard whether they wanted to or not. If they had anything to do with the skulling, she'd be sending them on a one-way trip to the Dark Reaches for all eternity before the night was over.

THE SHIP TRIED to outrun them, and of course they couldn't. They refused to reply to comm attempts. Within range, the *Unity* trapped them in a web-beam array. Now the rogue was caught. There was no escape.

"Unidentified Drakken vessel, this is the Triad Alliance ship *Unity,*" the bridge officer said. "How do you read?"

Finally a reply: "Get off our freepin' ass. We didn't do anything."

"Cooperation is in your best interest."

"Go fuck yourself, Coalition scum, eh?"

Finn pressed a finger to his mouth. He'd not been any less arrogant plying the Borderlands of old as the Scourge.

Brit stood by. "This sounds rather familiar," she said dryly.

"I never swore—not to you, at any rate."

"I swore at *you*," she reminded him.

"Enough to make a space-hand blush."

"I made you blush? I doubt that very much."

Their lingering glance was ripe with sexual promise. Then they seemed to remember where they were and walked apart.

Yarew was observing him. Finn fought off but listened to a prickle of alarm. This man and his intelligence background was not who Finn wanted learning about his nights spent with Brit. "The admiral and I have history," he said, making light of the moment to defuse what the man thought he might have observed. "Here in the Borderlands. She never caught me, and it bothers her still."

He heard Brit make a soft, derisive snort. "I simply let you go the way a fisherman releases a too-small fishlet back to the sea."

Hadley laughed at their banter then contained her amusement as Yarew glared at her.

"I'll talk to them," Finn offered and took the comm. "This is Warleader Finnar Rorkken. I'm the first officer. State your identity."

"Rorkken?" the vessel commed back. "A Drakken name."

"Aye. I'm in the Triad forces now. Drakken, Coalition and the Shrine of Earth all serve together."

Silence met his statement. They may have heard of the Triad, but had feared reports of its inclusiveness were lies to capture and imprison them.

"State the levels of your supplies—food and water."

"What food and water? We got nothing. No money. Let us go. We didn't do anything."

"They're underplaying it, of course, to get away," Finn told Brit and Yarew. "I'd guess their supplies are, in fact, low. They have at most a week's worth of supplies before they go hungry. We never had much more than that, even in the good times. They've probably come out to these remote parts to find something to steal without too much consequence."

"Or kill?"

He shook his head. "Not these. They're harmless."

"If I'm letting you board that ship, Warleader," Brit said, "you had better damn well be right."

CHAPTER SEVENTEEN

"LET'S GO." Finn finished suiting up. He and the others, armed to the teeth, boarded the shuttle. The rogue vessel was still caught in the array, helpless. Its weaponry was disabled. The *Unity*'s computer had taken over the ship's computer, rendering it useless. The rogues could fight back if they wanted, hand-to-hand when Finn and the team boarded, but it would be futile. They'd be destroyed. Finn knew the rogues were desperate, but they weren't that desperate. Despite their flashes of arrogance and pride, at this point, they'd want to avoid punishment and prison time. He could offer them a way out of both.

Rakkelle hopped into the pilot chair and buckled in. "Y'all ready? Here we go!" With ease, she cut loose from the ship and spiraled down to the rogue, looking tiny in the immense shadow of the *Unity*.

They entered the array. While it held fast to the rogue ship, it allowed them through. "Ease her in," Finn directed, "and sidle up to her…like that, aye."

"Ooh, I like sidling. Nothing beats a man who tells

me what he likes." Rakkelle cut power and drifted close. A tunnel-tube extended from the shuttle bay and covered the boarding hatch on the rogue. "Sealing...now." She shook her hair and grinned. "Done. Docking com-*plete!*"

"Check weapons," Finn said, taking the safety off his pistol. "Don goggles."

After everyone complied, Rothberg moved through the tunnel first. He tapped on the hatch with his rifle. It made a metallic clang. "Send your captain to open this up," he ordered, his weapon drawn. "Or we blow you the freep out of the sky."

That last part was unscripted, Finn thought, shaking his head. Rothberg was a pirate at heart.

"Aye," said a tired voice from inside.

Rothberg went flat against the tunnel sidewall. The door opened and a warm stench drifted out. Rakkelle inhaled then let out a mournful sigh. "Skins. How I've missed them...the softness, the smell, making love in them."

Rothberg tossed a 360-degree viewer through the open hatch and returned to his position pressed to the tunnel sidewall. Immediately Finn had a picture in his goggles of the scene inside. Five worn-out men sat around the small bridge in tattered uniforms and stained leathers. Two men wore no shirts at all. Their skin gleamed with sweat. Finn knew why. It cost money to properly ventilate a ship. They were probably running at emergency air levels—on purpose. Over time it affected you. He remembered.

"Do not move." He walked in, holding his rifle, followed by the others. The men simply sat, defeated. Their features were pinched with hunger and hopelessness, their tattoos standing out starkly against sallow skin.

"Thought you were Drakken," one said.

"He's got tattoos," another pointed out. "That be Drakken ink."

"But he don't look Drakken."

Finn's transformation must have been more complete than he'd realized if these men questioned his origins. First, he'd exchanged his leathers for a shiny new uniform. Then, sometime after beginning his affair with Brit, he'd removed the beading and braids from his hair. Though he hadn't yet cut his hair, he'd been considering it. And he bathed every day now, most days more than that.

Rakkelle paced around the bridge, somehow catching every man's eye. Her round little butt swayed as she inspected the pilot station. Her rolled-up sleeves revealed the tattoos on her forearms. One ear was so decorated with jewelry around the entire rim that the skin was barely visible. She wasn't wearing a bra and had a habit of arching her back and thrusting her chest forward, too, making the most of what little she had, a move not missed by the men. She might be in her Triad uniform, but she was still very much a Drakken in appearance.

Disapproving, Finn frowned. He'd have a talk with her later about that. It was high time they made an effort to blend in, especially in light of the terrorist attack, and those like Yarew, who in their narrowmindedness were all too happy to use old sins to excuse discrimination.

Bolivarr collected the weapons while the men were otherwise distracted by Rakkelle. "Who's the captain here?" Finn demanded.

No one immediately answered.

Finn tapped the muzzle of his pistol against his open hand. "We start cooperating or we start shooting. It's as simple as that."

"She's dead."

Finn's attention swung to the tall, thin man who'd spoken. He recognized the voice as the one he'd spoken with on the bridge. "My wife," the man explained. "We had a skirmish on a supply run, and she…" His hands were folded in his lap. Dirt was crusted under his nails. His skin hadn't seen a bath in who knew how long. He was a grieving man. The fight that had kept him and the others on the run was draining out of him before Finn's eyes.

"Come on now," Finn coaxed. "We'll take you on board and feed you a hot meal, and—"

"I don't really care what you do to me." He stood, holding Finn's gaze. "Shoot me right here. I'd rather join Kallea in the Dark Reaches than be forced to live as a Coalition pet."

Rage and shame flared in Finn, but he shoved it aside. It was the Drakken way to bicker and start a fight. Violence won more respect than authority. In the old days he'd be expected to fight it out to hold on to his honor. It was better to kill than to live with an insult hanging over your head. However, the man who once would have fought for his honor the way an animal fights for a meaty bone seemed light-years away from who he was now. He was civilized. Not a Coalition pet.

"We're taking you in," he told the raiders. "You'll be questioned and then transferred to a refugee camp. From there you'll be repatriated as a Triad citizen and relocated. You'll have choices. You can even join the Forces if you want to."

Rakkelle had moved back to his side. Bolivarr stood guard on his other. "The food's good," Rakkelle said. "Your nights are your own." Her voice became throaty, her tone inviting. "And I can tell you, I ain't anyone's gods-be-damned pet, neither." She rested a hand on her hip and thrust it out, her eyes smiling and seductive. Even Rothberg was watching her with a dark, assessing gaze, caught by Rakkelle's sexual spell. "I like to keep pets of my own, though. Aye, and more than one. Maybe we'll talk again when you're cleaned up and fed, eh?" She blew them a kiss.

The widower, Finn noticed, paid Rakkelle no

mind. He was too busy aiming his resentment at Finn. Transferring anger made grief easier to bear. He'd seen it happen too many times.

"Erikk?" one of the men asked the widower. "We should go with them. Food, a comfy skin…"

Rakkelle bit her lip. She wanted to tell them about the absence of skins, but had the good sense not to give the rogues another excuse to avoid coming aboard.

One by one the men rose, all of them casting hopeful gazes in Rakkelle's direction. The captain-by-default folded his arms over his chest. "I'll stay."

"If you don't come now, you'll be towed. We've got an emergency call to respond to," Finn said and made a show of sniffing at the stuffy air. "Conditions aren't too good in here. You'd best come aboard while you have the chance. I don't know when we'll be able to get you food or supplies, or transfer you over to the ship."

"Don't care about that."

"Warleader, get them rounded up now," Brit ordered in his PCD. "We've wasted more than enough time."

"I've got four men we're bringing aboard, Admiral. The fifth man wants to stay."

"Denied. He comes, too."

"You heard the admiral," Finn said to the widower. "No one stays. Everyone goes."

"I'll get my things," the man said. He turned and disappeared into another part of the ship.

The thought of stopping the man went through his mind. He motioned to Bolivarr to watch the corridor in case the man went freepin' crazo when he turned his back. "Let's move," Finn said, urging the bedraggled crew onto the shuttle where they gazed around in open awe. Finn remembered how he used to be amazed by the relative wealth and richness of the Ring and the *Unity*.

"Get them seated," he told the team, "and I'll see what's happened to the captain."

"Sir, you'd better come." Bolivarr stood near the stern of the vessel, his pistol at his side. Finn pushed through the narrow corridor. Rooms on either side lacked doors. Skins hung from the ceiling. A half-empty bottle of sweef and small glasses sat on one table. He caught the acrid aroma of a sweef still brewing somewhere on the vessel. Foul stuff, he thought. Well, more so than usual. It brought back memories he didn't care to have brought back. Homemade sweef would rot your tongue on the first taste. Aye, numbing the way for the rest of what you wanted to drink of it.

Depressing as hells. The captain wanted *this* over what he could have in the Triad? Once he saw what he was missing, he'd never want to go back.

"Hey, mate," he called after the raider. "You can't have that much to pack. Get yer ass in motion. You've got a shuttle to catch."

He waited a beat for a response.

"Bah. I've got half a mind to leave him here and—" Finn came to an abrupt halt. A body lay rocking in a skin. Blood dripped to the floor, spattering Finn's shiny Triad boots. Freepin' hells. The man had gone and shot himself.

TOWARD THE END of Brit's shifts and before the beginning of his, Finn had taken to walking the ship, top to bottom, bow to stern. He knew that Brit maintained the same daily habit. It was the way of ship captains, he supposed, walking your ship, knowing the scents and sounds, getting the feel of her, just as he'd gotten the feel of Brit as the days had passed. Hunting the terrorists by day, making love at night, he knew her physically. The woman inside remained elusive, however. Bit by bit, she was opening up, although certain topics were forbidden, namely the years prior to her entering her beloved Royal Military Academy.

Tonight, in the hours before they reached Goddess Reach, he walked for a different reason than to know his ship. He walked to know himself.

Coalition pet. The words haunted him. He'd spent many a year bleedin' the Coalition, driving them crazy in the Borderlands then later as a warleader known for rendering useless comm stations throughout the border worlds. Deep down, he knew the other side had it better—better food, better shelter, better technology, better leaders—but jealousy for what the Coalition had never fueled his fight. No, he simply did his job as it was assigned to him. When the chance came for more, he'd risked everything, giving up his command, so his crew could have a better life. In return, he'd won a better life for himself—one with a future, not the dead end that would have awaited him as a Drakken warleader.

He turned up yet another corridor on this massive ship. He should be resting, aye, but was too restless to do so. The encounter with the rogues—now resting safely in the brig after Yarew and his intelligence team had pumped them for predictably little useful information—left him questioning not himself but "his people" as Brit referred to them earlier. *Coalition pet.* Why didn't they see him as a symbol of success, an example, something to aspire to? Fools! If they were content to scrape bottom in the Coalition's upwardly mobile galaxy, they'd be left behind.

Not his crew, though. They were smart. The men and women from the *Pride* knew he'd given them a hand. They'd pull themselves up the rest of the way.

His aimless stroll took him to the area of the ship where most of the crew quarters were. In the least desirable location, on the least desirable deck, the space-hands lived. As on the *Pride,* he mostly stayed clear of the space-hand quarters, leaving some semblance of privacy to the men and women who lived here. Who wanted their captain breathin' down their neck?

A distant roar of voices caught his attention. He strolled closer, curious. Down one corridor, a crowd gathered outside an open door. All Drakken, by the looks of it. Someone flew out the door and the crowd shoved him back inside. What the hells was going on? Finn headed in that direction.

Several in the corridor noticed his approach. "Captain's here!" the warning call went out.

The crowd scattered. "Halt!" he bellowed. "Don't be leaving yet." Long strides carried him closer. The nearer he got, the clearer the guilty expressions were on the faces.

"Captain," the men greeted, shuffling and clearing throats.

"That's Warleader," he corrected, annoyed that so many of his former crew stubbornly insisted on "forgetting" that fact. "What's the noise about? What's going on in there?"

The men in the corridor stepped back to allow him through. Inside the small room, men scurried to right fallen furniture, a table and chairs. They'd been given nice quarters and this is how they treated it? One space-hand used a bloody rag to clean his face. Finn didn't need to see dice to know what they'd been up to.

"You're playin' grabble?" he snarled. The game he'd banned.

"Aye…" The men recoiled at his fury. Zurykk pushed his way through the crowd clustered around the door. He was clutching a fistful of the fabric from Silubakk's collar, the former civilian who was now a space-hand thanks to Brit's promotion, as he shoved him along in front of him. Silubakk had a swollen lip and a bruised eye.

"This one tried to get away," Zurykk said, pushing the space-hand into the room.

"Isn't grabble banned, or was I dreaming I gave the order?" Finn asked the crowd.

The silence was thick and tense.

"Well?"

"Banned, sir," or "We weren't supposed to be playin', Cap'n," and "We didn't see the harm," were grumbled amidst various mutterings and coughs.

"Didn't see the harm?" Finn bellowed, outraged. "Didn't see the harm in disobeying a direct order?"

"The nanomeds heal ya so fast," Markar said in a shaky voice as he tried to explain. "You don't stay hurt for much more than a day."

Finn didn't want to know the thought process behind it. He was so freepin' furo, he wanted to beat the men within an inch of their lives. Ever conscious of how Drakken were perceived—violent, antagonistic beasts—he resorted to hitting the table with the side of his fist instead. The men jumped. "You have no military discipline. You smell like you haven't bathed. You keep to yourselves and don't try to assimilate into Triad culture."

"Assim…?" he heard one of the space-hands ask another in a whisper.

"*'Assimilate,'* you grains-for-brains bore-head. Integrate, blend in." Didn't they realize the danger of being Hordish in a Coalition world? When those like Yarew were spring-loaded to wipe the Horde from the face of the galaxy? All they needed was an excuse. Being so outwardly Drakken would make it easy. Their survival depended on adapting to their new culture, not fighting it.

"You act like the animals the Coalition thinks you are. And maybe you are barbaric beasts, because all attempts to civilize you have freepin' failed! You're no better than the rogues we got down in the brig." He rubbed his fist, pacing a few steps then turning back to them. He knew what he had to do. "We're starting over."

He snatched a bottle of sweef off the floor and pulled out the cork, upending it into the sink. The pungent odor filled the stuffy room, adding another element to the mix of sweat and blood. "I want it all gone by morning. And, no, not by drinkin' it."

A surge of groans and "but, Captain"s erupted.

He sliced a hand through the air, silencing them. "Until you show me I can trust you as working, contributing members of this crew, no sweef. If I hear of any violations, if I hear of a single one, you'll be confined to quarters. All of you." He glared at each space-hand in turn. "We'll start by teaching you a taste of that tonight. Zurykk."

"Aye, Warleader."

"Get the word around. No one leaves their quarters but for work and orders until I say otherwise."

"Aye, Warleader."

Finn felt let down by his former crew in so many different ways that for once he didn't know what to say. Leaving them with only his disappointed silence to ponder, he exited the room.

"Captain." Zurykk jogged after him. "Warleader, I mean," he corrected as Finn turned around to frown at him.

"Do you think it's a good idea to take everything away like that?"

"Everything?" He waved a hand at the ship, the sparkling fittings and the top-notch materials. "Compared to our last ship, this is paradise. This is the best life they've ever had. They don't seem to care too much, going at each other like animals, marinating what's left of their pea-ball brains with sweef."

"When I say everything, sir, I mean what makes them Horde. They've got no skins, no sweef, no grabble, and they're living on a Coalition ship."

"A Triad ship."

"But, sir, even you said we shouldn't take away too much too soon. You said they're still Drakken in Triad clothing. You told the admiral that. You told her to give them time. If I may say so, they're still needin' that time, sir."

"Zurykk, man, you've lost the thread here. They disobeyed me."

"I know they shouldn't have been doing the grabble."

His former second-in-command said it in a way that had Finn wondering how much he'd known about. It got him thinking, too, how out of touch he'd been with all of them. He knew where his focus had been, and it wasn't on them. Aye, he'd been wrapped up in his relationship with Brit, wrapped up in his new duties, but, gods, he ought to be able to turn his back; he ought to be able to trust them!

"They're worried what they're going to lose next," Zurykk continued. "The tattoos, their beads."

"Humph." Finn thought of how close he'd come to cutting his hair short in the past few days. His aim was to look more Triad. *He don't look Drakken*—the rogues had treated him as if he were an aberration, not an example.

Was it the truth?

Finn scrubbed a hand over his face. Regardless, he had his crew to deal with. "I gave them an order, Zurykk. They chose to disobey. That's mutiny. They'll stay confined to quarters until I say otherwise."

"Aye, sir."

Finn left his friend standing in the corridor. The words *coalition pet* taunting him.

EERIE SILENCE ENVELOPED the cloud-shrouded world of Goddess Reach. In the shuttle headed planetside with Warleader Rorkken, the rest of the Cupezikan team and three extra hands, Hadley gripped her holstered pistol. If need be, she was ready to use it. At the academy, she'd been trained for combat operations. Since graduating, she'd never used any of her combat training. She hoped it came back fast. She was well aware that the admiral had sent her planetside on Cupezikan because it was supposed to have been a routine mission. Goddess Reach clearly wasn't. She'd make doubly sure she didn't screw up.

The descent was bumpy. Rain lashed the windows. "When we land, we'll break up into pairs and spread out looking for survivors. Note anything of interest and report back to me. Barrientes, you're with Odin. I'll be with Rothberg. And, Bolivarr, you go with Lieutenant Keyren." The warleader went on to pair up the rest of the team.

Hearing her assignment, Hadley tried not to ponder the little flare-up of nerves mixed with relief at being matched up with Bolivarr. The distress call had delayed her visit to Tango's quarters. Out of sheer awkwardness, she preferred to avoid the Earthling until that moment when they'd be able to be together. On the other hand, the wraith was proving increasingly distracting.

Stupid mood ring, she thought. *It means nothing.*

After landing, as soon as it was determined safe to exit, they tromped down the gangway and set off slogging through the mud in heavy boots as the team fanned out in all directions.

Rain came down hard. It was a miserable day. The settlement looked as deserted as Cupezikan had been. At first she'd had hopes of finding everyone alive. Now those hopes began to fade in the gloom of the day.

She and Bolivarr followed a winding, narrow, muddy trail into the hills. The data-vis showed nothing around except the heat-sigs of small indigenous creatures. Off to the left, some shrubbery caught her eye. She slowed to take a look. The wraith's quiet voice vibrated in her PCD. "What do you see, Hadley?"

"Broken twigs. Torn leaves."

The toe of his boot pushed at some of the leaves on the ground. "They're too new to have fallen on their own. They were knocked off when people passed this way. Days," he said. "Not weeks ago."

"Agreed."

"And this," he said, pointing off into the soaked woods with his rifle, "isn't the usual footpath."

"You're right." Hadley's pulse kicked up a notch. She considered herself a good observer, but the wraith's ability to see signs she couldn't was amazing. She tried not to think about how he got that way— hunting...assassinating—and shook off the visions of a darker, scarier Bolivarr from years past. "It may be where the settlers were forced on a death march to be skulled. Or, it may be an evacuation route to a shelter."

Bolivarr fingered a leaf then threw it down. "They are hiding in a shelter."

"You sound so sure."

"My hunches are always right." His dark gaze

held hers until she trembled, something the expedition suit didn't allow him to see, thank the gods, before his focus veered back to the trail. Silent, he took off walking, and she followed.

What about her hunches? Her gut instincts? They were good, she knew, but she wished she could be as confident about them as Bolivarr was. And Admiral Bandar, too. The admiral attributed her successes in battle to listening to her gut. Hadley had best do the same if she ever hoped to be as good a commander as her hero.

The muddy track ended at a mass of discarded brush piled up next to a hillside. "It's hiding something. An entrance?" She let high hopes buoy her along. Bolivarr grabbed her arm before she could kick away the brush.

"No, Hadley." He stalked around the immediate area, scrutinizing high and low.

"What are you looking for?"

"It's not widely known, but after skulling, landing parties were ordered by the battle-lords to leave behind booby traps to kill as many of the search-and-rescue people as possible."

She stood in place, drenched and holding her breath, wondering what she'd stepped on or was about to step on. "That's lower than low."

"It is what it is. I don't agree with the method."

"I know...." Somehow she did know. Underneath his intensity was an inexplicable gentleness that she was just beginning to notice.

She stood impatiently as rain poured down. It was dribbling along the seams of her suit as if looking for a way inside. Bolivarr's inspection of the area was quick. Eerie as it was, he seemed to know exactly what he was looking for. When he didn't find it, he let her assist him in clearing away the brush. A metal door had been dug into the hillside and shut tight against invaders.

She and the wraith exchanged a triumphant glance.

"You talk to them," he said and attached an aural amplifier to the door. "They'll hear my accent."

His Hordish accent.

"This is Lieutenant Hadley Keyren from the Triad Alliance Ship *Unity.* We answered your distress call. I sure hope you're alive in there, because, goddess, it's wet out here."

From behind the door, the sound of muffled, surprised shouts and weeping told her that her fervent wish had come true. Then, the door cracked open an inch, letting out the odor of warm bodies, sweat and a smell she'd not encountered in a very long time: the odor of foul, soiled diapers. A nano-layer could keep the waste lining clean only so long. "It's going to be all right," she soothed them as Bolivarr turned to speak into his PCD: "Warleader, they're alive."

FINN CIRCLED the perimeter of the chaotic scene as settlers poured out of the shelter none too happy about his presence or Bolivarr's. A quick call to Brit and another shuttle was dispatched. They'd brought only one, never dreaming they'd find survivors. It was good to see there was still a reason for hope in the galaxy; not everyone died. The downside was the survivors gave verbal proof that Drakken had attacked this settlement. It was exactly the kind of arrogant act to incite old enemies to retaliate. He doubted the Drakken had the ability to fight back in a real way—the warlord, Lord-General Rakkuu, and his son were dead, and most of the battle-lords dead or imprisoned—but a bloodbath was a real possibility. Drakken innocents could find themselves cast in the light of suspicion and killed, all in the name of security.

"Get them formed up in two groups, one for each shuttle," he told Barrientes.

"Yes, sir." The Earthling moved through the crowd.

Drakken! The settlers' frightened gazes screamed. *Horde!* Only Keyren and the non-Drakken amongst the expedition team and their forceful reassurances kept panic at bay. The Triad may have been widely announced, changing the face of the galaxy's ruling governments, but to the average Coalition citizen the idea of playing nice with Drakken was viewed with suspicion—suspicion that this latest round of attacks would amplify. What happened here and on Cupezikan would undermine the peace process, if this was in fact still peace. It was looking an awful lot like war.

Ensign Odin helped an injured woman hobble past

Finn. She clutched a tiny babe to her breast. "Oh, heavens help us," she muttered, trembling as they walked by him. The stares she cast his way were wild and tear-filled. As soon as they were safely away, the settler broke down into wrenching sobs. Odin consoled her, awkwardly patting the woman's back.

Finn scowled. So he was a "monster" to their people and a "pet" to his own. Damn it all, which was it? Would he ever belong anywhere, or was he doomed to be an outcast forever, always on his own in the world, the war orphan nobody had wanted? The Drakken who aspired to things well above his station? *And women above your station, too?*

He'd begun to consider himself a Triad officer, worthy of Brit's company. He was proud of his rank and position. A few terror-filled glances from the settlers dropped him right back where he used to be.

Finn kept his stream of dark thoughts hidden, watching over the team as they herded the bedraggled group to safety. Lieutenant Keyren joined him, typing on her data-vis.

A second shuttle appeared through the rain clouds, screeching to a soft landing in the field. "Tango," he called. "Get your shuttle ready to go. One up, and one down, until everyone is off this planet."

"Aye, sir." The Earthling had responded with "aye" as a pirate would. Finn sensed it was a way of showing him respect, regard that he'd seen growing in the pilot as the days had passed. Tango even threw in a Drakken salute before he walked away to get the shuttle ready for launch.

"*This* is the proper salute, Tango," Finn told him, bringing a fist to his chest.

"If that's the way they want us to do it. But we U.S. Air Force types used to do it this way." He returned a snappy hand slice to the forehead before giving in and pounding a fist to his chest in the Triad salute, which was no different from the Coalition salute.

Finn acknowledged the Earthling's attempt to bridge the gap between them with a grin. At this point, he'd take allies wherever he could get them.

He went in search of Rothberg, whom he'd put to the task of an accurate head count. A group of settlers was headed his way, led by Keyren. The group parted like a brothel's velvet drapes, allowing him a wide swath through. He shook his head. At least they didn't scream.

Rothberg stood with the settlement leader. The man appeared unruffled by Finn's presence. He was all business. Little wonder this group survived, Finn thought. They had a capable leader.

"How many do we have, Commander Rothberg?"

"Sixty-six, Warleader. That's a final."

"Our records show you at fifty-six," Finn told the leader. "That's ten more than we thought."

"Three are newborns," the leader said with a happy smile. The settlers would keep multiplying, too, Finn thought, having noticed several pregnant women. "The other seven adults are strangers—or were before all that time we spent holed up together. They were on the way to their settlement when they were attacked. They crash-landed here and begged sanctuary."

Finn was instantly alert. "Where's the ship?"

"Under about ten slogs of mud out in the fields. All this rain, we haven't had the chance to get out to see it. They warned us that Drakken were raiding. Good thing, too. As it was, we had precious little time to pack up and hide. We barely got a distress signal out before they blasted apart our comm. We don't know how many came a'raiding. We were underground by then and didn't dare take a peek."

Finn nodded. "Admiral Bandar and the ship's staff will want to hear what you told me just now. Understand? Once we're aboard, I want you to pull those seven out of the crowd to be questioned." They had valuable information, leading, he hoped, to the skullers.

"Admiral Bandar, as in *the* Admiral Bandar?"

"Aye. The one and only."

"The legendary," Hadley put in, proud.

"That's going to cause quite a bit of excitement amongst my village, more so for the adults. For the children the chance to see a galaxy-class starship is a wonder all on its own."

"You'll all be there soon enough." Finn rounded up Rothberg, Bolivarr and Keyren. "Let's have a look at that ship." They trudged off through the rain. "Admiral," he called to the *Unity* on his PCD.

"Warleader."

He steeled himself against the effect her voice had on him. He wanted this day to be over. He wanted to be in bed with her. With Brit, he was anything but a gods-be-damned pet. "News," he said. "Apparently they've gained seven adults in the past few days. All of them fleeing a Drakken attack." He dragged a hand over his face. His Triad expedition suit was light-years more comfortable than his old, scratchy, smelly Drakken sweater, but he'd rather be dry. Too many years spent huddled soaking wet and cold in a warehouse had left him despising wet weather. "I'm going to ID the ship. It was a hard landing—under ten slogs of mud the settlement leader says." He yelled above the roar of Rakkelle's shuttle lifting off. "Your first shipment of refugees is on the way. All the children are aboard."

Brit made a soft noise of displeasure. "I'll give the docking crew fair warning."

Finn ended the call. "I don't think the admiral sounds quite ready for little ones aboard."

Lieutenant Keyren got a funny look on her face and glanced away, saying nothing. Finn wondered at that. He'd never stopped to ponder whether Brit enjoyed children as much as he did. He'd assumed she would, even though her career, like his, had prevented her from having any of her own. Was he wrong? For some damned reason, he pictured her as a mother. He pictured her with their child.

Rorkken, you sentimental fool, he berated himself.

"Let's get this mission wrapped up and our asses off this planet. With the *Unity* watchin' over us, the danger of a surprise attack is nil, but an attack is still possible. We want to be on the bridge if that happens."

True to the settlement leader's word, the crashed ship sat buried in mud. It would take hours to dig the vessel out. Rothberg went down on one knee, scraping away muck. "I'm going to get us in." He moved his gloved fingers along a seam and paused, withdrawing one hand to scratch his chest. "It feels like I've got a mosquito in my suit."

"Mosquito? What's that?" Hadley asked.

"A pesty Earth insect. They b-bite." His hand moved faster now, up and down as if he were making a parody of scratching an itch. Then a deep, shuddering, guttural sound came out of his mouth.

"Gods be damned," Finn growled, taking a running step toward the man. "He's convulsing!"

CHAPTER EIGHTEEN

ROTHBERG SAGGED to the mud. Finn caught the man and dragged him away from the ship. The Earthling's body was stiff and jerking. It took all his weight to hold the man down. "Get me a med kit!"

Hadley ran to the shuttle. Finn pulled off his glove and wedged it between Rothberg's teeth. Blood foamed around his lips. He'd bitten his tongue. His lids fluttered, revealing the whites of his eyes.

Bolivarr crouched next to them. "I know what this is. I know what to do."

"Do it, then."

Rothberg seemed to be in the throes of the worst agony imaginable. Bolivarr tore open the man's uniform and hunted with his hands until he found a small red mark on his chest. He lowered his mouth to the tiny wound. Rothberg's convulsions bucked him off. "Keep him down, Warleader."

"Trying." Finn struggled to get a better grip, leaning his whole weight on the strong Earth soldier while keeping the glove in place so Rothberg wouldn't bite off his tongue.

Bolivarr's cheeks moved in and out as he went back to sucking at the wound and pushing inward with his index fingers.

Hadley returned with the med kit. She searched for a mouth guard and took care of exchanging the glove for the guard. Suddenly, Bolivarr came up on his knees and spat something into his hand. It was a thin, bright blue cylinder.

"What, pray goddess, is that?" she asked.

"Booby trap." Bolivarr worked spit in his mouth and again spat on the ground, repeating the action several times. "Poison," he explained in staccato gasps. "Designed for timed release to make death the most prolonged and the most agonizing it can be."

"Did you get it out in time?" Finn asked.

"It's only a quarter gone. I don't know."

"Did *you* swallow any?" Hadley asked, a note of panic in her voice.

"I don't think so."

She murmured what sounded like a prayer.

Rothberg went limp. Swearing, Finn started resuscitation. "His color's going blue," Hadley said urgently. "Try the heart-starting patch." She dug the item out of the medical kit, pressing it to the man's chest.

It didn't work.

"Come on, man. Come on." He kept pumping the chest cavity and filling the man's lungs with air until it was apparent the heart had stopped. He drove his hands through his dripping hair. "Damn shame…"

"Breathe," Bolivarr said, taking over.

"Bolivarr, he's gone." He covered Bolivarr's shoulder with a gentle hand as the wraith worked to revive Rothberg. "There's nothing you can do."

"I should have checked for booby traps first." He kept pumping, even after Rothberg's color deepened to a darker blue. "I didn't think this ship would be rigged. I didn't think."

Hadley's heart twisted with Bolivarr's pain. "It's not your fault," she said. Her voice seemed to break his frenzied, futile efforts. "He didn't die because of you."

Bolivarr sat back on his heels, his eyes utter desolation. "Wraith, taker of life…"

He thought that of himself? To feel that way would be awful. Aching with Bolivarr's pain, aching from the loss of a friend, she pressed a hand over Rothberg's heart. She thought of the time in the officer's-club restaurant when he'd dressed up in costume to serve the Earth food. Doing it all for a friend. Goddess, Tango was going to take this hard. How were they going to break it to him?

Something jumped in Rothberg's chest, under her palm. Hadley jumped back. He inhaled a shuddering, raspy breath and moaned.

Hadley grabbed Bolivarr's arm. "Not taker of life," she corrected. *"Giver.* He's alive!"

TANGO SPRINTED from the shuttle bay to the medical ward. "Fuck it! What happened to him?" he demanded, distraught as Rothberg was carried, unconscious on a smart-stretcher.

Hadley intercepted him. "Booby trap—a poisoned dart. Bolivarr saved him."

Neither the wraith nor Tango acknowledged Bolivarr's act. She wished it were different. *Wraith, taker of life.* Inside that composed exterior was a man struggling to make sense of who or what he was.

Swearing up a storm, most of it in a language she didn't know, Tango tried to muscle his way into the exam room, dragging Hadley in his wake.

"If you care about the man," Dr. Kell warned, "you'll stay out of the way, Major."

"You'd better take a look at Bolivarr, too, Dr. Kell," she suggested. "He had the dart in his mouth."

"I'm fine," the wraith said, seeming to fade away even as she watched him, becoming quieter, more shadowlike. The man of emotion who'd thought he'd lost Rothberg had disappeared.

"Have him check you all the same," she said.

Tango wouldn't budge from the triage room door, where inside his friend lay prone on a table, surrounded by medical personnel. "Dice, wake up. Come on. This ain't funny." He stood, helpless, as Dr. Kell closed the door in his face.

"Dice!" He pounded once on the door before Hadley got him away.

She grabbed his arms. "Pray. That's the best thing we can do for him right now."

His brown eyes shimmered with held-back tears as he pulled her close, and almost off her feet. His whiskers scraped the side of her neck. "He can't die. He can't."

"They'll do everything they can for him. At least he's alive. At least we've got that." Hadley held him close. Warmth spread through her with the knowledge that she could comfort him, and that he'd sought her out for that comfort.

"Hey, Earthling Flyboy. Sorry about your friend. I know what it feels like, and it freepin' sucks." Rakkelle stood nearby with her pilot gloves clutched in one hand. She'd hooked her jaw-length black hair behind an ear decorated with jewelry and micro-tattoos. Black shadow smudged the rims of genuinely sympathetic eyes. She probably was well-versed in what it felt like to lose or almost lose a friend. Admittedly, she and the other Drakken had witnessed more death and destruction than Hadley ever had or, hopefully, ever would.

Tango looked up. "Thanks, Rocky."

Bolivarr had faded once more into the background, a shadow. It made Hadley a bit uncomfortable that he watched her very public embrace. Good thing she'd left the mood ring stored in her quarters while gone on the mission. It would be a rainbow of colors if she were wearing it.

Tango tugged on her hand. "I'll go crazy standing around waiting to hear something, baby girl. Let's get out of here."

"I can't. I have to be at the debriefing with the ship's senior officers." For the first time in her life she cursed her duties.

"But I need you," he said under his breath. She squeezed her eyes shut out of guilt. "I need you with me tonight. Baby, please. I can't be alone."

Her heart filled to overflowing at the rawness in his tone. "You won't be. Not for long."

"How long you gonna be?"

"I'll try to get out as soon as I can." There would be a lot to cover in the debriefing; she wasn't too confident that what she'd promised Tango was true.

Tell him no. Tell him you can't.

His lips brushed her ear. "I'll be in my quarters."

"All right." That was that. Tango needed her, and she'd be there for him. She avoided looking at Rakkelle as she walked away. As far as she was concerned, the woman might have had him for one sweef-fueled bar-kiss. Hadley would have him for everything else. Now, and for a lifetime.

BRIT ADDRESSED HER STAFF in the conference room that still reeked from the seven unwashed refugee men that Yarew debriefed there and released only moments ago. "There was little of interest for us beyond tales of being frightened and chased by a Drakken cruiser. I'm disappointed but not surprised. This is what happens when you have civilians giving you data. To them all ships are either good or bad.

Identifying characteristics like ship numbers and names are not of interest and thus not remembered and passed along."

The seven did answer one question for them all, however: the attackers weren't mere raiders. The Drakken Horde was back.

They would be stopped.

A sense of purpose filled her once more as she pushed back from the table. "Star-Major, have Triad intelligence send a team to Goddess Reach to excavate the crashed ship and recover data from its onboard computers."

"Yes, Admiral." Yarew was inputting the request as she uttered it.

"The data will give us what we need to track the attacking ship—if it wasn't cloaked." By then it might be too late for whomever the raiders targeted next. Silence around the table told her the others shared her feeling of dread and helplessness. She detested this part of the hunt most of all: having the quarry slip through her fingers, unable to stop them before they inflicted more pain and suffering. She made a fist on the table which, she saw in her next breath, Finn had noticed.

His eyes were shadowed, as were everyone else's. She knew how exhausted she was only because she could see it in the faces of her crew. And in her lover's.

She tried not to think about how, with one look in those observant, soft brown eyes of his, she wanted to fall into his embrace and lose the world. Every cell in her body ached for him, and the hours they'd have in bed later. Not so much for the sex, though she hungered for it, but for the way he held her so very close afterward. Sometimes she fell asleep pressing her lips to his warm skin. Would she ever be able to sleep alone again?

She steeled herself against the desire. Tender feelings for a Hordish man with the possibility of the Triad splitting apart in civil war were at minimum a distraction, and a black mark on her judgment as a commander on the other end of the scale. Neither was acceptable.

End it now. Ah, but how? It had come down to him and war. Not too long ago the choice would have been an easy one to make. What in hells was she going to do? She didn't want to give him up. She couldn't continue the relationship with him if political tensions increased, either. To do so would be professional suicide.

Her PCD chimed. "Admiral, this is Dr. Kell."

"Go," she said, transferring the call to her data-vis so the others could hear.

"Commander Rothberg's vital signs are stable. I'm keeping him in an induced coma until I can flush the poison from his system. It's going to take some time due to cellular bonding."

Poisons that gripped you by the throat on the molecular level, she thought darkly. Leave it to the

Drakken to perfect such evil. Yes, but they'd done so using stolen Coalition technology. She hoped it could be used to counter the effects of the poison. The entire ship was pulling for Rothberg's recovery.

Kell said, "I'm told Battle-Lieutenant Bolivarr removed the source of the poison before it emptied— at the risk of his own life. I'd say that saved his life."

"He most certainly will be recognized for his efforts. Keep me advised, Doctor."

"Yes, Admiral." The call ended.

"Hadley, confirm that you already sent my request to headquarters for a Goddess Courage Medal for Bolivarr?"

"Yes." The girl looked uncomfortable. "It was refused."

"For what reason?"

"It just came back with a stamp—denied."

The attacks were already having the predicted effect. She could picture the meeting under way on the Ring at that very moment, where she'd appeared virtually soon after reporting the evacuation of Goddess Reach. Everyone but the Goddess Herself had been there: Prime-Admiral Zaafran, Supreme Commander Neppal, Supreme-second Fair Cirrus, the new Prime Minister Belduin and an assortment of Earthlings she didn't recognize. Only one elderly Drakken statesman was in attendance; like an old, neutered former attack hound, once a threat but rendered harmless now.

Zaafran had leaned forward at the meeting table, light-years distant on the Ring, and folded his hands on the glossy surface. "Keep up the good work," he'd told her. "Until our force presence in the Borderlands is at acceptable levels, you're our main defense."

Brit kept her snort silent. The Triad's best defense? With a green crew of mixed heritage, one-third of whom were on the "other" side, commanded by a woman who hunted Drakken by day and slept with one at night.

She rose, gathering her data-vis. "We'll keep analyzing ion echoes. It's not an exact science, unfortunately, but even a trace will give us something to track. Meanwhile, it's been a long night. If there's nothing else, this meeting is adjourned."

When no one spoke up, she departed the room.

She walked onto the bridge as she had for each of the countless days over the past fifteen years since she'd taken command of a starship. Not once during any of those intervening years did she ever face the sight she did now.

Startled, horrified, she halted. Squealing, energetic children swarmed over the bridge. Several of them fought to climb onto her command smart chair. Berkko, the watch officer, laughed as he carried a joyful little boy on his shoulders…a little boy with dark, ruffled hair who looked all too much like Dellan. The sight hit her like a gut punch.

She gripped a console to keep her voice steady.

"Lieutenant Berkko." Her teeth were clamped together. "There are to be no children on the bridge at any time."

The officer's smile faded. "Yes, Admiral. They were so scared. Coming here really cheered them up…." His eyes widened at her rising fury. "Yes, Admiral." He lifted the boy over his head. "Right away, Admiral." He and some of the other Coalition officers herded the children off the bridge.

Outside, the misty planet of Goddess Reach filled the forward window. Brit stared at it, hands squeezed together behind her back, until she'd tamped down the urge to send the settlers back home *immediately*. "Warleader," she snarled. "Get headquarters on the comm. Have them forward a location where we can offload the settlers. This warship is no place for them."

"Aye, but this is a diplomatic vessel, too, is it not?" he quipped. "Prime-Admiral Zaafran thought so."

Brit shook her head and stormed toward her office.

Baffled, Finn watched her go.

"The white box," Lieutenant Keyren murmured.

He turned. "What white box?"

She kept her voice very low. "When you're next in her quarters, look around—about this high and wide—you'll see it. It has the answers you seek." Blushing, she added, "You didn't hear it from me."

As if the conversation had never happened, she departed the bridge, leaving him staring after her in curiosity.

CHAPTER NINETEEN

BRIT MET FINN at the door to her quarters. She'd bathed and covered herself in scented oils, which was all she wore when she ran into his arms and wrapped her legs around his hips. His laugh of surprise and delight ended when she sealed her ravenous mouth over his.

They fell to the bed. Four hands helped him out of his uniform. He rolled her on her stomach, flipping her hair out of the way to kiss his way up from her tailbone to the base of her neck. She couldn't wait any longer to have him. Coming up on her hands and knees, she showed him without words what she wanted. What she *needed*. One strong arm looped under her belly to hold her in place. In the next instant, he'd buried himself inside her.

Pleasure shot through her like a star-flare. Moaning, she rocked with him as his magic hands caressed her breasts and more. All day she'd waited for this, for him.

They started out easy and slow, savoring the sheer

feel of one another. It didn't stay slow for long. The more frenzied she became, the harder he drove into her. It didn't take long to climax, and when she did, the intensity was blinding.

Nobody made her feel as he did. Nobody.

Treasonous thoughts.

"Ah, sweetheart, my love..." Finn said. Fevered, he groaned as he lowered his head to the crook of her neck, his big body covering hers, his teeth scoring the rounded top of her shoulder. She felt the sting as he lost control. Finally, his heat pumped inside her, amplifying the small aftershocks she still felt.

They collapsed together onto the bed. "Gods be damned, woman," he gasped. "You sure have a way of welcoming a man home from work."

She smiled as she turned in his arms. Propped over her, he found her mouth for a long and lazy kiss. "Mmm," they both murmured against each other's lips.

Finn stroked her hair, gazing down at her, his eyes sweet with mischief and affection. It melted her. How did he *do that?* Instead of fleeing his tender, no-defenses gaze, she let herself drown in it. An ache swelled in her, something she had not felt in so very long. *Love.*

Mentally, she reeled backward from the realization. This wasn't love. It was sex, only!

Brit, you're a blind fool. Her gut had been telling her as much every time she lamented the loss of her once-infallible control. She never wanted to listen. She didn't want to acknowledge the truth: her feelings for Finnar Rorkken were the reason why the barriers between her emotions and the outside world had thinned dangerously. No matter what her reasons for not wanting it to happen, he'd invaded her heart and soul. He'd tiptoed in stealthily and steadily over the weeks, fortifying his position while her guard was down; that's what he'd done. Now he was part of her. Ripping him out would take a piece of her with him. She knew how much loss hurt. "I need some wine. Would you like a glass?"

As she climbed out of bed, he lifted himself into a semireclining position, propped on his elbows. "No, thanks. I'd like to know what that was all about, however."

"What was *what* all about?" She opened the bottle and poured a glass full of wine before turning back to him.

"You opened up to me, there in bed, when we were looking at each other. I saw *you,* Brit. Then you shut down faster than a Borderlands money-changer stand in the middle of a crack-down raid."

"I don't know what you mean. I was thirsty."

He got out of bed. The determined look in his face worried her. He crossed the room with purpose, seeming to search for something on the tables and shelves. Naked, magnificently so, and covered in the scars and tattoos she'd learned to overlook, he picked up a holo-cube to view. "Where was this taken?"

"A resort world in the Arrabaranna Archipelago."

"Ah. You enjoy the tropics?"

"Very much so."

"There are many holos here. Where did you find the time to vacation?"

"Shore leave is mandatory for commanders— once a year, barring any major offensive."

"Enforced fun. So you'd pack your bags and head off to the sea and sun. Alone?"

"Yes, alone." Worried, she sipped more wine. He was veering dangerously close to asking personal questions. *Did you think you could avoid it forever?* "Why do you ask?"

He shook his head at her. "I want to know you, sweetheart. I want to know why a woman as wonderful as you tells me she isn't good."

She focused on her glass of wine. "I'm difficult to get along with."

"Yes, sometimes you are." His eyes sparkled. "And so am I."

"I am a very private person…"

"Aye, I see that."

"…completely dedicated to my career."

"Which is something else I admire about you." He continued to stroll around her suite, picking up items from her travels, looking at and replacing each one. Then his gaze tracked to her desk…and higher. "Why, that's an interesting box." He reached for it.

Her heart lurched. "Finn, no."

She'd allow him anything—*anything*—but not a peek inside that box! "Those are my things." She set her wineglass down, spilling some, and pulled the keepsake box out of his hands, bumping into the smart chair as she backed up. Thinking she was ready to sit at her desk, the damn thing did as it was programmed to do: it glided into position and stopped— in the precise spot to trip her. She lost her balance and fell backward to the floor, landing, legs sprawled, on her butt. Not a very graceful position for a nude woman. She'd managed to hold on to the box, but the lid came loose and fell.

Her sharp muttered curse tore through the sudden silence. *No!* She threw a hand over the box. Exposed was everything she'd never wanted anyone else to see. Secrets she intended to take to the grave. Horrified, she fumbled with the lid, trying to get it closed.

Oblivious, Finn was laughing. "Here, I'll help you up." He hoisted her to her feet, allowing him an unimpeded glimpse inside the box.

The fluffy pink, gaily decorated blanket.

The pair of tiny shoes.

"What's all this?" he asked.

Shame heated her face even as indignation choked her. She grabbed for the lid; he grabbed her wrist. "These are my private things." *My private hell.*

"A baby blanket?" His eyes bored into her, demanding more—demanding the truth, answers she didn't know how to give, having avoided them for so long. "Baby shoes?" The note of disbelief in his tone crashed through the wall she was so desperately trying to hold up around her. What wall? He saw everything. With him she felt utterly exposed, and not because she was naked; it was because of that damn box.

"Brit." His grip on her wrist tightened. "There's no need for secrets between us."

Wasn't there? If she were to tell him of the methods she'd chosen to assuage her grief, the killing she'd ordered in the name of vengeance and masked as military necessity, what would he think of her then? She shouldn't care, but her feelings for the man made that impossible.

And yet, she wanted the demons out. Out! No one really knew her. She walked alone. *So damn lonely.*

"You're hiding something."

Like her entire blasted life! "I told you—I'm a very private individual."

"Cut the freepin' crap, Brit. The next thing you're going to tell me is that you're not a good person."

She wanted to throw her hands over her ears but he had too firm a grip on her wrists. "Damn you."

"Why? Why damn me?"

"You're opening me up, and I don't want to be opened up!" The first tears rolled down her cheeks. Damn it, but she hadn't wanted to cry in front of him.

"Brit," he coaxed, unrelenting. "Tell me about that box."

"These were my babies' things," she blurted out almost accusingly—and to his open astonishment. "I had two children—and a husband. They're gone. Dead. This…this is all I have left of them."

His hold on her tightened—not to keep her in place this time, she knew, but with the shock of her confession. "I'm sorry. Gods, I am so damned sorry."

"Gods? Bah." Her laugh reeked with so much bitterness that even she recoiled from the sound of it. "There are no gods."

Finally yanking free of his hold, she slid the box onto the desk and went in search of her wine, finishing the glass in two deep swallows. Let the numbing begin. Sex used to do that. Sex before Finn. Being with him made her *feel* rather than deadening her.

More wine, then.

His large hand closed over her wrist, stopping the sloppy pour. "Use me for the pain, Brit—not the drink." She jerked away but he curved his other hand around the back of her skull and crushed her against him. His heart thundered under her cheek. "Use *me*."

"I did use you, Finn! At first, that's all it was. And then…" *You fell for him.*

"It changed," he supplied.

"Yes!" She tried to fight him off, to push him away, even as she hungered for his strength. Her struggles got her nowhere; he gripped her too firmly.

"I won't let you go, woman. Best you give up trying."

His quiet confidence and the underlying tenderness in his warrior's body broke through her resistance and she crumpled against him. "I don't want you to let me go," she whispered. There it was. That particular secret was no more, at least. What about the rest?

His hand stroking her hair was like a drug, stripping away her defenses, making it oh, so tempting to release what she'd kept bottled up inside her. To end the reign of secrets. "Open up, Brit. Tell me. I want to know—I want to know *you.*"

And learn just how personal she'd made the war? That revenge had driven her entire career? Would he still whisper "sweetheart" and other fluffy endearments once he'd learned the truth?

Tell him. Get it over and done with. She was many things. Coward wasn't one of them.

"We lived on Arrayar Outpost." In the hopes of remaining detached, she tried to distance herself from the reciting of what she'd never told another soul. "It was a religious settlement. We maintained the old ways of the goddess. I was raised in that life, a simple life. All I wanted was to be happy, and I was. We were."

Finn glanced away as if he were loath to imagine her content with another man, even a husband.

"We had a son. Dellan was two standard-years old. I was pregnant again, nearly midterm. That day, the day I lost them, I left Dellan with Seff so I could travel to another outpost with a friend. It was so rare for me to do something that adventurous."

Despite her wanting to remain aloof, she went soft with an image of how she used to be. "I was a quiet, pious girl who preferred to stay close to home. But a seamstress in another settlement was known far and wide for her work. I asked her to make a blanket and some shoes for the coming baby. I needed to fetch them before I became too pregnant to travel. My friend and I returned home, and no one was about. The cottages were empty. The market, too. It was so strange. We wandered through the village, calling their names. Then we found them."

As dark and bitter as bile, the old memories clamored for release. She fought for control, fought to continue. "They were in the temple…everyone, dead. Broken crystal everywhere. It pierced my sandals. I didn't feel it. Later, my feet required reconstructive surgery. I didn't care! I only wanted to find Seff and Dellan. There were so many bodies, Finn…." Her stomach rolled with the memory of the smells: the peculiar stink of Drakken—from their sleeping skins she now knew—and the odor the release of bodily fluids made when someone died. The smells would live inside her until her last breath.

"I found Seff with the men," she whispered. "But Dellan…Dellan…" It was the part she'd never wanted to think about. She'd spent a lifetime avoiding the images that represented every mother's nightmare. She pressed her fist to her stomach to be able to finish. Finn waited as if expecting the worst. It was the worst. "My son had been herded away with the other children. There he was, lined up with the rest of them, little bodies all in a row like dolls. He died alone, Finn. No one to hold him, no one to comfort him. No mommy to hold his hand. To them, to the monsters, my son was just another settler to skull."

Finn's entire body jerked. His once-smiling eyes were dark with anguish and shock. "Freepin' hells, Brit. You lost your family in a skulling raid? Why didn't you say anything?"

The tattoo inside his bicep was in her view: the black bird of prey stamped on the side of every Drakken vessel. She averted her eyes. He noticed and swore, jamming a hand through his hair in appalled disbelief. "That's why you ran into the bathroom after we made love the first time. Because my kind massacred your family. You realized what you'd done with me, a Drakken, and you couldn't bear it. You couldn't bear me."

What could she say? It was true.

He strode away to grab his fallen uniform. He shook it out, as if to get dressed and leave.

"Stop there, Rorkken!" she cried. "You wanted to hear this then you're damn well staying until the end. Then you can make your decision whether you want to leave or not." She stopped to catch her breath. "Not before," she whispered. Not before she told him everything.

He stopped but kept his back to her as she began again. "Then the contractions started. The baby was coming. My friend tried to help but it was too early. There was nothing to be done. I got to hold my daughter, you know. Just that once. My little girl. She was so tiny, so perfect. I kept her shoes. I'll always have her shoes…."

The muscles in his back bunched and he turned around. "How can you stand to look at me, Brit?" He held his arms out to the sides, showing her his scarred and tattooed warrior's body. Then his arms dropped until they hung at his sides. *"How?"*

Naked, he was utterly open, vulnerable, his good and kind soul bared. It touched her—*he* touched her—deep inside, in an inexplicable way that no one else had been able to do. Maybe because he'd risen above difficult beginnings…or that he'd somehow held on to his honor while surrounded by monsters issuing monstrous orders. Or maybe it was how easily his deceptively sweet, smiling gaze seemed to cut through the layers covering who she really was. And how he always seemed to know what pleased her in bed, enthusiastically amplifying that pleasure without skimping on his own.

She murmured, "When you look at me that way,

Finnar, it reminds me of all the reasons I fell in love with you."

He found the nearest chair and sat down, hard. For once the smart chair obeyed him but he didn't stop to notice. "When we first met in Zaafran's office, I thought you recognized me." His voice sounded flat. He spoke to the wall, not her. "I saw your shock. Now it makes sense. I resemble one of the Drakken who attacked your village."

"No. At first sight you resembled my dead husband."

He jerked around in surprise.

"It was your eyes. One look and you ripped me wide-open. All of a sudden, I could feel again. It was horrible, and wonderful, and I didn't know what to do about it. I didn't know what to do about you. No one's ever fought so hard to reach my heart, a heart I thought was dead. I didn't know I could ever feel this way again. I hated you for it." She swallowed, whispering, "I love you for it."

He groaned and strode back to her, taking her upturned face in his hands. His love for her was as clear as an Arrayan sunrise. "Finn, what are we going to do? I don't know how this can work."

"You've got the same damn problem I do, sweetheart. Our hearts and our heads are tellin' us two different things." He drew her tight against him. They clung to each other, swaying. "What happened after Arrayar, sweetheart? Where did you go? Who took care of you? Tell me how the girl who thought going to another settlement was an adventure became the greatest admiral the Coalition has ever known. And the most feared, I'll add. There were more Drakken soldiers than I could count who wanted a piece of you. I'd hear them talking in the bars. I'd hear the comm chatter. All of them wanted to catch ol' Stone-Heart. They wanted to be the ones to break you. It would not have gone well for you if you were ever captured."

She knew it, as well. If the disintegration of the Drakken Empire had done anything at all in her favor, it had taken away the threat of being taken prisoner by a vengeance-lusting battle-lord. "I don't know why I survived Arrayar. I was the only one out of two hundred and seventy-seven people."

"Your friend?"

Brit shook her head. "I lost a lot of blood. I passed out. Allas must have thought me dead. There was no other reason she'd take her own life. When I next opened my eyes, I was in a hospital. I woke a different person, Finn. A different girl."

As if he sensed the gravity of what she was about to tell him, he slid his hands to her shoulders, easing her back to search her face as she told him, "I thought, if the gods wouldn't stop the raids, if they refused to defend the innocent, I would. After that, I hardly shed a tear. I had purpose. When my wounds were healed, I pursued an appointment to the Royal Galactic Military Academy. I never looked back. I never formed any lasting, personal attachments. If I wanted sex, I bought it on shore leave. The love of my life was vengeance, Finn. *Vengeance.* It consumed me. Every Drakken I killed took me one step closer to avenging my family's deaths. Some have called me a master strategist, a genius tactician. It was never that complicated. I had but one goal— killing the most Drakken that I could. I've never told anyone this, not a soul, but I used to feel nothing, nothing at all when they died. You made that damned difficult, Finnar Rorkken. No, you made it impossible. You should hate me for not seeing your people as human, just as I hated your kind for the same crime. Tell me you hate me. Blast it all, tell me and I'll understand."

His hand was splayed on the back of her head to hold her close. She drank in his scent, everything about him, as his heart thudded under her ear. "Sorry, sweetheart, no can do. I've respected and admired you since our days back in the Borderlands, but never more than now. I know what you've struggled with. I've seen it in others who've suffered terrible personal loss. I've seen them seek answers in drink or drugs or sex, sometimes all three. Revenge is just as much of an addiction. You need more and more to reach the same high. The problem is that the satisfaction is fleeting. It's never enough, and it doesn't change the past. If you accept that, you'll break free."

His words made sense. For the first time, she held out hope that a day might come where she might feel normal again. Human. "It doesn't mean I'll let the skullers we're tracking get away."

"By the gods, we'll find them and keep them from doing it again. Aye, by the very gods you so despise who have been shoving us together since the beginning—first to chase each other in space, then on the decks of this ship. One way or the other, they were determined to get us together, and they did."

She nodded as his thumb wiped away a stray tear. "Yes, they did."

His brilliant eyes glistened with emotion. "Blast it all, I love you, Brit. Aye, I've fallen, hard, and I don't know what we're going to do about it."

That made two of them.

SHE WAS SO LATE! The debriefing had taken forever. Poor Tango. Hadley showered and changed into a simple dress of pale sky-blue. It was one of the only pieces of civilian clothing she had on board. The rest were home, hanging in the closet in her girlhood room.

Leaving her hair brushed loose, she took a small box of sweets she'd saved from her last shore leave and hurried up to Tango's room. She knocked, waited. No answer. Then she rang. Still no answer. It made her heart twist to think of him disabling the door-bot chime to go to sleep, uninterrupted and all alone. He'd been so upset.

Her position as Admiral Bandar's executive officer gave her some perks and allowed her some secrets. One of them was the command code for all doors to personal quarters on the ship, a way inside in case she had to reach someone in trouble quickly. Tango fell into that category in her opinion. His best friend was badly hurt, and the girl he liked would have appeared to have stood him up.

She input the master code and pushed the door open. "Tango?" she whispered. It took a second for her eyes to adjust to the darkness. Then she realized it wasn't quite dark. A single candle burned, illuminating the beanbag chairs and a bare butt…a pumping bare butt gripped by pale, slender legs. The sound of panting and grunts sank in next.

She gasped, realizing what she'd interrupted, and with whom. Rakkelle's cadet uniform was flung over a chair along with Tango's socks.

Hadley stumbled backward, hitting a chair. Suddenly, the butt stopped pumping. Tango glanced over his shoulder and swore.

Hadley ran.

FINN FOUND Dr. Kell in the infirmary. "How is he doing?"

"Commander Rothberg's condition remains unchanged, I'm afraid."

His arms folded over his chest, Finn observed the unconscious officer through the glass separating him from the rest of the med ward. "We're all pulling for the man. And praying."

"That will be what gets him through, Warleader, if anything does. That, and his will to live."

"Aye…" He turned back to the physician. "If you have the time, I would ask a favor. A personal medical favor."

"What's that, Warleader?"

"There's a tattoo…" Finn pulled up his sleeve, exposing his left bicep and the Drakken eagle imprinted on his flesh. "I was wonderin' if you would take it off."

As was her habit for years, Brit walked the corridors in between shifts. Finn's words replayed over and over in her mind: *Revenge is an addiction…. You need more and more to reach the same high…. Satisfaction is fleeting.* His hypothesis demanded consideration that she couldn't afford right now. Hunting the skullers required too much of her focus.

For now, however, she was off duty and could let down her guard and indulge in a bit of silliness, including a daydream or two about her lover. The shuttle docking area of the ship was peaceful now that all the settlers and their cargo were aboard. Finn had organized a practice drill earlier but it, too, was over and the docks and nearby corridors were silent. The hum of a well-run ship soothed her. More than that, a deep contentment had overtaken her, even in the midst of the ongoing hunt for the skullers and the turmoil it had caused in the Triad.

She was in love, and someone loved her back. It had been so long since anyone had loved her that she hadn't realized what she'd missed. In closing herself off to the possibility of love, of connecting with another human being, she'd suffered more than she'd had to after Arrayar. Was that what dear Seff would have wanted for her? No. He would have wanted her to be with a man like him, one deserving of her love in return.

A man like Finn.

A flush of happiness overtook her. All alone, only her boots echoing in the empty corridor, she smiled.

The back of her neck prickled suddenly. She slowed her pace, taking in her surroundings with all five senses.

Someone else is here.

She was halfway turned around when something *whoomphed* over her head, enclosing her in suffocating darkness. The stinging rush of meds entering her bloodstream dropped her to her knees and then to the floor. She never had the chance to scream.

CHAPTER TWENTY

YOU'RE A LIGHTWEIGHT, Hadley told herself and finished her second cocktail anyway. The bartender had made it for her, special. She wasn't sure what was in the tall glass this time, but it was such a pretty color. And strong. Yes, strong. She wanted strong.

Dizzy, she took another swallow and searched the bar for likely targets for her night's plans. She was going to get laid. If Tango could screw without a care then so could she. Yet the image of Tango thrusting between Rakkelle's thighs made her sick to her stomach.

She gulped down more of the drink.

A tall, lean form slid gracefully into the chair next to her. She squinted at Bolivarr and smiled. "Cloud shadow," she said.

"You're drunk."

"So I am."

He leaned forward, folding his arms on the table, his voice dropping lower. "I thought you'd be with Tango."

"He's an asshole," she blurted out. "He's a man-whore." People nearby stared at her. She turned even redder, if that were possible.

"Rakkelle," he guessed.

"Slut!"

"The Drakken nonofficer personnel are confined to quarters—Warleader Rorkken's orders. Rakkelle's risking her hide by being out of bed."

"Oh, she was in bed—just not hers." More accurately, it was the beanbag chair. Probably where Tango planned on doing her, too, and nearly did.

"I went to his quarters and she… And he…" Hadley grabbed for her drink. Bolivarr took it away. "Hey!"

"It means nothing to her," he said.

"It meant something to me. Didn't she know I was interested in Tango?"

"You told anyone who asked that you weren't." He paused. "Were you?"

"No. Yes." She pouted at her fisted hands, and the mood ring that had turned from gray to deep purple in the minute since Bolivarr had joined her.

"I named our grandchildren," she murmured.

"You don't even have children yet."

"That's the thing. I got too far ahead of myself. It's a Taloan trait. Talo, that's my homeworld." She squinted at his bemused expression then at the bartender, snapping her fingers, trying twice before she managed a decent snap. Her fingers didn't seem to be working right. "Another…whatever it was you mixed last time."

"Hadley. You don't need more to drink."

"Why? Because I'm drunk? I like being drunk." Her giggle attracted the attention of a few Earthling officers at the next table. Earthlings. She scowled at them and they turned away quickly.

"Yes, because you're drunk." He leaned closer. "Very drunk." He smelled good. Not of cologne but of his own unique scent. She liked his scent. A lot. Why hadn't she ever noticed how good he smelled? She bent forward and sniffed deeply, sighing, then caught herself before she tipped out of the chair.

Bolivarr sighed, too, but for a different reason, she suspected. "You need to go to bed."

"Since when do you tell me what to do?"

"Since I have become your friend."

"Friends with an Imperial Wraith. What would my mother say?"

"She'd say she was glad he thought to get you out of the bar before someone else took you home." He snatched her hand and pulled her up, despite her protests, hauling her against his hard, lean frame as he led her from the bar.

A few people whistled and clapped. "What are they so happy about?"

"They think I'm getting lucky."

"Lucky?" He steered her deftly through the corridors, seeming to know exactly where her quarters were. "Oh…you mean *lucky*." She blushed all over again.

"Trust me, as much as I would like it, I won't be."

He lifted her hand to her door panel. She fumbled with the security code and let them in.

He took her by the hand and led her to the sink, opening her storage cabinet. "Where do you keep your metabolizers?"

"I don't have any." Metabolizers were for people who drank and needed to speed up getting sober, either to avoid a hangover or to not show up at work drunk. "I never drink."

"Thank the gods," she heard him mutter. "Water will have to do." He filled a glass at her sink. "Here, drink it down."

She wobbled on her feet. Bolivarr caught her. Her arms draped over his shoulders and her face landed on the side of his throat. She inhaled and smiled against his warm skin. "How come you smell so good?"

"Because you're drunk." He peeled her off and helped her to her bed, pulling down the quilt before laying her down.

"If it's because I'm drunk then how do you explain the ring?" She thrust her hand at him. "See? It's purple. It means romance. *Passion.*"

His mouth seemed to fight a smile as he wedged the tips of his fingers in his pockets. A lock of hair fell over his forehead, softening away the hard lines of his face. "I thought you said it was broken."

"I lied." She giggled. "Me and you—that's too crazy."

He glanced away. "Here's your water. Try to drink

some." He loomed over her, helping her to sit up. He held the glass to her lips, insisting she have a few sips before he set the glass by her bedside.

"You have nice hands. Nice hands and a nice smell." She giggled again. "You're just really nice."

She stretched, rolling to her side and bringing her knees higher. It seemed to make him uncomfortable. She remembered she was wearing a dress, giving him a view all the way up her bare thighs. "Oops." She tugged the skirt lower over her bottom.

His hands were wedged even deeper in his pockets now. "Are you going to be all right if I leave you here alone?"

"You're leaving?" She pouted.

"I have to, Hadley."

"Why?"

"It's not proper for me to be here."

"Why?"

He exhaled. "Man…woman…*bedroom*."

"Getting lucky…?"

It wasn't her imagination; he blushed. "Something like that," he said. He pulled off her shoes and lifted the quilt over her. Warmth swelled in her chest at his tender gestures. Warmth swelled in other places, too, places that hadn't reacted at all to Tango's kisses but should have. All Bolivarr had done was tuck her in bed.

Tango's flirting had been exciting. It was nothing compared to a guy being nice, making sure she was okay. She realized then she'd almost made a very big mistake. "Had I gotten out of the meeting a couple of hours earlier, it would have been me on my back under Tango on that beanbag chair."

"Ah." It was the oddest thing—it was as if her remark disappointed him, and she didn't want to do that.

"I've never done it with him," she quickly admitted. "I've never done it...with anyone." She clamped her teeth together. It was the liquor talking. She wanted to die of embarrassment.

Bolivarr pondered her with a shy yet masculine smile. "I hoped that was the case."

"Why?"

"Because a first time should be special. Because I thought— I..." He shrugged. "Not that I ever anticipated having a chance with you, but if I ever did, well, I wouldn't have wanted to be the only one of us without experience."

"You're a *virgin?*"

"Let me put it this way. I don't remember having sex, or not having it. If I'm not a physical virgin, I'm a mental one."

"You never slept with anyone on the warleader's ship?"

He shook his head.

"Not even with Rakkelle?"

He laughed. "No. She never tried, actually. I must not be appealing enough."

"She's crazy. Or blind." Blushing, she bit her lip. It was the liquor talking again.

His reaction made her shiver. "It wouldn't have made a difference," he said quietly. "Celibacy is a decision of my own choosing. If I did sleep with someone, I was afraid I'd bond. I don't want to bond until I know who I am. There is still a big gap in my memories."

"So, it's the truth then."

"Of course it is."

"Yarew thinks you're lying to cover up crimes you committed for the warlord."

Rare anger flashed in his eyes. "Yarew has his own crimes to worry about."

"What do you mean?"

"Watch him, Hadley. I don't trust him. That's all I'll say for now."

Awkwardly, they studied each other.

"Thanks for escorting me out of the bar," she whispered, squinting as the room rotated slowly. "It was very nice of you."

"It wasn't all altruism."

She swallowed. "Really?"

His voice was deeper now, and slightly hoarse. "I thought it might give me the chance to be with you, alone. I've wanted to do that for a while now." He let out a surprisingly raw, quick laugh. "I don't even know if I should be having this conversation. I could be married."

Her heart was beating faster. With each excited thump, she became more sober. "I hope you're not."

"I don't feel married," he admitted.

"Who says we have to rush into anything more than friendship?"

"Because other than the children we took aboard today, we're probably the only virgins on the ship?"

"I am," she corrected. "You're undetermined."

He didn't laugh exactly but his dark, enigmatic eyes glittered with amusement. Then their smiles faded in sudden awareness that was mutual and unmistakably sexual. He might not remember his sexual history, but he had a hot gaze that she felt to the core. It was the kind of look that made her want to strip off her clothing without second thoughts. She'd wondered how people could get naked and not be overcome by self-consciousness. Now she had a clue.

Bolivarr sat on the edge of the bed. "I need to leave."

"I know. Not yet."

He brushed his warm palm over her cheek. "You are beautiful, Hadley Keyren."

Dizziness swept through her, and not from the drinks. Impulsively, she surged forward, threw her arms over his shoulders. Closing her eyes, she lightly pressed her lips to his. It was the liquor kissing him, not her, she assured herself but suddenly she wasn't so sure. She expected the tingle of warm, sensitive skin touching warm skin but not the earthquake that went through her.

"Goddess," she whispered in surprise, tasting him again.

When she moved back, his greedy gaze lifted from her mouth to her wide-open eyes. It looked nothing like Tango's hunger. That had been predatory. Bolivarr's was desire mixed with hope and a good deal of doubt and shyness. He probably looked a whole lot like her.

"I might be married," he warned again, his hand sliding around to her back.

"You don't feel married." Their mouths were so close now that their breath mingled. "If you did, you wouldn't be doing this."

He kissed her. Fully. Hugging her close. He might claim he didn't remember being with a woman, but he sure seemed to know what to do. When her mouth opened under his, it was like putting oxygen to fire.

And nothing like kissing Tango. It wasn't that Bolivarr had more skill; it was her reaction to him that made all the difference, and the absence of fear that he'd try for more than she was comfortable with.

She took his hand and laid it upon her breast. "Touch me," she invited. "Everywhere."

"Hadley." His voice sounded strained. "You're drunk."

"Not that drunk."

"Drunk enough." He pulled his arm away and took her face in both hands, resting his forehead against hers. "There's no rush. You said it yourself."

"Not so drunk that I can't see my own stupidity. My stubbornness, actually. The mood ring was never broken. It told the truth from the beginning. I just refused to listen. It reflected what my gut was telling me. I kept ignoring my instincts with Tango." *And with you, Bolivarr.* "I won't let that happen again. From now on, I will trust my instincts." She took the liberty of kissing his ear. "You're beautiful, too, Battle-Lieutenant Bolivarr."

His breath shuddered out. Then his body went rigid.

He sat up abruptly, his fists clenched. Shock widened his eyes. "N-no…"

"Bolivarr. What's wrong?"

"No!" He squeezed his eyes shut, his facial muscles constricting. Shaking, he brought his hands up to cover his face. "Stay a-away, Hadley. Don't touch. P-please." He tried to stand but fell.

"Bolivarr!" She recognized the signs now. The poison that took down Rothberg must be reacting now inside him, too. Bonding to his cells, multiplying, replicating. *Killing.* "Medical!" she shouted in her PCD. "Emergency—Lieutenant Keyren's quarters. *Come now.*"

BRIT WOKE to the agony of someone backhanding her across the face. She jerked with the shock of the hit, refusing to cry out. Admiral Brit Bandar did not yelp in pain. She tasted blood, felt it running from her nose to her mouth. It sprayed as she sucked breaths in and out. Screaming she could control. Her respiration she could not.

"Careful," someone cautioned. "We're not supposed to make her ugly."

Brit went still. He had an accent, a Hordish accent. A deathly chill spiraled through her. She'd been captured by the Drakken.

But how? How had they gotten her off the *Unity*? She had a vague memory of a bag being thrown over her head and that was all. Was she still on her ship? No…it felt different. She'd spent half her life in space. She knew a vessel by its feel. Less air pressure meant a smaller ship.

Her vision cleared some. She was sitting tied to a chair in what looked to be a prison cell. Several men dressed in Imperial Navy uniforms milled around, a startling, unexpected sight, and one she'd thought she'd never see…like this.

As their captive.

It took a moment to gather her wits and for her attention to swing around to the Hordish officer crouched in front of her.

His eyes were vivid green. His cheek was scarred. It looked like a fresh wound. Few Drakken had access to the healing technology of nanomeds. Yet, this man wore battle-lord rank. A battle-lord would have the wealth and means to smooth away scars. Unless…he got his promotion by default. Hatred choked her. He was a coward *and* a liar.

"Congratulations on your promotion," she said smoothly. "It's easy to jump ahead in rank when everyone in front of you dies or is captured."

He lifted his hand to slap her again. She almost flinched. He noted it and smiled. "You won't be so hard to break, Stone-Heart."

There were more Drakken soldiers than I could count who wanted a piece of you. I'd hear them talking in the bars. I'd hear the comm chatter. All of them wanted to catch ol' Stone-Heart. They wanted to be the ones to break you. It would not have gone well for you if you were ever captured.

Thinking of Finn's words would serve only to psych her out. She needed to stay clearheaded; she needed to keep fear at bay. "This won't help the Drakken assimilate into the Triad. My kidnapping is going to cause a backlash. Is that wise at this stage in the peace process?"

"Assimilate?" He hissed the word. "The Drakken and the Coalition will never be at peace. They will never be as one. Ignorant bureaucrats, thinking unification is the answer to war. Power is the answer. Absolute power."

"Drakken power?"

He wrapped her hair around his fist and pulled her half off the chair.

"Thought so," she muttered.

"Starting with you—in our control."

"Having a fleet admiral in custody gives you no edge. Ransom is never paid. Deals aren't made. Not even for me."

"We shall see. In the meantime, you'll serve as a little entertainment between the skullings."

Her stomach rolled. But there was something off here, aside from the obvious. She just needed a minute to wrap her mind around what was happening....

He jerked her forward. The bones in her neck made muffled pops. She tried not to wince at the flare of pain. "You'll amuse me for a bit, then I'll send you back home. Your broken body will inspire fear and awe. A Drakken specialty, yes? It will go a long way to resurrecting our former glory." His smile widened. "Meanwhile, let's play until you begin to bore me. You're not boring, are you?"

He forced her face close to his. His kiss was hard, merciless, the pain it caused her fresh wounds sharp. Stupid Drakken. She sucked his lower lip between her teeth and bit down hard.

He roared, shoving her away. The chair slammed into the wall. Pain exploded in her head and everything went blank.

"ADMIRAL," Finn paged, trying to reach Brit. She didn't answer her PCD. He caught up to Lieutenant Keyren as she ran alongside Bolivarr's smart-stretcher. The sight made him queasy. Young officers taken down in the prime of life was unfortunately getting to be a common sight on this ship. "Where is Admiral Bandar?"

"I thought she was on the bridge."

"No. She's late for her shift. Changeover came and went—she never showed. She never called in. I left Yarew in charge, thinking she was here with you and Bolivarr."

"I haven't seen her since the debriefing, Warleader. Have you?"

"Aye." He gave her a sharper look. "I saw her and the white box."

The girl paled. "Goddess. Do you think—"

"No. The end result was good, very good." He touched her arm. "Thank you," he said with gratitude.

The stretcher veered into the triage room, where Dr. Kell immediately set to work on Bolivarr.

"I think it's the poison," Keyren cried.

Kell had Bolivarr's vitals on-screen within seconds. An analysis of his blood scrolled across a datavis. "It's not the poison."

"What is it, then?" the lieutenant asked.

"To put it in a nontechnical way, something strange is going on in his brain."

Finn jerked his focus to the scanner the doctor moved over the unconscious wraith's head.

"There were signs of abnormal brain waves in his initial examination," the man said. "They're gone."

"Is it bad?"

"Quite the opposite, I think. My feeling only.

It may have been due to some sort of thought-suppression technology. I've heard of such techniques employed by the Drakken." An awkward glance in Finn's direction told him the doctor had only belatedly remembered Finn was, in fact, Drakken. It was a good thing; the doctor thought of him as crew first. It was more than he could say about some of the other Coalition officers, namely Yarew. "It's not unlike what was done to our REEF assassins before the procedure was banned. If the suppression has malfunctioned, Bolivarr could very well recover his memories after this."

Lieutenant Keyren made a sound of pleasure, grasping Bolivarr's hand. She murmured under her breath, "He didn't feel married."

"I'll have none of that," Dr. Kell said, shooing the young officer away. "Go, go, both of you. Out of my exam room. I'll comm you as soon as I hear more."

They obeyed, leaving the physician to his work. "Call the admiral," Finn directed Keyren.

"Admiral Bandar, Lieutenant Keyren." She repeated the call to no avail. "She's probably on the lightball court. She always takes her PCD off when she plays."

"When she's supposed to be on duty? That would be unusual." Then again he'd upset her with the contents of the box, and the memories that accompanied it. Could she have had a delayed reaction? "Find your uniform and get dressed."

"Yes, sir." The girl bobbled a bit on her feet.

"Have you been drinking, Lieutenant?"

Her blush gave him his answer. Probably drinking and carousing. But with Bolivarr? The night was getting stranger and stranger. "Get yourself a metabolizer from the infirmary and help me search for your commander."

A SWEEP OF THE SHIP, and two visits to Brit's quarters had Finn gripped with worry. She was nowhere on the ship, it seemed.

"Admiral Bandar, report to the bridge," the commbot intoned up and down the corridors. Finn had set the ship-wide call on automatic. It had been paging for half a standard hour now. There was no freepin' way Brit could miss hearing it. She was either ignoring the calls, or she'd disappeared. The former was doubtful. The latter was insanity.

"How can the commander of this ship simply vanish?" Finn demanded, storming onto the bridge. Leaning his weight on his hands, he hunkered down over a data-vis, scanning the comings and goings of the evening. "I show a shuttle launch at twenty past the last hour. Who was it?"

Yarew joined him at the data-vis. "That wasn't part of your exercise?"

"No." A chill ran down Finn's spine. "The exercise ended the hour before. You knew that."

"I actually did not." The intelligence officer's eyes

were cold. *Drakken,* they sneered. *Horde.* "I was off duty and sleeping—as I should be now, if not for you and our admiral traipsing about the ship, and you being where you have no right being."

Finn grabbed his uniform shirt in his fists, about to throw him backward when good sense came back. He opened his hands, releasing the officer. The entire bridge crew stared at him. *Drakken! Horde!* He knew what they were thinking, and he couldn't blame them, after witnessing his aggression. Then there were the Drakken staring, too. He'd punished them for acting Drakken and what had he gone and done? Acted like a barbarian himself!

He maintained a steady tone, if anything for his own people, his teeth gritted. "The fact is, Star-Major, Admiral Bandar is missing. I would like to see you with some sense of urgency about locating her."

"I am feeling urgency. The difference is that I'm professional about showing it."

Finn's fists clenched. With effort, he kept them at his sides, despite Yarew's deliberate provocation. This wasn't the deck of a Drakken warbird, or a pirate ship. This was the TAS *Unity,* and he was damned well going to act as if he belonged here. And there were more important issues at hand than a troublesome intel officer. The focus must remain on locating Brit.

"Run a check on every crew member," Yarew directed the watch officer. "I want to know who was where at the time we estimate contact was lost with the admiral. Report all abnormalities to me."

Better, Finn thought.

"Get me an ion wake trace on that shuttle," Yarew continued, putting Finn's mind further at ease.

Rothberg and Bolivarr were the two crew members he'd have chosen to send around the ship hunting for answers. Both men were in comas. Who could be used instead? He didn't trust Yarew, and many of the other crew members didn't trust him.

Zurykk. Finn had scarcely utilized his former second-in-command since coming to work on the ship. Brit's disappearance changed all that. He lifted his hand to his PCD. In light of the feeling of dread in his gut, it was time to call on his oldest friends if he stood half a chance of seeing Brit again.

CHAPTER TWENTY-ONE

"THE ADMIRAL ISN'T the only one missing," Yarew said, shoving a data-vis in front of Finn's eyes. "Seven settlers are gone."

The seven latecomers to Goddess Reach. Freepin' hells.

"They didn't outrun a Drakken ship. They *were* Drakken. They connived their way aboard in order to kidnap Admiral Bandar."

"Drakken… How could I have missed it?" He should have been able to spot a Drakken, with or without tattoos and pierced ears. Had he distanced himself so much from his past that he could no longer recognize his own kind?

The thought was disturbing as all hells.

Yet… "Maybe, Star-Major, a better question is how you missed they were Drakken. Maybe they weren't."

The intel officer snorted. "And you accuse *me* of bias?"

Finn rubbed his face with an unsteady hand. Wishful thinking wouldn't return Brit to him. He couldn't wrap his mind around the idea of her being held prisoner by the Horde, not after learning what he had about her past. Not after hearing how many Drakken wanted to punish her for years of military successes against them. "How did they manage to board one of our shuttles and fly it away, not knowing the departure codes?"

"They had inside help from your people."

Finn narrowed his eyes at Yarew's accusation. "Not my people. Not mine."

"Are you sure, Warleader?"

"Aye, I'm damned sure."

"Perhaps you'll reconsider once I show you the results of the crew bed check. Cadet Pehzwan shows out of her quarters at a quarter past. She never returned. She is the only crew member not accounted for. I'm putting in an order for her arrest."

"Zurykk," Finn said. "Find Rakkelle."

"Security," Yarew said. "Locate Cadet Rakkelle Pehzwan and take her into custody. Charges— treason."

"Disregard that order," Finn told security.

Yarew's gaze smoked with outrage. "I outrank you," Finn informed him briskly and in a tone that invited no argument. "Zurykk, find Rakkelle."

"Follow that order, and I'll have you arrested, too, Zurykk," Yarew snapped.

Zurykk paused, caught in a tug-of-war between the *Unity*'s two senior officers.

"Star-Major." The threatening note of warning in Finn's voice grabbed everyone's attention, and most notably Yarew's. "If there are arrests to be made, I make the call."

"I have evidence enough to arrest all of you Drakken."

"Don't go there, Star-Major," Finn warned. It wasn't so much that Yarew accused him of treason as it was he'd lose the ability to help find Brit if he was sitting helpless in the brig.

"Cadet Pehzwan is missing under suspicious circumstances, Warleader. Will you keep me from finding her and questioning her, or will this be mutiny?"

"She was with me," a voice called out in an Earthling accent.

Major Barrientes strode onto the bridge, his uniform wrinkled, and looking as if he'd dressed hastily. "I can vouch for Rakkelle. She was in my quarters. All night."

Next to Finn, Lieutenant Keyren cleared her throat softly. A sideways glance showed her to be blushing furiously, her eyes downcast.

"And we're to believe the word of one Earthling who can't hold his alcohol?" Yarew demanded. "I override your order, Warleader, based on threats to galactic security. The arrest will be made."

On the holo-monitor, two guards left their station, headed in the direction of Rakkelle's quarters.

"She was with me." Tango turned pleading eyes to Hadley.

"He's telling the truth," the lieutenant said after a moment's hesitation and with some reluctance as her gaze locked with Tango's. "She was with him during the time in question. I saw them together."

"Pehzwan drops in for a screw in order to have an alibi," Yarew said, dismissing Tango's claim. "So what? Everything else lines up. Note, Warleader, I have made a career of putting together facts and drawing accurate conclusions. A highly successful career. I have every reason to suspect Pehzwan assisted the seven settlers in abducting Admiral Bandar. The cadet is a shuttle pilot, a former civilian trusted with a level of security she probably shouldn't have been given."

"You question the admiral's judgment in doing so?" Finn glared.

"Yes," he said. "Yes, I do. I question her judgment in other things, too."

Yarew knew what was going on between him and Brit, Finn realized. Lieutenant Keyren had suspected it, as well. Was there anyone on the ship who hadn't figured it out?

"Our admiral has somehow been taken off a ship in a shuttle that requires proprietary codes to leave the docking bay, Warleader. How else do you propose that this happened?"

"I don't know." Finn scrubbed his bristly jaw. Nothing was clear anymore. Brit was missing and he could do nothing to help her but chase after ions and play a guessing game as to who took her and why. Every moment he wallowed in confusion, she remained in danger, mortal danger. He'd die if anything happened to her. *Think,* he urged himself. *Think hard.*

"Hey! Get your freepin' paws off me, you goons." On the holo-vis, the guards were pulling Rakkelle out of her quarters. Dressed in a flimsy long tank over bare legs, she looked thin and helpless against the much-larger men. Aye, but she fought back with her whole heart, nearly unbalancing one of the guards.

Lieutenant Keyren ran off the bridge. She'd liked Tango. Had the knowledge of his tryst with Rakkelle proved too much for her? If so, he was disappointed in the officer. He'd thought her more professional that that. Stronger.

Finn stalked across the bridge to the navigator's panel. "Any signs of the shuttle?"

"Looking, sir."

"Look harder."

Zurykk was right behind him. "Are ya going to let them arrest her, Captain?"

"For gods' sake, I'm not your captain!"

"No, you sure ain't. Not anymore. Abandoning yer own people. Maybe it's them who got to her? The Coalition. Did ya ever think of that? They've more to gain in war than in peace. They always have."

They've more to gain in war than in peace. Finn had been telling Brit no different for weeks now.

The Drakken people benefited from a cessation of hostilities. Some Coalition die-hards couldn't abide by that. Too many years of assuming a victory would be replete with a final drive to the Empire's center, leaving billions dead, a civilization broken. The way it had happened instead was a toppling of the warlord from within, a people's victory—done for the Drakken by the Drakken. Not so satisfying if you were on the conquering side.

He thought of how he'd taken the skins away from his crew, how he'd banned grabble and then the sweef, too. He thought of how hard he'd come down on them, and for what? For being what they were supposed to be? They weren't monsters. They were Horde. The terms weren't mutually exclusive, no, but neither were *Coalition* and *monster.* Cruelty existed on both sides. Wherever fanaticism existed, so did hate. What had happened to him? What had he done?

"Aye," he admitted under his breath. Zurykk's eyes grew wide. "Harboring prejudice against my own people makes me the same as that bastard," he whispered. Blind bigotry that may have cost Brit her life.

Finn turned away from a relieved Zurykk to face Yarew. His epiphany filled him with calm and purpose, helping him to see more clearly what had transpired since he'd come aboard the *Unity.* Yarew had been working at cross-purposes with him since the moment he'd set foot on this ship. "I gave you a piece of metal I found on the sand on Cupezikan. I asked that you investigate. What came of it?"

The question appeared to shock the man. He'd taken the piece and hoped Finn had forgotten it; that fact was painfully clear. "It belonged to a Coalition weapon, didn't it, Star-Major?"

Yarew's face darkened. With fear or with fury, Finn didn't know.

"Well, Vinn?"

The entire bridge was silent, listening in on the conversation. "We will continue this discussion in the office, Warleader." Yarew sneered.

"No. We will continue it here in front of our crew. Our unified crew. Where is that item?"

"I discarded it. It was nothing."

"You threw away evidence?" With Brit now likely being tortured and possibly killed because of it? Finn girded himself against the acute pain filling him with images of the love of his life hurt and bleeding. She wouldn't give in to her captors and it would cost her. "You didn't want that piece to be found because it proved rogues were behind the attacks. Rogue Coalition, not Drakken!"

Gasps went around the bridge.

"They took her and handed her over to Drakken raiders, Yarew. You allowed it to happen. You want the unrest it will cause."

"This is unacceptable, Warleader! This is mutiny. Security—take Warleader Rorkken to the brig."

No one moved. They didn't know who to follow. A telling sign, that.

"You debriefed those seven settlers privately before we did. You logged your findings in a report. What did you leave out?" Finn slammed a hand on the holo-vis table. "What did you leave out?"

"WATCH HIM, HADLEY," Bolivarr had warned her about Yarew. *"I don't trust him. That's all I'll say for now."*

He'd been right, Hadley thought. Yarew was hiding something. He knew what happened to Admiral Bandar and she was going to make damn sure no further harm came to her hero. For that she needed Rakkelle.

It was a crazy risk. Hadley could be wrong, and it could mean the end of her career. The trouble was, she was betting on being right. She'd been ignoring her instincts too much lately and learned the hard way the consequences of that. It was time to trust her gut. How many times had Admiral Bandar emphasized the importance of following her instinctive feelings and not a rule book? More than she could count. Now she *was* following her gut—maybe straight into hell.

Goddess keep her.

Hadley hurried down to the brig deck, where Rakkelle had been brought. A guard stopped her before she got past the watch station. "Admiral Bandar's orders," she lied calmly, years of practice behind those three words. "Cadet Pehzwan is to be confined to her quarters, not the brig."

"Admiral Bandar said that?"

"We're in contact with her now." Hadley could lose her career over that lie and be convicted of treason if her actions endangered the admiral or the crew of the *Unity*. Somehow, she knew she was on the right path. Or maybe she was just stubborn. Goddess no, she was right. *Trust in yourself.* As a shuttle pilot, and one prone to flying "outside the box," Rakkelle had to know how to "ping" another shuttle, and that's how Hadley intended to locate the missing shuttle—and the admiral! To the uninformed, pinging was merely a locate-and-avoid feature designed for collision safety when shuttles zinged in and around a larger ship. But there was another use for it: locate and *find*. The pilots on the *Vengeance* would talk about playing hide-and-seek, illegally. The best pinger always won. She prayed with her whole soul that Rakkelle liked to win as much as Hadley suspected she did.

The guard noted the event on his data-vis and let her through. In one cell, the Drakken raiders they'd brought aboard sat around a table. They looked clean and fed and bored. Hadley jogged past empty cells until she came to Rakkelle's.

The pilot turned to her in shock as Hadley tapped in the door release code. "You're coming with me," Hadley urged. "We've got to stop a war."

CHAPTER TWENTY-TWO

THE ENGINEER'S URGENT VOICE sliced through the tense standoff on the bridge. "Sir!"

"Yes," Yarew said at the same time Finn replied, "Aye."

"A shuttle just departed Bay Six. Pehzwan input the docking release code."

Rakkelle. She was escaping. Had he been that wrong about her? He thought he knew his instincts better than that. "Put them on-screen," Finn bellowed.

The image came to life on the large holo-vis. "Rakkelle," he yelled in disbelief. "What in the freepin' hells are you doing, woman?"

She smiled her impish grin, wriggling fingers at him as the shuttle pulled away.

Yarew spun to the weapons officer. "Blow that damned shuttle out of the sky."

"No!" Finn shouted. "I override that order. Lieutenant Keyren is with her."

Yarew's head jerked back around. "By the gods, she is."

Hadley's blond head was side by side with Rakkelle's dark one. "If you can't find her," Brit's assistant said, "we will." She reached up, closing the connection. The holo-vis went dark.

"THEY'LL SHOOT US DOWN," Rakkelle said, shrugging. "Oh, well. I always figured I'd go out in a blaze of fire."

"They won't shoot at us."

"Yarew's a trigger-happy son of a bitch."

"Warleader Rorkken isn't. He won't let him do it."

"Don't be so sure. He's not too happy with us Drakken right now."

"I'm here. He won't hurt me if he thinks it'll hurt the admiral."

"Yeah?" Rakkelle's glance was perceptive. "I thought there was something going on between those two. The warleader looked like a lovesick hound puppy every time she called his name."

She flipped the shuttle on its wing, banking around hard. Then she slammed the throttles forward and they were off. "Lucky Bandar," she mused as they raced away from the huge ship. "I'd have wanted a little bunk time with the good warleader myself. He never would. Propriety, he'd tell me. Didn't seem too important to him with Bandar, though." She made a noise of annoyance.

"You'd want bunk time with anything with a cock," Hadley muttered as her mood went south. "Or maybe I'm limiting you too much. Maybe you go both ways. Don't ask me, though. I'm not interested."

Rakkelle sighed. Her small hand tightened over the throttle. "He needed a fuck, Hadley."

"I would have slept with him last night."

"He didn't want that. He wanted a fuck. Don't you understand? He didn't want love. He didn't want *feelings*."

An image of Tango's pumping bare butt returned. She winced. "Was he any good?" She couldn't believe she'd asked but sick curiosity demanded she find out what she'd missed.

Rakkelle shrugged. "I've had better."

"Bolivarr?"

The pilot laughed. "Hells no, not him."

"Why not?" Hadley blurted out, vastly relieved to learn what he'd told her was true. "He's hot."

"The wraith is the kind of man who falls in love." Rakkelle shuddered. "Love. It's freepin' annoying. You can't shake 'em loose. Then when you fuck someone else, they start screamin' at you. Who needs it?"

Hadley looked over at her. "You've never been in love?"

"Nope."

"Neither have I." She thought of Bolivarr recovering in the hospital, sleeping now, at the last report, and wondered if her loveless status was about to change.

That was, if she survived this last-ditch search for Admiral Bandar.

All they had to go on was a shuttle ping, a faint ion trail and a prayer. What they were going to do when they tracked it to the source remained up in the air. Raid a fortress? Fight Drakken hand-to-hand? Hadley steeled herself as she touched a hand to her pistol. If that's what it took, she would.

"Ooh! We've got a ping-back already."

"Yes…" Hadley whispered, sitting up.

Rakkelle changed heading. "It's damned close, too. What did they do, hand-deliver her back to us?"

Hopefully not dead. Hadley's hopes chilled.

"Freep me. Look."

On-screen a shuttle floated in space. Hadley zoomed in on the craft. "Goddess. It's her." Fear spilled over, cold and sickening in her stomach. Seemingly naked under a blanket thrown over her midsection, Admiral Bandar was slumped, unconscious, in the pilot's seat.

"STAY BACK!" Finn shouted to the others, clustering around the docked shuttle that Rakkelle had towed in. He wanted some level of privacy for Brit as he entered the shuttle with a large, soft robe.

She was naked and smeared with dried blood across her torso and between her thighs. He wanted to die, seeing her condition, but her nanomeds were making fast work of any external wounds. They were unable to help the internal ones, however. Only he could do that. She'd been beaten and raped and gods knew what else. He'd spend the rest of his life helping her heal from this, he vowed.

"Finn," she murmured to him, lifting a weak hand.

"Ah, sweetheart. I've got you. You're safe now, love." Fighting his swelling emotions, he wrapped her in the robe and extricated her from the seat, carrying her through the corridors to the med ward.

A cheer went up as they passed. The crew loved her; there was no denying that.

Yarew trailed the group along with his Coalition cronies. As long as Finn held Brit in his arms, he was safe from arrest.

"Everyone out," Dr. Kell ordered.

Brit's hand brushed Finn's uniform. "He stays."

"You heard the woman, Doctor. I'm stayin'." Even if Brit hadn't spoken her desire to have him at her side, he wasn't sure he'd have left.

"Finn…" Brit's fingers scratched weakly at his uniform as the doctor began his examination.

"Hush now." He stroked her hair back from her forehead, feeling his chest fill with rage at her attackers. He better understood the hate she felt after Arrayar—and he hadn't even lost her.

"Call headquarters," she said thickly. "Tell Zaafran. Now."

"I will. We'll tell him. Soon."

"No. Now. No time." As weak as she was, her voice held the power and confidence of command.

Captains never wanted to care for themselves. It was a fact of ship life. "Patience, sweetheart. We have to concentrate on you now." He stroked her hair, aching at the sight of her bruised cheek. How good it would feel, crushing the windpipe of the man—or men—who did this to her, aye, and in his bare hand. Monsters. For Brit, knowing her background, it would have been a singularly horrifying experience. He still couldn't fathom how she got free of them. "We'll find them, we'll hunt them down. Have no fear of that."

"Contact Zaafran." Brit's fingers found his collar and pulled. For her condition, she had an amazing amount of strength. "That's a freepin' order, Warleader."

Finn sat up in shock. She was half-alive and issuing orders as if she were on the bridge.

"They weren't Drakken. Not Horde. They were Coalition."

Finn jerked upright. Gods, he'd been right. The so-called settlers were Coalition troublemakers pretending to be Drakken.

"He needs to know before people die for it." She swallowed. "Before Drakken innocents die for our sins."

Dr. Kell heard her, too. He put down his scanners. "You say we did this to you?"

"Fanatics did. They kidnapped me to start a war. They knocked me around a bit, they spoke in mock accents. It was all a show to make me believe they were Horde."

"She wasn't raped," the doctor confirmed. "There's no sign of penetration. No foreign bio-cells."

Brit's eyelids fluttered. "Thank gods. I didn't know. I was beaten unconscious...."

"Are you absolutely certain, Brit?" Finn asked. No matter how much he'd like the blame to be on the other side, the truth was too important. Galactic peace was at stake and gods knew he wanted to see the end of war. He was born in war; he wanted to die in peace—many, many years from now, a content old man. "How could you tell?"

She let out a small laugh. "Easy. They didn't stink of those awful skins."

CHAPTER TWENTY-THREE

PATCHED UP and back in uniform, Brit took command of the bridge. Only a few bruises told of her scuffle with the fools who'd kidnapped her. Lingering weakness dragged at her, but blazing anger made it easy to ignore. "Star-Major Yarew—report!"

He appeared in the entrance of her office. His skin was pale, his body language broadcasting his discomfort. Good. The more he suffered, the better.

"How are you feeling, Admiral?"

"Much improved, thank you." She sat back in her smart chair. "At ease, Star-Major." She waved at the seat opposite her desk.

Swallowing, he nodded in gratitude and sat down. The chair lurched sideways, spilling him.

Brit brought her hands together, resting her fingers against her lips to keep from laughing outright. "One would think after all these weeks on the *Unity,* you'd have mastered the art of sitting down."

"I have—there's a malfunction, apparently," he blustered as he leveled the chair.

She leaned forward. "Bullshit."

His face lost what little color it still had. "Admiral?"

"Evidence of your tampering with the smart chair programming was easy to find, once engineering knew what to look for. You've been scrambling the codes for Warleader Rorkken since he set foot on this ship."

He opened his mouth to protest. "I—"

"You will not speak without permission," she snapped in her coldest admiral's voice. Rising from the desk, she clasped her hands neatly at the small of her back. The entire bridge crew looked on through the glass. "A little inter-civilization rivalry is to be expected at a war's end. While I don't approve of your rigging the chairs, it hurt little more than the warleader's pride. It was mischief, plain and simple. Yes?"

He swallowed. "Yes, ma'am. My apologies."

She stopped in front of the officer, making sure she held his gaze in the steel-hard grip of hers. "In contrast, giving proprietary codes to traitors looking to destabilize the galaxy is treason."

"But, Admiral, I—"

"Permission to speak *not granted!*"

The smart chair rocked as he tried to stand.

"Nor is permission to stand," she hissed coolly. "You'll be doing plenty of both once your war crimes trial commences in the High Royal Court on Sakka. You had us believing in a terror threat that caused us to depart the Ring prematurely, unprepared and understaffed. You knew the attacks on the settlers were committed by Coalition masquerading as Drakken. You aided and assisted them, all while keeping information from me, your commander. You are what's sick with the galaxy. You, who hate to the point of blindness. The war may be over, but ridding the stars of the likes of you is only just beginning." Her voice turned even colder. "If I've learned one thing in my life, it's that monsters come dressed in many different uniforms."

As do angels. Brit turned to the bridge where three sharp, Triad-uniformed guards waited: one Drakken, one Coalition and one Earthling, just as she'd requested. "Take him to the brig," she ordered the guards.

"But I acted in the interests of galactic security," Yarew pleaded with her, a guard tugging on each arm. "I did it for our future. Our glory."

She replied with a brief, disgusted wave of her hand. "Get him off this bridge and out of my sight."

As Yarew was led away, the main holo-vis came to life, revealing a grand view of the Ring. The image dissolved into one of Prime-Admiral Zaafran. He nodded. "Admiral."

She nodded back. "Prime-Admiral, sir."

They'd been in and out of discussion ever since the drugs the mock Drakken had pumped her with had faded enough for her to think clearly. "The conspirators are in custody," he informed her. "And Yarew?"

"The same."

"Excellent." Zaafran's expression softened to one of respect borne of their long years working together. "I owe you, Brit. We all owe you. The entire galaxy. Or maybe," he said, his dark eyes crinkling in amusement, "we owe your nose."

She laughed at the irony. "I never forgot that smell. When it struck me that the odor was absent on their ship, I knew the cowards weren't really Horde. The one masquerading as a battle-lord was particularly pitiful. He injured his cheek just to appear scarred!" All so she, the most well-known of Drakken haters, could be "rescued," telling all of her story of horror, making her an unwitting accomplice in what would have amounted to a full-scale massacre of Drakken, and likely civil war.

The thing was, she'd never been very good at being unwitting…except perhaps where falling in love with Finnar Rorkken was concerned. That had blindsided her.

As the holo-vis went dark, she aimed her smile at Finn, who was sitting comfortably in a smart chair that now listened to his every whim. His eyes twinkled with mischief. *My rugged, wicked boy.* She'd been hunting Drakken most of her adult life. Now it was time to settle down with one.

She turned away to brush a hand along the window as she took in the vista of stars. So many worlds. Once, they were like pebbles to be turned over to see what vermin lay hidden underneath. She was done with that; her hunt for Horde was over. All the killing in the world wouldn't bring back Seff and the children. Twenty years of battle and she was no closer to erasing that loss. Love would make it easier to bear. Love would help her *heal*.

Finn appeared at her side. Her hand brushed against his but did not take it. They were, after all, professional military officers on duty. A furtive, tender touch was all they'd allow themselves. "It's over," she said as they gazed out at the stars. "My mission is complete."

"Am I hearing you right, love?" he asked under his breath. "Is Admiral Brit Bandar considering retirement?"

"Not exactly. Prime-Admiral Zaafran has a plan for me—for us." She pressed a finger to her smiling mouth. "I'm hoping you like it, too."

HADLEY WAS AT Bolivarr's bedside as soon as Dr. Kell cleared him for visitors. "Try to keep his heart rate down," the older man pleaded before letting her go inside. Grumbling something about frisky young people, he went to attend to Commander Rothberg, who was improving steadily. He'd recover fully.

"I heard your memories came back." Nervously, she perched on the bedside chair.

"Dr. Kell says it was the kiss."

"Really?"

He smiled. "He didn't say. But that's my guess."

She wrung her hands. "And…?"

"I'm not married."

She expelled a loud sigh of relief. Then she lowered her voice. "What about being a virgin?"

"That's for me to know, and for you to find out."

"Bolivarr," she protested.

His smile was almost regretful as he shook his head. "I guess I'm not."

"The girls must not have been too memorable, though," she said with a small pout.

"Not at all. Not like you."

"But we haven't…"

"I hope to remedy that one day."

"'One day' sounds so far away." She'd hoped he'd put her out of her virginal misery much sooner.

"When we arrive in port, I have to travel to the Royal Military Hospital on Sakka. I had a suppression device installed. It's blocking secrets I'm not supposed to remember. They—I—want to know why."

"The people who put it in you are probably dead." It made her sick to think of beautiful Bolivarr used as a tool for the warlord, much like the coalition's now-banned REEF assassins.

"They probably are, Hadley. I want it out. I don't want anything they made to be inside me. I want a normal life." He reached for her hand, holding it between his as he rubbed her fingers. "I don't know how long I'll be. I might need surgery. There will be recovery time, perhaps therapy, depending."

"I'll wait for you," she whispered. "I will."

Joy flashed in his dark eyes that were so much more animated now that the suppression device had malfunctioned. "Besides, I promised to help out with your, ah, little problem," he said with a mischievous slant of his mouth. "If you'll want me to."

"My first time will be with you, Bolivarr." Despite Dr. Kell's warnings, she leaned over the bed to kiss him. She wasn't halfway down when the wraith pulled her down the rest of the way to his mouth.

His pulse must be off the charts, she thought, because hers sure was. Goddess, the man could kiss.

"Uh-oh," a male voice said.

In an Earthling accent.

Hadley sat up, smoothing her mussed hair off her forehead. "Hi, Tango."

The pilot was clearly flustered. "Rothberg kicked me out of his room for some cute little star-lieutenant. So I stopped by to see how Bolivarr was doing. I guess good, huh."

She smiled sweetly. "Really good."

"Good. Great." He backed toward the door. "I'll leave you two to your, uh, visit."

He disappeared out the door. Bolivarr and Hadley looked at each other and laughed.

BRIT ORDERED Hadley to her office. "It's about time you got here," she said sternly when the girl arrived.

"Sorry, ma'am. Is there something I can get you? Water? Wine?"

Hands clasped behind her back, Brit paced in front of her desk. "I understand that you and the war-leader had a conversation about my white box." She stopped, eyeing the girl. "And what was in it."

Hadley seemed to crumple. Then she recovered, standing taller. Good, Brit thought. She'd showed a lot of grit on her brilliantly conceived and executed mission with Rakkelle, but she still needed to develop more spine. She would, in time. "Yes, ma'am." Hadley pressed her lips together. "I looked in it only once, the day I moved your things from the *Vengeance* to here. I'd worked for you for so long, but I never really knew you. I wanted to."

No one knew her before. Now, yes. Then, no.

"You are my hero, Admiral. I'd never do anything to hurt you. What I did was wrong, snooping, seeing things I didn't understand."

"Sit down."

Hadley all but fell into a smart chair. Then, with her gaze on the stars, Brit told her of the keepsakes in the box, of Arrayar and what transpired in the years afterward. No, not the worst of the details, but enough for the girl to understand who she was. Enough to know her.

Hadley sat quietly in the chair. Sorrow creased her forehead and tugged on her mouth. "It makes my presumptuousness in opening the box—and telling Warleader Rorkken about it—all the more appalling."

"Because of what you've done, I'm going to have to send you off the *Unity,* Hadley."

The lieutenant's shoulders sagged, and again she recovered. She stood, nodding. "I understand, Admiral."

Brit walked toward her. "Put out your hand."

The girl hesitated.

Brit sighed. "I'm not going to bite it off!"

Hadley extended her hand. She looked ready for her punishment. Brit dropped two epaulets into her palm. "Congratulations, Captain. You're the new commander of the *Cloud Shadow.* You often told me of the clouds on your homeworld, and how they raced across the sky. I thought the name would fit a small, swift vessel."

Hadley's mouth had dropped open. With the tip of her finger, Brit pressed on her chin, closing it. "No, it's not the most awe-inspiring ship name as ship names go, but we did all right with the *Unity,* don't you think?"

"Yes, ma'am," she whispered. "Oh, my goddess. My own ship. My own command."

"One that you richly deserve, owing to your brave and timely actions the day I was abducted. She's a small cruiser, but many don't ever have the chance to command a ship of any kind."

"I know, Admiral. Oh, I know." Hadley brought

the epaulets to her lips and kissed them. "You've made my day, Admiral. You've made my *life*."

"I wouldn't go that far."

"No, you have." The girl's blue eyes shimmered. Then she threw her arms around Brit.

Brit closed her eyes and hugged her close. Her daughter would have been close to Hadley's age, had she lived. Gently, Brit took the thought and tucked it away. It was time to start a new life.

CHAPTER TWENTY-FOUR

One year later

THE GROUNDS OF THE Royal Galactic Military Academy were as lovely now as they had been the day Brit arrived as a new cadet, over two decades ago. Then, suffering from post-traumatic stress and grief that weighed on her day and night, she'd found it difficult to appreciate her surroundings. Now in her position commanding the venerated, centuries-old school—and as a woman healing—she saw beauty in everything around her.

"Admiral!" Her chief of faculty made her way through the gardens to where Brit strolled on her walk, much the way she used to walk the decks of her ship. Only this evening, she was headed home—to a land home, and a husband. "Prime-Admiral Zaafran and Prime Minister Belduin have arrived in their quarters. Shall I tell them dinner is half past sept-hour?"

Her tenure as headmaster brought many celebrities to the academy. As well, Finn brought in his own share of those eager to dine with him. Heading up a brand-new position as chief of Drakken recruitment, he'd attracted a wealth of qualified candidates. Traveling far and wide, he worked to transition those in Drakken refugee camps to enclaves in cities, where, he hoped, they'd ultimately blend into the general population. Finn considered his life's work helping the Drakken integrate without losing their identity.

"Half past, yes," Brit replied, glad that tonight Zaafran would join them. Many interesting visitors made their way to the academy but she enjoyed the dinners with old friends the most.

"I'll let them know." The woman smiled and hurried off. They could have communicated via data-vis or PCD, yet the interaction had occurred in person. It was still so old-fashioned here. Hi-tech comm was used more often than not in cases of emergencies only. It was fine with her.

Brit stopped to watch new cadets drilling on the lawns. Others soared overhead in fighter-craft, roaring past in tight formation. Drakken, Coalition, Earth, they'd graduate to command a military vastly different from the one she had.

Finally, she turned in the direction of home. Not that she was opposed to whatever new adventures and opportunities life might present, but working with the next generation of galactic cadets and setting down some roots was her focus for now. Roots. It had a nice ring to it, that.

LATER THAT NIGHT, after the guests had gone, Finn made love to her. It had never abated, the chemistry between them, but tonight had seemed somehow sweeter, even more loving than usual. It had a different purpose.

They'd set out to make a baby.

When they were finally ready to rest, Finn leaned over her in bed, his kind, smiling eyes shining. Savoring the silence, the way they could talk without words, she reached up to caress him. He still wore his tattoos, save one, the Drakken bird of prey. She'd encouraged him to keep the others so he'd never forget his origins, just as he helped her to come to terms with her past. She'd even started a data-note to her parents, whom she'd located not long ago. She'd reach out and see what happened.

"Moonstruck," he said as he gazed down at her.

She laughed. "What's that? Not a name for our child, I hope."

"It's how your former executive officer says I act around you. She took time to tease me when I ran into her at Yirshmokk Port after the summit meeting."

"She did?" Brit smiled. It was always nice to hear of Hadley. The girl was as green as a captain could be when she took command of the *Cloud Shadow,* but she was learning fast. Her future was bright.

"Aye. On her homeworld, Talo, 'moonstruck' means being so crazy in love that nothing else matters."

"I'd say that's an apt description of us. Crazy. Insane. Ill-advised."

Finn chuckled as he bent down to kiss her.

"And perfectly perfect," she murmured against his mouth.

"Aye…" Chuckling, he nibbled his way to her ear. She heard her wedding earring clicking against his teeth. "That's exactly what I told her." He drew her close as he rolled to his side.

Once Finn Rorkken got hold of "something good," he never let it go. He reminded her of that fact every time he held her near all night long.

As he did now.

Warm with contentment, she closed her eyes, smiling when he gently, protectively, rested his hand on her belly. It was a moment beautiful for its simplicity: the man she loved holding her, and perhaps a newly created life snuggled safely between their warm bodies. It made all the years she'd served the Coalition worth it. Her military service had brought her to Finn, as his had to her. Now she and her rugged, wicked boy would have a baby, and their child would grow up in peace.

REQUEST YOUR FREE BOOKS!

2 FREE NOVELS
FROM THE ROMANCE/SUSPENSE
COLLECTION PLUS 2 FREE GIFTS!

YES! Please send me 2 FREE novels from the Romance/Suspense Collection and my 2 FREE gifts (gifts are worth about $10). After receiving them, if I don't wish to receive any more books, I can return the shipping statement marked "cancel." If I don't cancel, I will receive 4 brand-new novels every month and be billed just $5.49 per book in the U.S. or $5.99 per book in Canada, plus 25¢ shipping and handling per book plus applicable taxes, if any*. That's a savings of at least 20% off the cover price! I understand that accepting the 2 free books and gifts places me under no obligation to buy anything. I can always return a shipment and cancel at any time. Even if I never buy another book from the Reader Service, the two free books and gifts are mine to keep forever.

185 MDN EF5Y   385 MDN EF6C

Name _____ (PLEASE PRINT) _____

Address _____ Apt. # _____

City _____ State/Prov. _____ Zip/Postal Code _____

Signature (if under 18, a parent or guardian must sign)

Mail to **The Reader Service:**
IN U.S.A.: P.O. Box 1867, Buffalo, NY 14240-1867
IN CANADA: P.O. Box 609, Fort Erie, Ontario L2A 5X3

Not valid to current subscribers to the Romance Collection,
the Suspense Collection or the Romance/Suspense Collection.

Want to try two free books from another line?
Call 1-800-873-8635 or visit www.morefreebooks.com.

* Terms and prices subject to change without notice. N.Y. residents add applicable sales tax. Canadian residents will be charged applicable provincial taxes and GST. Offer not valid in Quebec. This offer is limited to one order per household. All orders subject to approval. Credit or debit balances in a customer's account(s) may be offset by any other outstanding balance owed by or to the customer. Please allow 4 to 6 weeks for delivery. Offer available while quantities last.

Your Privacy: Harlequin is committed to protecting your privacy. Our Privacy Policy is available online at www.eHarlequin.com or upon request from the Reader Service. From time to time we make our lists of customers available to reputable third parties who may have a product or service of interest to you. If you would prefer we not share your name and address, please check here. ☐

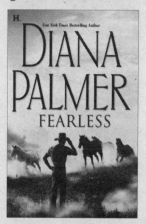

SUSAN GRANT

77192	MY FAVORITE EARTHLING___	$6.99 U.S. ___	$8.50 CAN.
77106	YOUR PLANET OR MINE?___	$5.99 U.S. ___	$6.99 CAN.

(limited quantities available)

TOTAL AMOUNT	$ _____
POSTAGE & HANDLING	$ _____
($1.00 FOR 1 BOOK, 50¢ for each additional)	
APPLICABLE TAXES*	$ _____
TOTAL PAYABLE	$ _____

(check or money order—please do not send cash)

To order, complete this form and send it, along with a check or money order for the total above, payable to HQN Books, to: **In the U.S.:** 3010 Walden Avenue, P.O. Box 9077, Buffalo, NY 14269-9077; **In Canada:** P.O. Box 636, Fort Erie, Ontario, L2A 5X3.

Name: _____
Address: _____ City: _____
State/Prov.: _____ Zip/Postal Code: _____
Account Number (if applicable): _____

075 CSAS

*New York residents remit applicable sales taxes.
*Canadian residents remit applicable GST and provincial taxes.

HQN™
We *are* romance™

www.HQNBooks.com

PHSG0608BL